There was a faint crunch on the gravel behind her. Clarissa whirled around. Suddenly a man stepped into the framed archway. Against the lighter shades of the night Clarissa recognized the tall figure leaning on the heavy oak cane. "Adam?" she called, but he did not answer. Then, with horror, she saw him lift the cane high over his head.

She threw up her arms as the cane swished through the air, striking the vines beside her. She flung herself wildly to the side, and a choking scream tore from her throat.

Her mind could not accept the nightmarish reality of what was happening . . . could not believe that the man to whom she might have given her heart was now savagely trying to end her life. . . .

REST HERE, MY HEART

Maryhelen Clague

FAWCETT GOLD MEDAL • NEW YORK

REST HERE, MY HEART

© 1979 Maryhelen Clague

All rights reserved

Published by Fawcett Gold Medal Books, a unit of CBS Publications, the Consumer Publishing Division of CBS Inc.

All the characters in this book are fictitious, and any resemblance to actual persons living or dead is purely coincidental.

ISBN: 0-449-14284-1

Printed in the United States of America

First Fawcett Gold Medal printing: December 1979

10 9 8 7 6 5 4 3 2 1

*For my children
Billy and Sarah*

"For where your treasure is, there will your heart be also."

Prologue

"Please, darling. Won't you finish your tea?"

She saw the familiar hardness growing in his eyes, the grim pursing of his lips, and her heart sank. Turning his head angrily on the pillow, he clamped his jaws together in what she recognized as refusal. It would do no good to urge him now.

Clarissa sat back in her chair and lay the cup and spoon on the table beside the bed. "All right. I won't beg you. But you would feel better if you finished it."

She sat quietly for a moment, waiting to see if he wanted to speak. He seemed to be trying to draw his strength together, pulling the energy of his body into a thin thread that would give support to the words he found so difficult to form. Then, as she watched, he gave up the struggle before it was begun, and his eyes focused listlessly on some dark vision beyond the window.

In a nervous gesture Clarissa smoothed back her hair, which she had taken to wearing severely pulled back in a tight knot at the base of her neck. What was the use of trying to curl or crimp it anymore? Her attempts at fashion had gone the way of her useless dreams, into nothingness.

7

From the barn she could hear the bellowing of the cow complaining that it was past her milking time. She had put it off, knowing that once she started there would be a long list of things to be seen to: cow, horse, chickens, wood—all waiting for the indifferent ministrations of her own two hands. Glancing around the small bedroom, she sighed to herself. Well, at least Mina would be here today, and that would give her less to see to in the house. With a twinge of guilt she remembered that it also meant she could leave the care of her brother to someone else—the loathsome, embarrassing, demeaning chores that his needs required could for the space of one day be shunted off onto other shoulders.

For shame! she said to herself. How can I complain when the pain of it is so much worse for him! Then, to cover her thoughts, she spoke out loud:

"I'd better go take care of mother's cow. Mina will be here soon. Are you all right then?"

He was already drifting back to sleep. She leaned over the bed and saw the dark eyes flicker open for a moment, then shut out the world once again. The faintest lifting of a smile played on his lips. Perhaps he's having a pleasant dream, Clarissa thought as she lightly kissed his forehead. Poor Philip. Dreams were all that were left to him, while she, who used to be the dreamer of the two, had none left at all.

She came into the kitchen just as Mina was entering from outside. Her tight sliver of a mouth was more compressed than usual as she hung her tattered shawl on a peg and went right to stoking up the fire. The tiny appraising eyes took in every detail of Clarissa's neat figure and mentally tallied up the day's accusations.

Normally Clarissa would cringe under their severe gaze, but today she had defiantly thrown on her gray homespun with yesterday's mud still clotting the hem, and half combed her hair. What did it matter anyway how she looked? At least this unconcern with her appearance would rob Mina of her favorite criticism. She can't accuse me of dolling up beyond my station, Clarissa thought, too full of despair to enjoy even that minor satisfaction.

"And how is himself?"

It always amazed Clarissa how this recalcitrant old woman could make a simple question sound so like an accusation.

"He's sleeping. He's just finished breakfast. I'll be out back."

"Humph! Must not have slept too well, poor soul. You didn't forget to turn him?"

Clarissa stood watching her, letting the anger she felt pour out of her eyes, but keeping her lips closed against it. You'd like that, wouldn't you, you old hag! You'd love to say I'd been primping again, putting on airs while Philip got bedsores from my neglect. Well, I won't give you that satisfaction, you miserable peasant!

From the barn the insistent bellowing of the Jersey cow grew louder. "I didn't forget," Clarissa snapped and left the kitchen, throwing on her old serviceable cottage cloak.

Stepping outside, she paused for a moment on the stone stoop and pulled her shawl around her head, fastening the ends tightly across her shoulders. Beyond the barn a thin line of skeletal trees hid from her sight the familiar rocky fields where her father had struggled so hard to raise a few stunted crops. Mentally she pictured the frost-encrusted road which skirted their rotting fences to dip down the hill and into the village of Manhattan where skinny frame houses clustered protectively around St. Mary's Church. How many times had she imagined that road as it turned south down Manhattan Island, curving leisurely around Lord Courtenay's fine house, pushing on past the Bloomingdale Asylum, dipping and climbing between hills and creeks and elegant country estates finally to lose itself among the brick houses and clamorous traffic of New York City. How she longed to strike out and follow it all the way to Castle Garden on the Battery, never once looking back.

The clear, cold air was growing almost painful. A thin sprinkling of snow frosted the ground and crunched like slivers of glass under her feet. Thank God they had not suffered the severe snowfalls of former years, or she did not know how she would have managed to make a path between the kitchen door and the low barn thirty feet away. The shelter of its thick walls at least kept out the worst of the frigid wind, but the all-pervasive cold still managed to seep under her skirts and through the porous cloth of her cloak right into her very bones. Her mother's old cow turned and half glared at her as she pulled up the stool and began working its cold teats. With numb fingers she pulled at the cow's udder while the animal jabbed aimlessly at her with its back hoof.

Cows were supposed to be placid, docile creatures, but this one had a streak of meanness Clarissa had never been able to subdue. Her mother had actually liked the nasty thing and had soothed and babied the animal through many a morning such as this. But since her mother had died, an almost diabolical dislike had developed between Clarissa and the beast, a dislike that grew worse as the cow aged.

This morning the creature, with a kind of moronic sixth sense, picked up Clarissa's mood and made every drop of milk that much harder to extract. When the pail was half-full, the dim-witted beast managed to land one hoof exactly where it would send the pail flying, spilling the creamy liquid into the straw.

"Damn you!" Clarissa cried and brought her fist down on the animal's stupid velvet nose. The big warm body began to sway angrily, and Clarissa just managed to get out of the stall before she was pinned to the plank wall, narrowly missing a kick from a hind hoof as she darted into the aisle.

She leaned against the opposite stall, not even trying to fight back the tears. "I'll never get out of here," she cried aloud. "It's a prison and I'm caught here forever. I'll spend the rest of my life growing old trying to scratch a living from this miserable farm and tied to a cripple! I'll never be free!"

If only her father could be here to see her sobbing alone in this barn, what would he say? Would this finally turn him from the old nonsense of how she was meant to be a lady, how some day she would live in a fine house, be waited on by others, and pass her time in pleasant pursuits that left her hands clean and her fingernails whole?

That was the trouble, wasn't it? For years Papa had filled her head with dreams because he himself had been nothing but a dreamer. A dreamer of dreams and a singer of songs and a complete failure at anything practical.

In her helpless rage she hammered her fist against the post near her head. Why didn't Papa leave me alone? she thought grimly. Why didn't he help me accept the life of a drudge trapped in poverty and teach me never to want anything more? Why didn't Mama keep him quiet? Why did Philip have to get hurt?

At the thought of her brother she felt her rage dwindle and seep away into nothing. How much worse it was for him—chained to a helpless body for the rest of his life, barely able to mouth his pleading that someone let him die. Out of all the wonderfully useful mechanisms of his superb body, only one movement was left to his command—the restless, never-ceasing wandering of his eyes. How could she complain when he had to live with this?

Clarissa dug at her eyes with her apron. But she did complain, and her pain was real, only the degree might differ. As surely as Philip had destroyed his own body when he fell from that barn roof, he had destroyed her future as well. There would be nothing now but this never-ending weariness and drudgery for all the long years that stretched ahead.

"Missy! Missy!"

It was Mina's voice calling from the kitchen. Clarissa picked up the pail and hung it over a wooden peg. Let the milk go until tonight. Carelessly she flung some oats into the mangers and picked up a sack of dried corn to feed the chickens. The voice from the kitchen grew more insistent.

"Missy! Come here! It's himself!"

Oh, Lord, Philip again. Now what? Deliberately she opened the cloth sack and poured a portion of the grains into a woven basket. Yet even as she continued slowly with the chores a thin edge of fear chilled the shallow

11

skin of her neck. Suppose he had hurt himself somehow. Or had another of those horrifying attacks.

The genuine love she felt for her brother surged, blotting out her despair and rebellion. Quickly she set the basket down and started at a slow lope up the path to the kitchen. She had a brief glimpse of Mina standing in the doorway waving her arms before she disappeared back inside the house. Clarissa began to run.

In the big hearth the fire was roaring. Clarissa darted across the room to the open bedroom door and saw Mina bending over her brother's form on the bed. Under the coverlet the huge mound of his once spectacular physique already showed signs of shrinkage. Clarissa stood very still, seeing each detail of the blue-checked pattern standing vivid against the oatmeal-colored background.

Looking up, Mina stared at her over Philip's body, her eyes glaring like black holes in a skull.

"He's dead! Himself is dead," she croaked.

Clarissa stared back at her. "He can't be! Why, he just had his breakfast. It's impossible."

"I tell you he's dead. No breath, no heartbeat . . ."

Clarissa's eyes moved from the woman's accusing face to the serene stillness of her brother's countenance. His skin matched the background of the coverlet. The fine features might have been molded in marble, dignity in every curve and the faintest of smiles at the corner of the lips. Then back to Mina's homely features, which crumpled like paper before her eyes as a limp tear streaked the leathery cheeks. To her own horror Clarissa heard herself laugh. A thin, mirthless, hollow chuckle. Touché, my darling Philip. You finally got what you wanted.

At the unnatural sound that escaped her throat something seemed to coalesce in Mina's brain. "What did you do to him? What did you give him?" she cried hysterically.

The laugh died on Clarissa's lips. She stared at the old woman like someone in a stupor.

"What? What are you saying?"

A thin misshapen finger pointed toward Clarissa's face.

"You did it, I know you did! You hated him. You hated taking care of him! What did you put in the food? In the tea? It was you, I know it was!"

"Old woman, you're crazy! What are you talking about?" She shrank against the door frame.

"Unnatural sister, I'm saying you killed him, you took his life. Daughter of Babylon, thirstin' after Sodom! You killed him. You killed your brother!"

One

    "Would you like a cup of tea, Miss Shaw? So refreshing after your long ride from New York."

The chair into which he had placed her seemed to bump and heave as though she were still on the stage. She pushed her frozen feet closer to the brass fender and nodded toward the trim, white-haired man sitting across from her. Hot tea would taste heavenly after that long, cold ride. And it might serve to quiet some of the strain that always threatened to overwhelm her whenever she was faced with new places and strange people.

"How unfortunate," he went on, "that you missed the earlier stage. However, we have a simple supper planned, so it won't matter."

Cold as she was, she found it difficult to take her eyes off Judge Granville. The high, old-fashioned stock which enveloped his chin in wads of white silk made it impossible for him to turn his head without turning his shoulders also. With his elongated neck above his billowing, wide chest he reminded her vividly of one of the vain powder pidgeons who used to stroll through the farmyard. The blue eyes above the spectacles perched low on his nose held an awesome severity; yet his voice was kind.

14

Nervously she smoothed the faded brown merino of her skirt and tried to keep out of her voice the timidity she felt.

"I meant to stay the night at the North American Hotel where the stage leaves, but it was so much more congenial at Judge Williams' home that I changed my mind. I thought the carriage could get there in plenty of time, but the rain held up the traffic."

"I know that hotel—on the Bowery, is it not? Judge Williams' house would be far superior and a great deal more proper for a single lady alone in the city. However, you are safely arrived, and that is what matters most."

He reached for a small, cut-glass bell next to his chair and with a few sharp flicks of his wrist set up its delicate tinkle. Almost at the same moment the door opened, and the maid who had earlier shown Clarissa into the house entered the room.

"Nancy," said the judge, "you must have been standing beside the door."

"I thought you might be wanting some refreshment for the lady, sir."

"This is Miss Clarissa Shaw, Nancy, who has come to stay with us for a while. Her father was a kinsman of mine."

The housemaid in her spotlessly white, starched apron curtsied primly in Clarissa's direction. Under her voluminous cap her smile was as cheerful as the freckles sprinkling her nose. Clarissa almost got up from her chair, until she remembered that one didn't rise for servants. She smiled politely instead.

"Edwards has brought your box up, Miss Shaw. You'll find it in your room. Now I'll just go along and get that tea."

"Nancy takes very good care of us," the judge said with warmth. "You look quite frozen, my dear. Pull your chair a little closer to the fire."

"No, no, I'm all right." She wasn't, but she suspected that it wouldn't do to show it. An embarrassed silence fell between them as Clarissa glanced timidly around the room. When she first entered, it had struck her as the most elegantly beautiful room she had ever seen. Now, as she took the time to examine it closer, she began to sense the same incongruity that she had noticed in the house, Zion Hill, the first time she saw it. Like the house, the parlor was a strange mixture of luxury and shabbiness. A brass fender, polished to perfection, glimmered with the reflection of the incandescent flame in the fireplace. The silver sconces on the wall, the graceful candlesticks on the table, the fluted ruby-glass compote, and ornate ormolu clock on the mantel—all mirrored the shimmering light. Yet the carpet was worn almost to the floor in places, the fashionable Chinese wallpaper was tearing away from the wall at the corners, and the paint on the moldings was peeling away. At first glance it had all seemed so warm and pleasing, but when she looked closer, there was a decay within it that transformed the charm into depression. Clarissa shuddered and leaned toward the fire.

Judge Granville had slipped away into some reverie of his own, and the only sound in the room was the comfortable crackling and hiss from the fireplace. Then Nancy swept in again bringing a silver tray with china cups surrounding an incongruously homely fat, brown teapot.

"Ah, here we are," said the judge, at once all politeness. "This will warm you up in good time, Miss Shaw."

Nancy set out the cups and saucers and filled the brown pot with steaming water from a small kettle on a trivet by the fire. Then, quietly and efficiently, just as Clarissa imagined a good servant should, she left the room, closing the door behind her.

"I do hope you will not find life at Zion Hill dull after your stay in the city, Miss Shaw. We live very quietly here."

"I am quite accustomed to a quiet life, Judge Granville. At least—I was—before—"

He glanced up quickly, noting the sudden pain on her face. "Oh dear, my careless tongue. Please forgive me. I'm sorry about your brother."

His voice trailed off in embarrassment. Clarissa's cup rattled against the saucer as she hastily placed it on the table near her chair. "Thank you, sir," she said hesitantly. "And thank you for inviting me here. After what happened I could never go back to Manhattan Village again and, of course, I could not impose on Judge Williams indefinitely. I am so grateful that I did not have to seek a position—that was an ordeal I was dreading. That you sought me out and offered me this refuge—well, I just can't find the words to express my gratitude."

Judge Granville seemed to squirm inside the confines of his stock. "I'm happy that it suited you to come. Of course, though we had never met, you were not unknown to me. I even met your father once, years ago, when you were small. I thought because of our family connections in England we might be friends—that I might even be in a position to help him get established here. But he was a proud man and very bitter toward his family. He would have none of me.

"Over the years I heard reports of him and his family now and then, and finally, when your brother died, Judge Williams contacted me and kept me informed of your difficulties. Once they were resolved, I made sure you received my invitation. He entirely agreed with me that your place was here, and it was partly on the strength of his recommendation that I wrote to you. I feel sure that his confidence and mine will not be displaced."

He would never mention it, of course, but there had been a dim worry haunting the back of his mind. One never knew what to expect on taking a complete stranger into one's home. Yet, watching her across the hearth, he began to feel a sense of relief. Her quiet, well-bred manner and neat appearance made a pleasing first impression. She was not a strikingly pretty girl, but she had a subdued loveliness which suggested a gentle spirit with hidden resources of strength. Watching her quietly sitting there with the golden firelight tinting her thick auburn hair and setting her large brown eyes in shifting shadows, he grew more convinced than ever that he had done the right thing.

"Now have a little more tea while I tell you something of our life here at Zion Hill." He settled back in the creweled embroidered chair and, in a characteristic gesture, placed his fingertips against each other and gazed at her over them.

"As you know, for many years I had a rather flourishing career in the city. If I might speak boldly of myself, I might even say a distinguished career. But circumstances compelled me to give it up and take up a more secluded life out here in the country.

"I did not go into explanations in my letter, but there is perhaps one detail of our life here which I should explain now at the beginning. It might have some bearing on your decision to remain."

Clarissa watched him curiously. His self-contained exterior seemed all at once to shiver under some minor convulsion. Then the image was gone, and there he sat as sure of himself as before.

"I moved my family out here to Sing Sing," he went on, "because of the fraility of my wife. For several years now her health has been uneven. Generally speaking, she is robust, but she suffers at times from slight indispositions which quite incapacitate her. We find the peace of the countryside is most beneficial to her."

Clarissa was not sure of how to reply. "Will I be taking care of your wife?" she finally asked.

"Oh, no, no. She has a nurse of her own and keeps mostly to her own apartments. I don't wish to make more of it than I should. It is unfortunate that you could not have known her when she was better. A most lovely, gracious woman."

Nervously he smoothed back his thick white hair. "You will not likely see much of her. Now and then you may pass her moving around the grounds or the house."

She didn't know what to make of this. It sounded as though Mrs. Granville was suffering from some debilitating disease—perhaps the dreaded consumption. Could that perhaps explain the underlying unease beneath his casual words?

She shrugged it off. This home, any home, was welcome now, and an unusual factor like Mrs. Granville's

18

illness did not seem important enough to drive her back into the homeless world beyond the door of Zion Hill.

"I'm sure I shall be happy to meet your wife," she answered politely. "And if you would like me to read to her or anything like that . . ."

"No, that is not necessary. I appreciate your offer to help the children with their lessons, and of course, with the education your father gave you, you may be able to assist me with my correspondence at times. That will certainly be contribution enough for you to make to the Granvilles. Until such time as you decide to leave us, I would like you to think of this as your home."

His look was direct, but Clarissa sensed within it as much warmth as this dignified man probably ever permitted himself to express. "How can I ever . . ."

"Now that is enough of thanks." Deliberately cutting her short, he rose abruptly from his chair and took up the brass fire iron, stirring at the logs with unnecessary concentration. The scattering sparks caught her attention, and for the first time Clarissa noticed the andirons before the hearth. She had never seen their like before. They stood there, painted cast-iron figures of soldiers in the full uniform of the revolutionary war, presenting their long rifles "at arms" before them, and marching in silent, frozen tread, their boots balanced on splayed brass feet on the marble hearth. The painting was minute, down to the stern, unyielding facial glares under their conical pointed hats.

Turning from the fire, Judge Granville noticed her leaning forward to observe them more closely. "They are interesting, are they not?" he said. "They are antiques, actually from the period of the war for independence. They were once quite common in taverns and inns. If you look closely, you will see they are not Americans but Hessians. When the colonials sat before their fires, they rested their feet on the German allies of the British. Gave them some kind of satisfaction, I suppose."

Clarissa smiled up at him. The warmth of the fire and the comfort of the room settled around her like a blanket. It occurred to her that for a long time now her world had centered around herself and her own problems. She could barely remember when she had last been able to become absorbed in the world of the past. Looking at the andirons, she had a sudden mental image of some yeoman farmer—a ninety-day enlistee in General Washington's ragged army—taking a moment to smoke his clay pipe and warm his feet before the fire, perhaps upon these very andirons. It was a congenial, homely picture, a link with another world.

"Actually," the judge went on with more enthusiasm than he had yet expressed in their conversation, "this very house, or parts of it, were built before the revolutionary war. And the armies of both sides tramped every inch of these woods and fields."

He was all at once aware of how he had warmed to his subject and he smiled wryly at Clarissa. "Forgive me. I have a passion for history, which my exile in the country has only reinforced. How does my neighbor, Mr. Irving, put it?—'to escape the commonplace realities of the present and lose yourself among the shadowy grandeurs of the past.' He was speaking of the grandeur of Europe, but I think that for any student of history, the present is trivial and boring and the past congenial and glamorous."

"Please go on," she reassured him. "It's so pleasant before the fire, and I enjoy listening."

Her sympathetic response was all he needed. "I suppose your stage came through Tarrytown. It's an old village, settled originally by the Dutch, and it still boasts several old houses dating back to the previous century. Our own little village of Sing Sing is not so ancient, although we do have an old porterhouse which has stood for many years. Perhaps these andirons came from there originally. They were in the house when I bought it."

"Was your teapot also in the house originally?" she asked, setting down her cup. "It is as unusual as the irons."

"No, I brought this with me." Judge Granville picked up the brown china pot. The lustrous dark pottery took on a soft, tawny glow from the flames as he turned it in his hands and read the gold inscription that encircled it:

20

" 'In the midst of life we are in death.' That's from the burial service. A curious sentiment to inscribe on something as homey and comfortable as a teapot, isn't it? And rather gloomy too. They might just as well have turned it around, and it would have been just as true and much more comforting. It's very old, this pot. It belonged to my mother's aunt in England—she was Chapel and they tend to look on the dark side of things. She gave it to my mother when she married, and it crossed the ocean with her and her new husband. It has brought comfort to many a friend and stranger over the years, in spite of its morbid sentiments."

Clarissa murmured a response, but she was hardly aware of what she said. Lethargic with the heat and the stillness of the room, she was growing sluggish with fatigue. Glancing up, Judge Granville noticed for the first time the weary lines on her face. Of course, he thought, that long journey in a jostling post stage would be enough to drain all her strength.

"My dear, I fear I am tiring you excessively. I am sure you would like to rest a while before supper. I suspect that you are not of a strong constitution."

Afraid she had seemed impolite, Clarissa was about to protest when a short, brisk tap on the door interrupted her. Without waiting for an answer, a tall, elegant woman opened it and swept into the room in a cloud of dark green bombazine and exquisite blond lace. Her dark, thick hair was piled in a knot on top of her head except for two graceful spiraled curls on either cheek. Her slanted green eyes under heavy, pointed brows had a kind of feline beauty, but her mouth was thin and severe and seemed to have frozen into a perpetual frown.

"Papa." Her voice was as businesslike as her appearance. "I'm sorry to interrupt you, but Nurse Evans wishes to see you right away. Some urgent request of mother's, I believe."

"Augusta, my dear," said her father, rising hurriedly from his chair, "I'll go at once. This is Miss Clarissa Shaw, your cousin, who will be staying with us for a while. My daughter, Miss Shaw."

Clarissa rose and took Augusta's thin extended hand. The direct gaze which met and held her own seemed a little forbidding; yet Clarissa could not take her eyes away. This is the way a real lady should look, she thought. Graceful, chic, sure of her worth.

"I hope you will be happy with us, Miss Shaw, and that you will find Zion Hill a pleasant home," Augusta said in a resonant voice. The words were graciously polite, but the manner behind them was distant. Clarissa had the impression of a woman who knew exactly the proper thing to say but who didn't mean a word of it.

The judge was already starting for the door. "I should see what Miss Evans is wanting. Augusta, perhaps you can tell Miss Shaw about the family and then show her to her room. She is in need of rest after her long journey. I will see you at supper, Miss Shaw."

Before Clarissa could answer, he was gone, taking with him some of the ease and comfort she had begun to feel. Taking his place, Augusta settled herself stiffly before the fire and came right to the point.

"How much do you know about us, Miss Shaw? Forgive me, but at times Papa tends to digress so in his conversation that he leaves out the most pertinent data."

This clipped description hardly seemed to Clarissa to fit the confident, kindly man she had been talking with. In his own way he had at least made her feel welcome. The woman who sat opposite her, poised on the edge of her chair as if for flight, would hardly do the same or would want to. She was so erect, so unbending, that she gave the impression of sheer energy locked into a body and holding itself together by the power of its will. Still, she fascinated Clarissa who, with only the Ladies' magazines to guide her, imagined this dignified reserve to be the mark of a true gentlewoman.

"I had a letter from your father in which he mentioned his wife, two daughters, and the small children of another daughter now deceased. I told him I would be happy to help with his correspondence, should he wish me to, and to assist the children with their lessons. Not having a home of my own at the present moment, I was extremely grateful for his offer of one here at Zion Hill. At the same time, I wish to make myself useful in return."

She had sensed that Augusta would prefer a clear, direct statement and she could see by the minute relaxation of the tense body that her assumption was correct. The ghost of a smile settled on the thin lips.

"You are a friend of Judge Williams, are you not?"

Clarissa felt the color rise in her cheeks. "He knew my family," she murmured.

Augusta seemed not to notice her discomfort. "I'm sorry to hear of your recent bereavement, and I'm sure the family will join me in making you welcome here at Zion Hill. I don't know how much Papa has told you of our life here, but you should know that there are two other members of the family, my brother Adam, and the children's father George Clarendon. He has lived with us since my sister Jenny died."

With a deliberate gesture she smoothed the creases of her heavy skirt. "The children had a French governess while we lived in town, but she soon found the rural life here too quiet for her taste. Since she left I am afraid their education has been sadly lacking."

"Well, I am certainly not a governess," offered Clarissa, "but my father saw that I had a good education; so I may be able to help them in their studies."

"Yes, I suppose you may." The cold eyes turned toward the flames. "As for Papa's correspondence, you will find that I take care of the most pressing matters. There may be one or two smaller things which he can turn over to you."

"Oh, but I don't want . . ." She colored again. Augusta was making it obvious that her well-meant offer of help was unwelcome. How unfortunae that she had antagonized this formidable woman at the beginning of her stay. She sat there miserable and saying nothing.

From what seemed a great height, Augusta smiled down on her. "And now, I suppose I should warn you about Adam."

Again an expectant pause. "Adam?"

"My brother. You may as well be prepared for him. He

is a bitter man, Miss Shaw. You are likely to see little of him, so just learn to ignore his caustic tongue when you do. At supper you will also meet my sister Hannah, a timid little person not much given to conversation. If all this sounds too depressing, let me reassure you that my father has many distinguished friends both in New York and in the neighborhood who often visit us. We are not solitary nor are we completely out of the reach of civilizing influences."

Obviously Clarissa was supposed to be impressed. The distinguished friends were a compensation for the caustic and drab siblings. The cool, poised voice went on.

"The Hill itself is not large, but the estate covers several hundred acres. We farm a little, graze sheep, and keep several horses. We also have a small grape arbor."

There was no mention of the ailing mother. No doubt Augusta had, with steely efficiency, taken over the management of the household from her parent. Even now she seemed to read Clarissa's mind, and the unspoken subject hovered on the air between them. Then she went on, ignoring it.

"Nancy is our house servant, and Sally McCreary, the caretaker's wife, runs the kitchen. Simon Edwards is groom, and Mr. McCreary, the farm overseer. He and Sally live in a small cottage on the other side of the stables. We have other temporary help coming and going, but these are the main servants. That about completes the picture. Is there anything you would like to ask me?"

The questions that had been tumbling about in Clarissa's mind disappeared into the air upon this direct invitation, and she found herself looking blankly into the green, unsmiling eyes. Augusta waited through a heavy silence, while Clarissa could not, to save herself, think of a thing to say.

"Well, then," Augusta Granville said, rising, "I'm sure you would enjoy an opportunity to freshen up. Supper is at seven, evening prayers at nine. I'll call Nancy."

Angry with herself for letting this dominating woman so intimidate her, Clarissa rose to follow and was surprised to see Augusta turn back and once again extend her hand. With more warmth than she had shown at an. time before, she said, "I do want you to know, Miss Shaw, that we are all of us happy to get to know you, and we do hope you will feel that Zion Hill is your home."

At the unexpected words and the sincerity behind them, something of the self-consciousness Clarissa suffered melted away. She took the other woman's hand and with real gratitude murmured an embarrassed response. It left her feeling better about the house and the Granvilles, and by the time she followed Nancy upstairs, she was almost happy at the thought of a new life in such grand surroundings.

Two

Clarissa was enchanted with her small bedroom with its Wilton carpet and serviceable green floral-striped window hangings. The two large windows looked out on the front of the house over wide meadows stretching toward a border of birch and pine in the distance. Sheep grazed on the brown, stunted grass, huddling together in their mindless communes near a long wooden trellis covered with thickly twisted bare vines.

It was late March, so the scattered sentinels of beech, ash, hickory, and elm rimming the house and meadow were leafless, their gray skeletal branches swaying in the strong breeze blowing in from the river. The house stood on a hill, and from her window Clarissa had an especially fine view of the Hudson with its little whitecaps fringing the busy traffic of sloops and barges. The beautiful waterway was a convenient highway for produce and passengers flowing down toward New York or north toward Albany. Though Zion Hill was isolated, surrounded as it was by forests, and hemmed in by a sharp rise of ground behind it, still the busy river seemed to her a familiar and welcome link with her old home on Manhattan Island. In her mind's eye she could see again the old stone farmhouse where she had lived with her parents and her brother Philip, and the thought brought with it a strange nostalgia, all the more unusual because she had never expected to regret leaving the place. The old Dutch door with its top half open to the sunny pasture, the huge stone hearth flanked by rough plank settles, her mother bending over her eternal sewing, or her father over his books—she had been so anxious to leave them behind that she had never appreciated how dear they were or how much she belonged to them.

Yet all the happy times had been before: before the pox had carried off both parents; before that terrible accident which had turned her strong, lively brother into an embittered cripple; before . . .

Something of the old panic swept over her, and she pressed her hands against her ears as though to force the memory from her mind. Then as suddenly as it had come, it was gone, and she remembered she was standing in a quietly elegant room, looking out on a peaceful afternoon. Clarissa straightened her shoulders and spoke aloud to herself.

"I must put all that behind me. After wishing for it all these years, at last I'm living in a gentle home like a real lady and I'm going to enjoy it! I'm going to enjoy it thoroughly!"

It was a familiar device and most of the time it worked. She turned back to the room, and her glance fell on a small table nearly covered with a blue willow washbasin and pitcher which someone had thoughtfully filled. The cool water she splashed on her temples was like a mild shock, and it helped to restore her outward calm. She stared at her reflection in an oval mirror over the table, a white frame encircled with painted pink roses and green ivy. Large brown eyes looked back at her from a thin face heightened by rather prominent high cheekbones and a firmly shaped mouth. Her thick hair, parted in the middle and smoothed back, was wound into a braid which circled her head—decidedly not the fashion, but very practical and easy to arrange. Fatigue and strain had left deep shadows under her eyes and a leanness to her cheeks; yet

27

there was a subdued beauty there, all the more so because she was completely unaware of it. Staring into her own eyes, all she could see was the familiar reflection of her brother's, so like her own. Such laughing, dancing eyes changed almost overnight into a transfixed stare of anguish, pleading silently for release. . . .

No more of this! She turned from the traitorous mirror and with brisk practicality opened her traveling box, which had been left in the middle of the room. With furious concentration she began to take out her clothes, shaking out the wrinkles and smoothing the creases which were the inevitable result of traveling. It occurred to her that she should probably try to rest before the ordeal of facing the Granville family at supper, but although the bed looked inviting, she knew she would never be able to relax. So she busied herself about the room, hoping to use up some of her nervous energy in settling in.

The adjoining door was not completely closed, and some movement there caught her attention. With an almost unconscious intuition she knew she was being watched and she moved softly to the door to give it a gentle push. As it opened she saw great blue eyes staring up at her from under a mass of yellow curls.

"Hello," said Clarissa.

The child stared without answering, transfixed with a paralyzing terror. Well aware that she had blundered into her first meeting with the Clarendon children, Clarissa made an attempt to put him at ease by extending her hand and speaking kindly.

"I am Miss Shaw, your new teacher. Won't you tell me your name so we shall be properly introduced?"

The child looked down at her hand, then turned his large eyes back to her face. As he stared, his cupid's mouth fell open, and Clarissa saw for the first time the blankness behind the terror in his eyes.

With a sinking feeling she began to wonder if this was a normal child or an idiot. She reached down and took his hand, which felt soft as butter in her grasp. The boy glanced down for an instant at his little hand lying in her

28

own, then quickly yanked it away and thrust his thumb in his mouth.

"His name is Georgie."

The voice was hushed and it came from the deepest recesses behind the door. This would, of course, be Mary. Clarissa hesitated a moment. Should she try to peer through the dark shaft between the door and the wall—perhaps to make a game of getting acquainted? No, she thought. Better to be direct and get it over with. 'Cuteness' was not in her nature, and she suspected that children preferred to be treated with the same respect that adults took for granted. She moved past the boy in the doorway and into the room, her skirts swishing against the frame. As she closed the door the girl behind it pressed against the wall.

"And you are Mary?" Clarissa said, extending her hand.

She was about eight years old, and someone had taught her her manners, for in spite of her shyness she took Clarissa's hand and gave her a quick curtsy.

"I'm very happy to meet you, ma'am," she muttered. Like her brother she was a pretty child with long sandy curls that had been carefully brushed and ribboned. Someone had taken pains with her dress, a lustrous dark blue wool over starched eyelet pantaloons. Both children wore thick, white cotton stockings and black slippers.

Without speaking, they both kept their intense stare on Clarissa. Obviously they were afraid of her; yet their curiosity had driven them to the door connecting their two rooms. She felt an uncomfortable sense of what to say next. Should she matter-of-factly announce that she was their new governess and leave it at that? Plenty of women with far more experience than she handled new situations that way. But from the first mention of them in Judge Granville's letter, Clarissa had given a lot of thought to her new relationship with Mary and George Clarendon. She had looked forward to working with them and hoped to build a kinder relationship than one of a mere pseudogoverness. She had no one and they had no mother. In her secret heart she hoped that there might be

29

some little reservoirs of affection they might share with each other.

Now, facing them for the first time, she found them so withdrawn and unresponsive that she was at a loss where to begin. Glancing around the room, she pointed to one of the beds at the far end.

"You have a lovely room," she said. "Is that your bed by the wall, Mary?"

A derisive smile appeared fleetingly across the child's face. "No, that is Georgie's bed. Mine is the one with the green and white coverlet."

The room served as both playroom and bedroom. At one end were the two beds and a huge oak clothes press. The wall at the opposite end was taken up by a fireplace flanked by bookshelves. Before the hearth, near the wide windows which on a good morning would flood the room with sunlight, stood a large, round mahogany table, black with age and covered with a jumble of books surrounding a camphine lamp in the center. Across the length of the wall and just above the fireplace, someone had painted (for the edification of the children or to remind their mentor?) "BRING UP A CHILD IN THE WAY HE SHOULD GO AND WHEN HE IS OLD HE WILL NOT DEPART THEREFROM." The gothic gold letters marched across a pale blue background, their path entwined with tiny birds, white-tailed deer, and cloyingly cute squirrels carrying walnuts in their paws. The whole elaborate inscription was bordered in gilt fleur-de-lys. It looked to Clarissa like some second-rate artist's idea of a children's homily, and she thought it ghastly. Ignoring it, she moved over to the round table and began to leaf through the books. There were several large nature studies with hand-tinted drawings of birds and flowers, very lovely and very expensive. She recognized one or two school primers and story collections mixed in with magazines and annuals. Then her hand strayed to a small red leather volume which also had a familiar look about it. Knowing what she would see, she opened it to the title page where in minute black etchings against the yellow background a heavy two-handed sword stood superim-

30

posed against elaborately drawn thistle and broom. For a moment Clarissa was back before her father's hearth, and she spoke aloud, almost to herself:

> Midst furs and silks, and jewels sheen,
> He stood, in simple Lincoln green,
> The center of the glittering ring—
> And Snowdoun's Knight is Scotland's King.

There was an almost imperceptible movement behind her, the faint echo of an intake of breath.

"Do you know that?" asked Mary, amazement in her voice.

Clarissa turned, the book still in her hand. " 'The Lady of the Lake'? Oh, yes. My father and I read it many times together. It's one of my favorite stories. But surely—are you able to read it?"

"Well, I can't quite get all the words, but I do like it and it has nice pictures. Mlle. Montmorency, she was our governess in New York, she said I was a very good reader."

"My father visited Loch Katrine as a boy," said Clarissa, sitting down beside the table, "and he used to tell me all about it. I suppose that is why I love the story so. When he read to me about Inch-Cailliach or the Trosach's Glen, he could see it in his mind's eye and describe it to me. I felt that I could almost see it too."

"I like the part where Roderick fights with Fitz-James, but Georgie likes the stag hunt the best."

Mary slowly edged her way to the table, her anxiety forgotten in her enthusiasm for her favorite book. Her brother stayed stubbornly near the door until, curiosity finally getting the better of him, he sidled over near his sister. He didn't speak a word, but as Clarissa and Mary leafed through the little book, examining the drawings, he watched, his eyes moving between his sister's animated face and the pictures on the page. Clarissa began to feel that her first impression of the child had been wrong. Obviously he was following their conversation and at times seemed on the verge of joining them. But when she asked

31

him a direct question, he pushed his thumb into his mouth and turned his head away.

"He doesn't talk much," Mary casually explained.

"Does he talk to you?"

"Sometimes. We have good times together. Mostly I tell him what to do and he understands me. We have our best places, like the rock castle at the end of the sheep meadow and the cave by the old mine near the river. We pretend that I am the queen and Georgie is my slave."

To Clarissa's surprise she saw a look of pure pleasure diffuse the blankness of the boy's face at this humbling assignment. His gaping mouth turned up at the edges into a dimpled smile. Clarissa reached out and gently touched the thick, unkempt curls, but he instantly jerked away from her and went to stand behind his sister's chair.

"We find pretty things," Mary went on. "Rocks and flowers, and one time I found a real bird's nest—the whole thing just as the mother bird built it. It was in a bush, but not up so high; so I was able to climb up and take it down. I didn't break it at all. Do you think the mother bird built it too low and had to leave it?"

"Perhaps. Or some animal came around to disturb her. Perhaps a cat was too close. A bird will abandon a nest when that happens, sometimes with the eggs still in it."

"Did you ever find a bird's nest?" asked Mary. "Grandpa says that you used to live on Manhattan Island, and I thought that was all houses."

"Oh, no. At least not where I lived. My father had a small farm far above the city near the Harlem River. There are still many farms and orchards there and also a village. We had woods around our house, and when I was a little girl like you, I used to climb trees and hunt for nests too. If you follow the river all the way to the end, you will come to the city. There are no more farms there now, only houses and shops."

"Will you go back to live there someday? Do you have a mother and a father waiting for you?"

The question was asked with a child's natural insensitivity, but it gave Clarissa a bad moment.

"No," she finally answered. "I had a father and mother

32

and a brother too. But they all died. Now I will stay here with you at Zion Hill for a while. Would you mind that?"

Mary didn't answer her question, but she smiled secretively to herself, and Clarissa felt that perhaps the first hurdle in their friendship had been successfully cleared.

"We had a mother, but she died too."

It was a simple statement conveying no sense of tragedy or loss. Clarissa reached for one of the nature study books and began turning the colorful pages. Mary edged nearer and leaned against her arm, absorbed in watching the pictures.

"I can show you the nest," the child said tentatively. "It's here in the room."

Clarissa looked around but could see nothing resembling a bird's nest on the mantel or shelves.

"Is it here? I would love to see it if you want to show it to me."

"It's in our secret place," Mary answered, leaning closer to Clarissa and speaking in a conspiritorial voice. "We keep everything special there. Only Georgie and I know where it is. It's our secret!"

"Oh, well, then, of course it must stay there. Perhaps someday you will want to take it out and show it to me. I can wait until then."

Mary considered the matter for a moment, struggling between her desire to share a trophy with this new friend and her concern to guard the hiding place.

"I'll tell you what," she finally said. "You hide your eyes and don't look round, and I'll get the nest out to show you. What do you say, Georgie? Is that all right?"

Without waiting for an answer, she ordered Clarissa: "Now turn to the window and close your eyes tight—very tight!"

Clarissa followed the child's directions, smiling to herself. The children assumed that because her back was turned and her eyes closed she would not know what they were doing, but it was obvious they had turned her away from the fireplace, and when she heard the bricks sliding against one another, it was not difficult to guess where the secret lay. There was much grunting and straining and a

33

few more conspiritorial whispers amid the sharp grating of the bricks. Then Mary spoke.

"All right. You can turn around now."

There on the table lay the saddest-looking nest Clarissa had ever seen. The rough handling by childish fingers had almost destroyed the perfect symmetry into which the sharp straggling twigs had once been wound.

But Mary was very proud of it. "Isn't it lovely?" she asked, watching Clarissa expectantly.

Clarissa smiled at her. "Yes, it is quite beautiful. How proud you must have been to find it."

Even Georgie beamed as he touched the little twigs and traced with his finger the faint outline of its circled interior.

"I'm going to keep it forever," Mary sighed. "Always. All my life."

Clarissa watched the girl's loving gaze. This poor bedraggled nest is a treasure to her now, she thought, and she really believes that it will continue to be one in all the years ahead. She can't know how when children grow up they make treasures of such different things—money, land, power, even the clothes they wear. What do I treasure? she wondered. To be a lady. To live in a house like this. Never to dig my fingers in the dirt again.

"We have other things in our special place. Would you like to see some of them?"

Before she could answer, there was a short knock at the door, and Nancy bustled into the room.

"Excuse me, Miss Shaw," she said, "but it is almost time for supper downstairs, and I must be getting the young ones ready for bed. I was wondering if you needed me to help you dress? I see you have already met the children."

Clarissa rose hurriedly, a little panicky at the thought of Nancy hovering over her while she dressed. "We were just getting to know each other. Thank you, Nancy, but I can manage quite well by myself. Good night, children. I'll see you in the morning, and we can continue our talk."

34

"They're good children, poor motherless dears. Cast out with no one to care, God love 'em."

The cheerful maid swept both children to her ample bosom and planted a kiss on each small forehead, which they endured with stoicism. Then she turned to tidying the room, chattering about how impossible it was for young natures to keep things neat. As Clarissa watched her, standing near the doorway with that "no one to care" echoing in her mind, it occurred to her that Nancy was probably the mysterious someone who took such pains with Mary's curls and the children's clothes. There were other women in the house, of course, but somehow she couldn't see Augusta bothering with an eight-year-old's appearance. This warm-hearted, slightly sentimental creature clucking about the playroom had probably in her own way tried to make up for the mother they had lost.

"Heaven's alive, what's this!" exclaimed Nancy as she held up the straggling nest.

Mary gave a strangled gasp. She had forgotten it was lying on the table.

"Who brought all these filthy old sticks into my clean house?" said the outraged maid. Clarissa saw the stricken look on Mary's face as Georgie began to wail.

"Oh," she said, retrieving the nest, "that's mine. I wanted to show it to the children. I . . . I found it. Yes, at one of the stage stops. It's a bird's nest, you see, in very good condition. I thought we might study it."

"Study a shabby old bunch of sticks like that! Well, I suppose you know what you're about, but it looks a terribly messy thing to bring indoors. It's dripping twigs all over the carpet!"

"Here," said Clarissa. "We'll wrap it in my handkerchief and lay it on the mantel until the morning when we can take it outside. Will that be all right? I promise you after that you will never see it again."

Somewhat mollified to have the trailing sticks netted, Nancy grudgingly agreed, and Clarissa started back to her room. Catching Mary's grateful look, she knew that once Nancy was gone the nest would quickly go back into its hiding place. She was going to have to explain somehow that white lie about the stage stop, but on the whole, she felt that her first encounter with her two young students had not gone off too badly. Not badly at all.

Three

    As the hour drew near, supper with the Granvilles began to loom before her like a dreaded ordeal. Her anxiety grew as she changed her traveling dress into one more suitable for evening—a dark blue Guernsey with a wide neckline, decorous but not daring, which she covered with a soft white shawl. Taking down her single braid, she combed her hair into a twisted cone over each ear, a style which was closer to the fashion. Her mother's small filigree silver earrings were her only jewelry. She looked at herself in the glass, satisfied, yet miserable. To be going down to dinner dressed like this was an old ambition finally realized; yet instead of a dream come true it seemed more like a nightmare.

    Entering the parlor, she found Judge Granville and his daughter Augusta already there, the one pleasant and the other as dour as she had been earlier. Gradually the room filled as the other members of the family appeared. Most of them greeted her courteously and then turned to become absorbed in their own conversations, leaving her to discreetly observe them as they moved about the room. Hannah, Augusta's sister, was a shy, pretty young woman who looked to be in her middle twenties. Her embarrassment on meeting Clarissa was painful, but she bravely forced herself to inquire about the trip from New York, then retired quietly near her father. One of Augusta's "distinguished visitors" was also present—a neighbor, Mr. Ashley, a pleasant man whose round face was almost completely eclipsed by his great whiskers and thick beard. He entered the room deeply engrossed in a conversation with Judge Granville's son-in-law George Clarendon and so gave Clarissa only the most perfunctory of greetings.

Clarissa could hardly turn her eyes from George Clarendon, attorney-at-law and solicitor-in-equity. He dominated the room. A tall man with an almost classical Byronic profile, smoky gray eyes, and blond silky hair with sideburns, he had a dramatic elegance with drew attention like a magnet. She could easily imagine how all eyes—particularly female eyes—turned when he entered a room. As if appearance wasn't enough, he also possessed a resonant baritone voice which he used to an almost theatrical effect. How could this gorgeous creature be the father of that poor delicate vacant-eyed boy upstairs? What must he feel to have such a son? Was he kind and understanding, or embarrassed and resentful? she wondered. He seemed a man so completely in control of his own studied effect that he would have little sympathy for the less-favored mortals of this world. Even a son. Especially a son!

Yet, attractive as George was, Clarissa found the most interesting person in the room to be Judge Granville's son Adam. From Augusta's description she had pictured an older man, soured on life and living on spleen. She saw instead a young, neatly dressed, black-haired gentleman of some height with a wide generous mouth and dark eyes crackling with mischief. She was surprised to see that he wore a brace on one leg and walked with the aid of an elaborately carved hickory cane. Using his stick and dragging his leg slightly behind him, he still managed himself so well and moved with such grace that she guessed he must have been born with this deformity.

Clarissa sat quietly on a sofa against the wall, relieved that no one attempted to draw her out. In fact, they seemed to have forgotten she was there. Mr. Ashley, his voice rising, his pink face deepening to magenta, waved his spectacles under George Clarendon's nose and thumped his fancy striped waistcoat to hammer home his point.

"I tell you, sir, this is one time Calhoun is in the right. The sovereign states of the Union have the inalienable right to make these decisions for themselves without a lot of pusillanimous backwoodsmen interfering in what is none of their business."

"Oh, come now, Mr. Ashley. I'd hardly call Van Buren a backwoodsman."

"Van Buren. Bosh! He'll be no help. He's completely under the domination of the president. Just let King Andrew crook a finger and he'll come running along behind. New York means nothing to him anymore. I never thought to see the day when my sympathies would lie with South Carolina, but this is one time they most emphatically do."

George Clarendon smiled patiently. "I can't see why this tariff so offends you. After all, it is the cotton industry of the South which will feel it most. And surely you don't take issue with the evils of slavery."

"No, no. It's state's rights which are at issue here. Why should that rabble down in Washington City have the right to force up the cost of our own small industries? Just you wait until it's wool and not cotton at stake. When it hits you in the pocket, then you'll know what I mean."

Adam Granville limped up beside them. "In order for King Andrew to hit lawyers in the pocket, Mr. Ashley, he'd have to place his tariff on hot air."

George glared at his brother-in-law. "I was never impressed by your knowledge of lawyers, Adam, but I yield to none in my acknowledgment of your expertise on 'hot air.'"

Adam smiled wickedly at George, then turned back to their guest. "You'd do well to be more circumspect in your conversation, Mr. Ashley, or you'll have Old Hickory up here threatening to hang *you* from a lamppost!"

"That was all talk," Ashley blustered, smoothing out his whiskers.

Judge Granville spoke quietly from before the fire. "Not so, Robert. I'm inclined to agree with the senator that when Andrew Jackson begins to talk of hanging, you can begin to look for the rope."

"Old Hickory! Bosh! Damned backwoodsman elected to the highest office in the land by rabble. He'll lead us to ruin yet, just you mark my words."

"Rabble," said Adam in mock dismay. "What a way to speak of the great American electorate. Would you prefer rule by aristocracy? Yes, of course you would. You are a true-blooded old Tory, Mr. Ashley. You love the past, tolerate the present, and dread the future."

"Well, now, I don't know about that," spluttered Robert Ashley. "There is a lot to be said for the past. And if change must come, I certainly don't see why it has to be forced upon us from Washington. Let the states regulate their own changes. That was how the Union was founded."

"By the time our distinguished president is done with his stubborn quarrel with the banks, I think we may all have real cause for alarm," George added coolly. "We are already beginning to feel the effects of a depression."

Robert Ashley groaned. "That is all we need to bankrupt us all! It is the small farmer like your father and me who will take the brunt. We'll be the ones who are hurt, as usual."

Judge Granville sat forward in his chair, turning his shoulders to peer at his friend from above his high silk stock. "Robert, I hardly think you should put yourself in the same category as the small farmer. After all, you are a very wealthy man and, even if prices rise sharply, you are not likely to feel it too much. The small farmer, on the other hand, who depends upon his few acres and limited livestock for his livelihood—a depression could wipe him out overnight. He is the man you should pity."

"I pity myself," Mr. Ashley replied stubbornly.

"Dear me," Adam exclaimed. "If a depression does

come, what will happen to all of us idle young gentlemen? We may be forced to go to work!"

"Cheer up, Adam," said George with a hint of malicious humor. "There is always the army. I hear they will take anybody these days."

"I'll be in line, right behind you!"

The delicate peal of a small bell rang from the hallway. Judge Granville rose from his chair with a sigh. "It is said that Americans can talk of nothing but money and politics. Shall we leave both subjects here in the parlor while we go in to supper? Come, Miss Shaw. Take my arm."

Inside the exquisitely appointed dining room, Clarissa was surprised to feel a glow of pleasure when she was seated next to Adam Granville. Although the room was impressive, its gilded elegance added to her sense of unreality. The heavy drapes had been drawn across the floorlength windows, and the soft flickering gold from hearth and candle sconces fell on the gleaming silver epergne in the center of the long table. Above a marble mantel the still, painted eyes of a lovely woman looked down on the scene below. Almost overcome with fatigue and the strain of being a stranger in a roomful of people who are comfortably familiar with each other, she ate sparingly, dabbling at her corn pudding and cold chicken. She hardly spoke, except to answer when a question was directed at her, and in the back of her mind she found herself wondering just how much these people knew of her background. She was relieved that they did not seem interested in drawing her out.

Then Adam's voice startled her out of her reverie. She turned to see him watching her with a curiously intent gaze.

"You are very quiet, Miss Shaw. I trust our voluble family group isn't too overpowering."

The dark eyes seemed to mock her. She grew flustered, unsure of how to answer. George Clarendon spoke up, thoughtfully covering her self-consciousness.

"You must become accustomed to Adam's little sarcasms, Miss Shaw. It is typical of his outlook on life to ridicule whenever possible, and you will have to allow yourself a few days to become adjusted to it. It's something you learn to live with, like ice and snow in the winter."

"Or flamboyant brothers-in-law," Adam smiled back across the table.

"Adam! George!" Judge Granville intervened. "Please let's not spoil our young cousin's first night with us by this incessant needling which you two so enjoy. You've hardly eaten a thing, Miss Shaw. Won't you have some more blancmange?"

"That needling is something else you have to learn to live with, Miss Shaw," said Augusta from the opposite end of the table. "Like ice and snow in winter—" She smiled sweetly at George.

Robert Ashley leaned across the table toward Clarissa, his fork poised in midair. "Now, my dear, you must not take this family too seriously. I've known them for a long time. They like to have a go at each other, but actually they are quite devoted."

"The happy hearthside!" exclaimed Adam, turning his unsettling gaze back to Clarissa. "Nancy tells me that you have already met our young friends upstairs. Since their solicitous father doesn't ask how you found them, I shall. Did you get on?"

Clarissa glanced up in time to catch the quick flash of hostility George shot across the table at Adam. Feeling a little like a minnow caught between two pike, her cheeks warm with embarrassment, she forced herself to answer civilly.

"With a little help from 'The Lady of the Lake' to break the ice, we got on very well."

"Ah, Sir Walter," said Adam. " 'Harp of the North, farewell!' Moldering and long, yet those cantos do come in useful at the oddest places."

Clarissa watched his inscrutable face, and some of her first admiration for him began to waver. It was obvious that he was not really interested either in her or the children, and his comments were really meant to annoy his brother-in-law, nothing more. She was studying the strong

42

profile, wondering what went on behind those black eyes, when she heard Augusta speaking to her.

"How do you like Zion Hill, Miss Shaw? Do you find it comfortable? This is quite an old house, you know, and has an interesting history."

Clarissa hesitated, carefully laying down her spoon on the plate. The house was a great deal grander than anything she had ever lived in; yet its peculiar mixture of shabbiness and gentility gave it a lack of cohesiveness, as though it had been stacked piece on piece haphazardly without order or design.

"It's very . . . comfortable," she said lamely.

"Oh, come now," Adam broke in. "You must do better than that, Miss Shaw. A hayloft can be comfortable, after all. A grand country estate like Zion Hill should at least deserve the appellation 'gracious,' 'charming,' 'rustic.' Or is it possible that you see the wretched old place for the wreck that it is but are too polite to say so? In that case, I congratulate you on your sound judgment."

"Speak for yourself, Adam," answered Augusta. "Personally, I like living at the Hill. It is quiet and relaxing. The countryside is very beautiful, and it is so pleasant to be near the river. Even the house has a certain fascination."

"Now that is what I mean, Miss Shaw," said the cynical voice next to her. "Press Augusta long enough and you will eventually get her to admit how much she really misses the gay social whirl of New York and how truly boring she finds the country. But first we must wade through this veneer of polite platitudes."

Augusta glared at her brother.

"Naturally Adam finds this a bit trying, Miss Shaw," George spoke up, "since he has no polite veneer of any kind. Straight through to the bone is his idea of unpretentiousness."

Clarissa decided to ignore them both and turned back to Augusta. "It is a beautiful valley," she said. "I could see that riding up here today, even though the trees are still bare."

"Ah, yes, my dear," said Judge Granville, "but just you

wait until spring comes along about May. You will think you have died and gone to heaven. Such colors and such flowering trees—it is truly a sight to see."

"I almost enjoy the fall better than the spring," added Augusta as she laid her napkin beside her plate with a careful precision. "It is a different kind of beauty but quite breathtaking."

Adam lounged back in his chair and sketched patterns on the cloth with his knife. "Yes, it should be a revelation to you, Miss Shaw, since you have, I understand, spent most of your life only twenty miles away in exactly the same kind of countryside."

Mr. Ashley leaned toward Clarissa again. "This area has many old houses, you know. Some of them go back to the days before our war for independence and saw some stirring events during that historic struggle. I hope that sometime you will visit my home in Tarrytown, Miss Shaw. If you like houses with history, you will enjoy seeing mine."

Clarissa dabbled at the soft pudding in the bowl in front of her. "Was this house involved in the war?"

Judge Granville answered. "There was a farmhouse here, as I believe I mentioned earlier, but I know of no event in the war in which it played a part. Probably it was tenanted by some farmer who was able to carry on quietly without involving his neighbors."

"Or without having to offer his house to General Washington for headquarters," added George. "I don't know how he missed that actually, for the house is just near enough to the High Road to be convenient."

"Probably because it is between villages and the Post Tavern was more convenient," suggested Augusta in her carefully enunciated phrases.

Clarissa looked up to see Adam watching her, a cryptic smile on his lips. "Yes, but you mustn't think that we don't have our own little history, Miss Shaw. Zion Hill may not have been quiet during the war, but it saw its share of devilment later."

Augusta groaned as George said disdainfully, "Trust Adam to raise old skeletons and unpleasant subjects. Really, brother-in-law, couldn't you let our young guest have at least one night's peaceful rest before dragging up these old shades?"

Mystified, Clarissa looked to Judge Granville, who smiled reassuringly. "Pay no attention to Adam, Miss Shaw. He is referring to something that happened long ago, about fifteen or sixteen years ago. A man was murdered here at Zion Hill. At least, it was called murder, although it was never proved to be."

Clarissa felt the blood drain from her face. Gripping the edge of the table under the linen cloth, she braced herself against the wood, willfully freezing her features into an expressionless mask. The judge noticed at once how white she had become, but none of the others paid her any mind. Adam was unwilling to let the subject drop.

"Tell Miss Shaw the details, Papa. I'm sure she would find them fascinating, and after all, it is the only claim to fame that this old house can offer. Murder is perhaps a poor second to General Washington's head on the upstairs bedstead, but it has its own notoriety, don't you think, Miss Shaw?"

There was that mocking scrutiny again. He must know all about me, she thought as she stared back at him blankly.

"Let me tell the story, Judge Granville," said George. Clarissa was suddenly aware that she was twisting her napkin in her lap, and she forced herself to keep her hands still while George enthusiastically warmed to his subject.

"It all revolved around this strange man, Matthias the Prophet, a sort of self-appointed preacher who built up quite a following in the area a few years ago."

Though he had barely begun, Augusta broke in, "He must have had some kind of mystical power or else some great gift of oratory. Wherever he went, he made converts who were so devoted to him that they gave him everything they owned—all their money, property, and valuables."

"Now it's my story, Augusta," said George good-naturedly and turned back to Clarissa. "I prefer to think that he was simply a shrewd charlatan who knew how to

45

work on the weakness of his followers. After all, it is not difficult to find people whose mental quirks lead them to accept the influence of a dominating personality who then has them completely at his mercy. That seems to be what happened here. The house belonged at that time to just such a person, a Mr. Reddick. He and his wife, another disciple named Allen, and the good Prophet Matthias all set up housekeeping right here at Zion Hill where they established their 'church.' "

"Don't forget, George," said Augusta, "the most significant thing about the arrangement, namely that Mr. Reddick deeded everything he owned—which was much—including the estate, to the prophet. That was his undoing."

"How could I forget that? It turned out to be a great mistake because Reddick was murdered. His body was discovered by his wife stuffed in an old wall oven in the unused part of the house—the old kitchen of the original farmhouse."

"Very convenient for Matthias," said Adam laconically.

As it turned out, it never did him much good. The prophet was eventually tried for Reddick's murder, but there was not enough hard evidence to convict him. The deeds were declared invalid, and the trial finished his popularity forever. After that he drifted off into obscurity."

"Then came the real surprise," said Augusta, breaking in again. "It was discovered that shortly before his death Mr. Reddick had sold everything he owned except this house. The deeds were all worthless because everything had been converted into cash, and *that* was nowhere to be found. Mrs. Reddick accused the prophet of hiding it away somewhere, while he accused her and Allen of the same thing. No one ever seems to have discovered what actually became of all that money."

Judge Granville spoke up for the first time. "After that the house was empty for a long time. When I was looking for a quiet place in the country I discovered it and made it my home. The land is good, and although the house had been badly vandalized while standing empty, it has still, I believe, a certain charm which overcomes its sad history. So far I have never regretted my decision."

Clarissa thought charm was the last thing she would have associated with this house, and now she knew why. It must have been from the first that the shades of violence unexorcised had touched her own distress, carried like a canker in her heart. With a sudden clarity she watched the flame of the candles before her streaking from their golden nimbus like a thing alive, setting into subdued shadows the intent faces around the table, all with their eyes turned accusingly toward her.

Then George went on in his prosaic voice, and the image vanished. "The most frustrating part of the story lies in the fact that no one has ever been able to discover whether it was old Matthias or Mrs. Reddick who absconded with the money. Allen died shortly after the trial, but the other two, well, they just dropped off the face of the earth."

"Perhaps they ran off together," Augusta suggested.

"Not without the money," answered Adam. "It was wealth the prophet was after, not souls. Of course, we don't know what she was like. If she was young and delectable, perhaps he found something that interested him more than money for once."

"Adam, please! Remember there are ladies at the table," exclaimed the judge. "A shocking man, that dreadful prophet. His name actually was Robert Matthews, and he was no more a prophet than I am. He was a greedy, worldly, evil man masquerading as a man of God! And now, I think that is quite enough of criminals and murders. There are other, more edifying interests at Zion Hill, Miss Shaw. I forgot to ask you earlier, but, do you ride, by chance?"

Clarissa answered him gratefully. "Only a little. I'm not very good at it, I'm afraid. My father had a horse which I sometimes rode around the fields or into the village."

Next to her, Adam Granville leaned forward, rested his elbow on the table, and with his hand against his cheek turned his direct gaze upon her. His black hair fell forward over his long fingers. She found herself foolishly shrinking before those dark, enigmatic eyes.

"Tell me something, Miss Shaw. I understand you are going to be helping Jenny's children with their studies. It seems curious to me that a girl from a farm on Manhattan Island would have enough education to teach. It is something of an incongruity, is it not?"

Clarissa looked down at her hands in her lap. "My father was a gentleman, Mr. Granville, with a year at St. John's College, Cambridge. He had a good education and he made sure that my brother and I received one as well."

"Judge Williams thought highly of Clarissa's father, Adam," said the judge. "I understand they had many a lengthy debate on the merits of Burke versus Rousseau."

Clarissa smiled shyly at the judge. "Yes, there was nothing he loved so much as a good, roaring intellectual argument. He read voraciously and enjoyed keeping his mind nimble even though he worked the land."

"And did you join him in these debates, Miss Shaw?" said Adam, his casual manner belied by the intensity of his gaze. "Or were you too busy churning butter and spinning flax and such other pursuits common to farm women?"

Clarissa's shyness began to give way to the stirrings of anger at his mocking demeanor. "My father believed that women as well as men have the gift of good minds. He made no difference between my brother and me in that respect. We worked hard, but he saw that we took the time to read Locke, Voltaire, Bacon, and Paine. I've lived to be grateful to him for that."

"Oh, you must forgive my amazement. It's just that the idea of a woman discoursing on the merits of Adam Smith's theory of Economics or the inner workings of the steam engine—well, it boggles the sensibilities of smaller minds."

His arrogance infuriated her. She looked straight into his eyes and said, enunciating each word, "The smaller the mind the greater the conceit!"

"Ha, ha!" Augusta threw back her head, laughing. "Hoisted on your own petard, Adam dear. Oh, Cousin

Clarissa, I can see that you are going to be an asset to this family."

Judge Granville, coughing slightly, raised his napkin to his lips, hiding the smile which he could not suppress. Adam's face above his high satin bow flushed crimson. He sat back and folded his long hands over his knee.

"Done in, not by Burke or Locke but by Aesop! I suppose I deserved that, although it pains me to make the admission. I shall have to be more careful how I needle you in the future."

It was gracefully done. Clarissa felt that her own rudeness had been appropriately chastised as well. Remembering his crippled leg, she thought how so many of the pursuits young gentlemen enjoyed would be denied this man—and riding the most bitter loss of all. Perhaps that was why he had such a flippant manner and venomous tongue. It was his way of staving off pity before you had a chance to feel it.

"I don't believe it," said George, astounded. "An apology from Adam! Bravo, Miss Shaw. You must savor it because it will probably be the last. By tomorrow you will be on the same familiar footing as the rest of us.

"Actually," he went on, "Augusta is a really superb rider. You must let her show you some of our roads and trails. Andre's Cave—now you mustn't miss that. It's a capital jaunt, just far enough for a bracing ride but not so far as to fatigue you if you're not accustomed to horses. Augusta could go there blindfolded, couldn't you, my dear? Don't you think it would be a pleasant outing for the two of you?"

Augusta looked as though she could imagine nothing she would rather do less, but she answered politely.

"I would be happy to ride over with you some day, Miss Shaw. The cave is only a natural formation of rocks making a sort of shelter. Legend has it that the infamous Major Andre spent the night hiding there when he was trying to return to New York after his meeting with Benedict Arnold. Perhaps you could accompany us, George, and make it a family outing."

Watching the exchange between Augusta and George,

Clarissa felt not for the first time that evening like an innocent and unwilling pawn in some kind of game going on around her. She was grateful when Hannah spoke up at last with what seemed like a genuine invitation.

"I often drive into the village, Miss Shaw," she said timidly. "I would be pleased to have you come along when you need anything or if you would just want to see what Sing Sing is like."

Clarissa answered with real gratitude. "Thank you, Miss Hannah. I should enjoy that very much."

Hannah had barely spoken during the meal, and Clarissa now noticed for the first time how pretty and fragile she looked. She seemed quite overpowered by the other members of the family; yet, in her quiet way, she had more sincerity and lack of pretense than any of them. If she could get to know her, Clarissa thought, get beyond those great walls of reserve, she would probably like her more than the other Granvilles.

Later in her room, Clarissa stretched between the sheets of her comfortable bed and thought back over the evening. What a strange family. There seemed to be some kind of unspoken competition going on between them all the time, with the head of the family, Judge Granville, acting as peacemaker and umpire. They did not seem to like each other very much; perhaps that was it. Under their polite needling, which never quite became an argument, there lay a lot of unspoken hostility.

Suddenly, as she sank into sleep, it occurred to her that during the whole evening no one had mentioned Mrs. Amelia Granville, the wife and mother. Nor had she appeared.

Four

Clarissa was up early the next morning, still tired from the events of the day before and filled with the restlessness of waking in a strange room. Now that it was daylight she was eager to be out of the house to see what lay outside. Hurriedly she splashed a little water on her face and wound her long hair into a net at the back of her neck. Then, wrapping a thick woolen shawl around her shoulders, she slipped quietly downstairs.

She could hear Nancy and Mrs. McCreary moving around in the kitchen on the lower level, but the front hall was empty. Glad there was no one about, she moved softly through the hall and stepped out on the long veranda. Beyond the row of wooden columns supporting the overhanging roof of the porch, a few short steps led to the gravel walk running before it. To her left the walk curved around toward the rear of the house, but off to her right it stretched out across the wide expanse of green meadow rolling toward the pewter river in the distance.

She followed the walk, hedged with low, sculptured box and young maples, to the trellised arbor where she sat on one of the stone benches enjoying the freshness of the morning. It was warm for March, with the promise of

51

sunshine later on, although now the thick dew on the grass gave a leaden moisture to the air. How pleasant, she thought, to sit quietly like this before facing the Granville family again. She glanced back at the house, gray against the rising sun. How thrilled she had been when she came here at the thought of living in such a grand country estate. Now the house seemed only to epitomize for her the misery which had dogged her life since the death of her parents. Out here in the coolness of the waking morning and away from the confining walls of Zion Hill, the happier memories of an earlier time loomed a little larger.

Her thoughts were interrupted by the crunching rhythm of footsteps approaching along the walk. With a tinge of irritation, Clarissa looked up to see Judge Granville coming toward her, his short figure rigid with dignity even as he hurried.

"My dear, I hope I am not intruding upon your meditation," he said, almost apologetically. "I saw you walking here from the upstairs window and took the liberty of sharing with you the pleasures of this most excellent morning. I hope you do not object to company." Without giving her time to answer, he sat down beside her on the bench. "I love this time of day. It gives one such a feeling of expectancy—the promise of a good day to come."

Clarissa murmured a reply, and they exchanged a few mild pleasantries. Obviously he had been up for a while because he was fully and nattily dressed. The starched collar points above his silk, padded "pudding" reached almost to his ears, and it had taken some time to arrange those elegant folds of his huge neckcloth. Then her thoughts came back to what he was saying.

"Actually, Miss Shaw, my purpose in joining you here was not merely to discuss the morning. I wished also to apologize to you for . . . for our conversation at table last night. I am sorry that it distressed you—as I could see it did. My son Adam, you must have realized by now, seems incapable of using discretion in polite society. Indeed, he takes a rather devilish pride in avoiding it. I hope you will learn to pay him no attention. These old tales about Zion Hill were bound to come up sometime, but I do wish that

52

the old ghosts could have been let lie until you were more comfortable with us."

Clarissa pulled her shawl closer across her chest. "I was a little upset, Judge Granville, and I appreciate your explanation. I know that I must become accustomed to hearing of murders and trials without going to pieces inside, but I am not quite able to do so yet. In time I hope to be."

"It is very important that you do. And time will help. It is all still too recent."

She looked up at him, and he noticed for the first time how large her eyes were for her small face. "It would help," Clarissa went on, "if I were aware of just how much your family knows about me. You see, last night I could not tell if they were speaking to my experiences directly or if it was all simply a coincidence."

"They know nothing about your past, Miss Shaw, I assure you. To them you are a distant relation who has no other home and therefore is staying with us. Believe me, when these old stories come up, they are nothing but pure chance. You mustn't let them bother you. It is your own sensitivity which causes you so much distress."

"You've been very kind—" Clarissa murmured, feeling grateful yet somewhat chastized. If only she could believe it. If only she could overcome this feeling that everywhere she went, even in this house of strangers, people were pointing accusing fingers at her.

"There is one other thing, Judge Granville." Deliberately she rose and crossed the walk to stand beside one of the slender posts of the arbor, grasping the tough, leathery vine in her hand.

"My brother . . ."

"Please, Miss Shaw. This is completely unnecessary."

She turned and faced him squarely. "I loved my brother. I admit that his paralysis often caused me to despair, both for him and for myself, but I never . . . I never could have . . ."

"Miss Shaw, you were acquitted of any responsibility for your brother's death—a death which I must say was a welcome release from an intolerable existence. You must learn now to stop thinking that people are judging you. Good heavens, haven't we all had our trials in one way or another! Yours is at least behind you."

He ran his hand over his thick hair in an uncharacteristically nervous gesture. Clarissa, remembering Mrs. Granville, was all at once a little ashamed. He smiled thinly, reading her thoughts.

"I was thinking as well of Adam. He so bitterly regretted the loss of his good leg and he must live with that the rest of his life. So you see . . ." Rising, he offered her his arm.

"I suppose I am being selfish in the extreme, seeing everything through the veil of my own troubles," Clarissa said as they started back toward the house.

He patted her arm lightly. "That is a very wise insight, my dear. If living here at Zion Hill can help you put your own difficulties in perspective, well, it will be a good thing for us all. To drown in despair would be a tragedy for one so young. Now, let us talk of something else. I came across a little book last night which I should like you to read. It's the diary of a young man who served with the American army during the war for independence. It's quite charming and will afford you a very accurate picture of the times. It might even be useful in teaching the children about those momentous days."

"I would enjoy that. Thank you, sir."

"What do you plan to do with your young charges this first day? Start them right off in their studies?"

"I had thought rather to go easy, since it's our first time together. I would like to know just how far they've come in their books, but I hope to win a little of their trust before setting them to work."

"Some might say that is a little too easy-going for a proper academician, but I think you may be wise. After all, you are not strictly a governess, and they are good children."

"Mary is a charming girl, and Georgie is only terribly shy, I think. At least, that is how he strikes me."

"Oh, I assure you he is. So different from Adam who was a veritable devil at that age. Drove every governess we hired straight out the door! No, sometimes I wonder if our little Georgie is not too subdued for his own good. Perhaps you will be able to draw him out."

They had reached the end of the walk. Standing before the high walls of Zion Hill, Clarissa was struck once more with the utter shabbiness of the place. In the evening dusk of the day before, the house had seemed worn but welcoming. Now, close up, even the growing sunlight could not bring warmth to its million flecks of peeling paint and sagging tiles.

Judge Granville was looking not at the house but down toward the river, in the distance already dotted with the brightly colored sails of the Hudson sloops. A smile of satisfaction rested on his broad face. Watching him, Clarissa felt that he embodied something of the same incongruity. He seemed so sure of himself, a man who had come to complete terms with his world. Yet, behind him in this depressing house lay enough family problems to make the strongest man quake. Had he truly mastered them and found peace? To look at his quiet dignity and placid countenance one would think so. Yet, without knowing what it was, Clarissa could not help but feel there was something there which shouted a lie to the whole picture. She turned back toward the pitted walls of the shadowed doorway. Just like this house.

When they entered the parlor they found most of the family already gathered for morning prayers. Judge Granville had initiated this custom when his children were young, and he insisted on maintaining it, even though he suspected his now-grown children attended more from duty than fervor. Before he opened his well-worn prayer book to family prayers, the two young Clarendon children joined the adults in the room. Mary looked bright as a penny in a white muslin dress with a long pink sash and a pink ribbon in her golden curls. Her brother was dressed in a smaller version of his father's morning suit—long trousers and a little velvet jacket. Only a large black bow at his collar differed from the high collar points and exquisitely arranged neckcloth of the older man. Mary, without a glance at anyone else, went straight to her papa and kissed him on the cheek perfunctorily. Her brother seemed to quiver in his shoes as George Clarendon extended his hand and gave his son a manly handshake. Clarissa sensed something akin to disdain on the handsome features of the older man as he looked down on the timid, frightened creature who was his only son. After acknowledging the rest of the family and receiving in turn a pat on the head from Augusta, a warm embrace from Hannah, and total indifference from Adam, they retired to the sofa against the wall. As she sat down, Mary threw Clarissa a fleeting half-smile, then went quickly back to arranging her dress.

After the brief prayer service the children disappeared downstairs to take their breakfast in the kitchen, while the family moved into the dining room at the end of the hall. Still not hungry, Clarissa was relieved that everyone seemed anxious to be about the day's business and not interested at all in her. As soon as decency permitted, she escaped upstairs.

The entire morning was spent with the children, getting to know them and beginning to nurture the tender roots of trust which she hoped would eventually flower into friendship. Everything she had ever heard about governesses had led her to expect a wild, unruly session; yet she found that with these two, the problem was not to curb their high spirits but to draw them out from behind their wall of taciturn solitude. Their studies had not been neglected, but they had followed an erratic course—excellent tutors for a time followed by long periods of none at all. Mary had a bright inquiring mind which Clarissa felt it was going to be a pleasure to nurture, while Georgie, though he would barely respond with one spoken word, nevertheless seemed to follow intelligently any discussion between his sister and his new teacher. On the whole, Clarissa felt it was an encouraging morning.

Her efforts with the children were not in vain, for by the time they went downstairs for luncheon, Mary was urging Clarissa to take them for a walk that afternoon. She had expected to use that time for herself, but aware of the compliment the children were paying her, she readily agreed to join them.

"But I'll just have to make sure that your grandfather has no work for me in his study first," she said, retying Mary's sash.

"Oh, Grandfather will let you go if we ask him, I'm sure," said Mary. "You only just came here, and he should like you to see the farm. We can walk down to the river and we'll show you the old mine."

"Mine? There's a mine by the river?"

"Well, it's not a mine anymore. Now it's just a big cave and we play in it sometimes. But it was a real mine once. At least, that's what Grandpa said."

"I think I should like to see this mine very much, but let me speak to Judge Granville first."

"All right. But I'll ask him too. Just to be sure."

Whether it was because of Mary's influence or it was true that the judge had no pressing correspondence, she was sent off with the children readily enough. The promise of early morning had fulfilled itself in the bright sunshine which showered the brilliant green fields stretching toward the woods in the distance. The air was warm——that deceptive warmth which suggests that spring is almost here when in fact it is still a month away. Knowing this, Clarissa was still able to enjoy the hope it raised in her heart. Away from the house she found that she, like the children, was free of the tension that prevailed there. They walked for almost two hours, following a well-worn path through the trees to where a small stream bubbled its way to the river below. Then they paralleled the river through the forest which lined its edges toward a narrow clay path which wound back toward the High Road and the house, stopping along the way to peer into the darkened entrance of the old unused copper mine.

As if reluctant to go back to the house even then, they cut back across the meadow to the far side where they had started, and visited the barn and stables.

At the barn Clarissa met the steward of Zion Hill, Angus McCreary, a tall, cadaverous Scotsman with calloused hands and a thin smile. Aloof at first, he relaxed a little when he learned that Clarissa was accustomed to farms and he then took time to show her the way they handled the wool from the Hill's many sheep, shearing and baling it for delivery to the homes of the local spinners in the area.

The stable was not large, five stalls along each side and a wide paddock adjoining. At the familiar pungent manure and straw odors Clarissa felt a tinge of nostalgia. The children clambered immediately to one of the larger stalls where a mottled gray pony with a thick white mane was munching at the hay. Near the door Clarissa saw Georgia stop briefly to retrieve a handsome leather riding crop with a silver handle that was lying on the straw. Holding it tightly in one hand, with the other he lovingly stroked the pony's sleek neck. Then, to Clarissa's astonishment, he launched into his first direct conversation.

"This is Aunt Hannah's pony, Straw-boy. Isn't he pretty? I just love him."

Straw-boy seemed delighted at the unexpected arrival of company. He left his snack and began to nuzzle the children, expecting a treat.

"He's lovely," Clarissa said. "Affectionate and gentle, just what a pony should be and so often isn't."

"Sometimes Aunt Hannah takes us for rides in the cart," said Mary, reaching into the pocket of her apron and pulling out two small sections of a carrot purloined from the kitchen. "I saved these from the trash," she explained. "Everyday I try to bring something for Straw-boy when we visit him. Here, Georgie. This one is yours."

Greedily the pony nuzzled the boy's hand, setting him giggling at the tickling wet lips.

"You children are going to make that pony fat!"

Clarissa recognized the disapproving voice before she turned to see Adam framed in the doorway. She made a quick decision to meet his disdain with an aggressive cheerfulness and gave him a broadly smiling, "Hello."

"And look at you both," he went on, a scowl deepening his dark brows. "Your boots are covered with muck and your clothes are a disgrace. Furthermore, I found the

58

wicket gate left open again. That kind of carelessness will not be tolerated."

"Oh, that must have been my fault," Clarissa started.

"Don't make excuses for these children, Miss Shaw. That's doing them no favor. Young man, I'll thank you to take your hands off that crop. How many times have I told you to leave my tack strictly alone."

The riding crop dropped as though it had become a molten bar, and Georgie melted into the shadows. Clarissa could almost sense his trembling, and she felt the hot flush of anger on her cheeks. This would happen just when the boy was beginning to open up a little.

"Really, Mr. Granville. We have been for a long walk which is bound to leave them untidy, and I apologize for the gate. It won't happen again. I'm sure Georgie didn't realize—after all, the crop was lying on the ground and it does have such an attractive handle. And the pony—" She smiled feebly. "A little treat can't harm the pony, and it's such a pleasure for them."

She was fighting to keep her composure, but the sardonic smile her words brought to Adam Granville's face was almost too much.

"Miss Shaw," he began, slapping the crop against his gloved hand, "I'm sure you are well educated for a female or my father would not have asked you to teach these children. But your habits of mind are deplorable. Excuses for everything. The young must learn responsibility. You will not help them by trying to cover for their every mistake. A fat, indolent pony is not much good to anyone. There must be something more constructive these children could be doing."

It was useless to attempt to be pleasant with this man. "Perhaps you would prefer to see them put to work in the fields," Clarissa said icily.

He looked startled. "Well, as a matter of fact, most of the local children of their age have already become accustomed to hard work. It is only the idle sons and daughters of the gentlemen farmers who are allowed to fritter away their early years with whirligigs and dreams. Gainful employment never hurt anyone, I'm sure."

"And what gainful employment do you profit from, I wonder, Mr. Granville? I am not overwhelmed by the signs of your usefulness, but then perhaps they are hidden from the eyes of ordinary mortals."

A pink flush rose from her neck to her temples as she heard her own silly words. Once again she had allowed this irritating man to provoke her to rudeness against her will. Sparks flew from Adam's eyes for an instant, then faded almost as quickly as they had appeared. He watched her, a tight smile on his lips.

"So. Our mousy little cousin has spirit. I believe this is twice now that you have met my dagger with your parry. Touché for you, Miss Shaw. I retire, disarmed."

"Wait, please!" Clarissa impulsively moved toward him as he turned to leave. "I'm sorry I was rude both now and last night. But you are provoking, you know. Why should you begrudge these children a few years of pleasure? They will discover soon enough the burdens and responsibilities of life."

Adam glanced quickly at the children, his face unreadable. "Why, indeed," he muttered and limped away.

At the approaching clatter of hoofs Clarissa turned to see Augusta cantering up on a beautiful, sleek, black stallion. A marvelous horsewoman, her dark blue habit and smartly plumed hat were a perfect complement to her expert handling of the big horse. She reined up near a mounting block and dismounted, throwing the reins to Simon Edwards who was riding groom behind her.

"Rub him down well, Edwards, then turn him out to pasture. He's earned his pleasure."

She stopped momentarily to fondle the horse's nose and rub her cheek against the flat headbone. Her habitual glower was diffused by a soft smile. Then she saw Clarissa watching, and the dourness returned.

"This is Sultan," she said with pride. "I raised him from a foal. Isn't he beautiful?"

"He certainly is," Clarissa answered, hoping that she would never be asked to ride such a powerful and high-spirited animal.

Augusta caught up the long train of her skirt and fell in

beside Clarissa walking toward the house. Behind them the children trudged along, kicking at the gravel.

"Did I see you talking to Adam? Don't bother to answer. I can tell by the look on your face that you were and it was unpleasant as usual."

"He doesn't think the children should feed Hannah's pony, but I was unable to tell if his disapproval was inspired by concern for the pony or merely by animosity for the children."

"I can tell you that if the pony swelled up and fell down dead this instant, he wouldn't care a fig. He simply enjoys annoying people."

Clarissa shook her head. "It seems a strange method of finding pleasure. Is there nothing or no one he genuinely cares for?"

There was a pause before Augusta answered. "Yes. There was one person, once. And, although I don't mean to be making excuses for him, you should bear in mind that his accident has made him bitter. He is inclined to vent his anger at whomever is about."

"Was it an accident, then, that caused his lameness?"

"Oh, yes. He was young and a daredevil. He was trying to ride a really unmanageable horse, and it threw him, shattering his leg in the fall. Actually, he was very lucky. He could have so easily been killed. But my brother was never one to look for the good side of a thing when there was so much to be got out of the bad. You must try not to let him bother you. That is how I handle him. I refuse to be provoked. Then he and George are free to go round and round and enjoy it to the hilt."

Augusta's words carried an echo of bitterness; yet there was much in what she said. "You are probably right," Clarissa answered. "Actually, for myself I don't care how much he tries to hurt, but I am sorry that the children are made to suffer for his bad temper."

They had reached the low steps to the veranda. Augusta hitched up her train and started toward the door.

"Children should not be pampered. They might as well learn early that life is hard and cruel. I'll see you at tea, Miss Shaw."

61

Bemused, Clarissa watched her go. No wonder these children had retreated into their private world. And what was so hard and cruel about the life Augusta led? she wondered. She turned to wait for Mary and Georgie trudging up the path behind her. They looked so young and vulnerable. What kind of woman had their mother been? she wondered. Did they remember one warm, loving person now gone forever? It had only taken one morning for her to realize that when she was with them she thought less about her own troubles, in that way children have of drawing you out of absorption with yourself. In the long run, she thought, they may help me as much as I hope to help them.

It was almost a week before Clarissa had her first encounter with Mrs. Granville. She had almost forgotten about her except to wonder now and then what kind of illness would wither away a "generally robust" woman from her rightful place within her family.

Then one morning she was sitting in her room after breakfast when she heard a low, sing-song voice in the children's adjoining bedroom. It was all the more strange because she knew Mary and Georgie were below in the kitchen with Nancy. Curious, she laid down her brush and moved to the connecting door. A neatly dressed woman was sitting on the floor in the middle of the room, her skirts billowing around her, cradling Mary's French doll in her arms. Her long white hair was twisted into one strand which hung over one shoulder and down the front of her dark silk dress. Sensing someone was watching her, the woman glanced up, and Clarissa caught at her breath.

The face was that of a mature woman and incredibly beautiful. Her skin was like porcelain, her lips perfectly shaped. Green eyes, slightly slanted, looked out at Clarissa through thick lashes, very black in contrast to her white hair. She smiled and stretched out a beautifully shaped hand, clutching the doll and rocking back and forth.

"Good morning," she said in a cultured voice. "Who are you?"

It was the lady of the portrait in the dining room. Clarissa stepped closer, fascinated by the beauty of this creature and wondering why she was sitting on the floor. This curious lady had to be Mrs. Granville; yet, judging from her plump cheeks and ample figure, Clarissa saw that she was certainly no consumptive. Then, as she looked into the white face, she saw with a dreadful clarity the vacant blankness in the green eyes. A sudden coldness touched the back of her neck.

"I . . . I am Clarissa Shaw, Mrs. Granville. Your cousin from New York. I've come to stay with you for a while."

"Oh, well, I suppose that is all right. Only we must tell the queen. She must know, of course. She has to know everything."

The prickling chill spread down Clarissa's back. Mrs. Granville drew herself up, still clutching the doll.

"I am the queen, you know. Only don't tell anyone. It is a secret. Can you keep a secret?"

"Well, yes. I suppose so."

"You may kiss my hand," she said, regally extending her fingers only to yank them away. "You haven't come to take my baby, have you? You can't have my baby!"

Suddenly the empty green eyes went dark, and she jerked back, grasping the doll's head and twisting it.

"No, no!" Clarissa cried, concerned for Mary's doll. "Please. I won't take her. You can keep the baby."

"Oh, that's better then. The old queen, she spoke to me just yesterday. She speaks to me often, you know. It's not easy running an empire, and I must have her help. I just don't know how I could bear all the burdens, the decisions, if she did not tell me what to do." She looked blankly up at Clarissa again. "Why are you here? Have you come to take my baby?"

"No, no . . ." Clarissa took a step backward, inching toward her door, but with a sudden flash of her hand Mrs. Granville reached up and grabbed at her collar, pulling her face down near her own.

Her mood changed abruptly. "Isn't she pretty?" she

said sweetly. "Such a pretty baby. All my babies were lovely. Just like me, someone—who was it?—said . . ."

"She's very lovely." Clarissa tried to disentangle the fingers from her dress, her desperation to leave the room growing stronger every minute.

All at once Mrs. Granville released her grasp and sat back, a triumphant smirk on her face.

"Ha! That's a joke on you, my pretty miss. This is not a baby, it's only a doll."

Clarissa was completely taken aback. All she wanted now was to get out of the room, but before she could move, the woman grasped the doll by the neck and began bashing its china head against the floor.

"Think you're so smart, do you! Ha, ha! Bad! Bad girl! Punish you!"

"No, please don't break it . . ." Clarissa cried and reached to rescue Mary's lovely French doll from her sinewy hands. For someone who appeared fragile, the woman had a terrible strength, and in only a few seconds their struggle became a tug of war with the poor doll nearly ripped apart between them. Mrs. Granville's hysterical cries grew louder with every stubborn yank and pull.

"Stop! Stop this instant! What the devil do you think you're doing?"

At the ringing authoritarian voice both women halted at once. Clarissa looked up to see the doorway filled with a wide expanse of black broadcloth supporting a bloated red face, furious with rage. In that instant she weakened her grip on the doll, and Mrs. Granville tore it from her hands and threw it furiously across the room where it landed with a thudding clink of cracked china. Then, grabbing her long skirt, she threw it completely over her head and sat impassively, a dark, rigid figure on the floor.

Clarissa thought at last to flee the room, but the nurse in the doorway bore down on her too quickly. She was as forbidding as her charge was horrible. Her thin, graying hair was pulled back in a tight knot at the back of her head; her lips were an almost straight line in the heavy folds of her face. Her eyes were like tiny black holes, and they bristled with outrage and hostility. Leaning over the rigid woman sitting on the floor, she spoke in the voice of a strict governess reprimanding an unruly child.

"Miss Amelia, get up! Remember yourself! Put your skirt down and stand up like a lady at once, do you hear!"

Clarissa almost waited for Miss Amelia to receive a smart slap on the wrist; yet evidently the woman knew what she was doing. Amazingly, Mrs. Granville threw her skirt back down over her petticoats and slowly rose from the floor, her head hanging. Then, like a full-rigged warship going into action, Nurse Evans turned on Clarissa.

"Who the devil are you? What are you doing here and how dare you upset the madam like this? Haven't you got any sense at all?"

"Now just a minute. I am her cousin, Clarissa Shaw, and my room is just next door. I didn't mean to upset her, but it seemed such a shame to break Mary's doll."

"You didn't mean! Well, that's just what you have done. Look at her, crying and blubbering like a spoiled baby. I'll be lucky to get her calmed down by evening, and there won't be no peace for the rest of the day. You stupid girl!"

She grabbed the blubbering woman by the arm and began propelling her to the door. "Come along, madam. You are a bad, bad girl to have left your room. For shame! Naughty. Come now and have your breakfast."

"I don't want any . . ." Mrs. Granville whimpered. "Naughty, naughty. No breakfast . . ." and she broke into loud sobs.

Miss Evans tried to make her voice conciliatory, which, considering her tone, Clarissa thought was no mean feat. "Oh, stop that now. A little tea and you'll feel better. Merciful God! What a day we're in for!"

She glared at Clarissa. "The next time you find her loose like this, just you call me. Don't try to argue with her."

Through the doorway Clarissa could see Hannah, who had been drawn from her room by the noise. She went straight to her mother and, putting her arm around her shoulders, led her to a window seat at the end of the short hall. Gradually the distraught woman seemed to grow calmer under her daughter's gentle ministrations.

Moving over to where the nurse stood glaring down the hall, Clarissa made one more attempt to explain her perplexity in handling someone like Mrs. Granville.

"It's little enough you'll have to deal with her," Miss Evans snapped back. "I keep her out of everyone's way. She has her own rooms and hardly never leaves them. Now and then I turn my back—a body can't be alert every instant—and she's off like a willful child. But you don't need to do nothing—anything—if you find her. Just holler for me, that's all."

"But surely if I knew how, I could talk to her a little." Clarissa felt her protective instincts surging toward the poor senile woman as they had toward her grandchildren. But Miss Evnas was having none of it.

"Don't talk to her at all! I'm her nurse. I'll do all the talking she needs. You take care of the chil'ern and don't go meddlin' in what don't concern you."

At length she led Mrs. Granville away, while Clarissa and Hannah stood looking after them.

"Well, really. That's the most unsympathetic nurse I've ever encountered," she said to the small woman beside her.

"Her nature is not very kindly, is it?" Hannah replied. "Yet it can't be easy taking care of Mother the way she is now, a grown woman with the mind of a child. You look a little shaken, Miss Shaw. Why don't you come and sit on the window seat for a moment until you get your composure back."

Suddenly aware of her trembling knees, Clarissa gratefully accepted Hannah's invitation. If only Judge Granville had warned her. "Slight indisposition" indeed! Why, the woman was witless.

"You mustn't think poor Mother suffers, Miss Shaw," said Hannah as she sat primly down beside her. "She has her own apartments, but we each of us go in every day to visit her, and Papa spends part of each afternoon with her."

"It must be difficult for all of you to see her this way."

"It's heartbreaking. Especially for Papa and Adam and Augusta, who remember her as she was. She began to change when I was very young; so I have only the dimmest memories of her as herself. Yet, hard as it is for us, it must be many times more difficult for her. Are you feeling better now?"

"Yes, thank you. I am afraid Miss Evans was right in one way. I did behave stupidly. I should have let her break the doll. Next time I shall know better."

"Perhaps. But Miss Evans should have been watching Mother more closely. She is not supposed to let her out of her sight. Papa won't like it a bit, and I shouldn't be surprised if he reprimands her for her carelessness."

"Oh, dear. She'll probably hold that against me too. It's been a dismal beginning to the day all round."

"Well, the sun is shining, and Mother is back in her nest. Perhaps the rest of the day will be better."

"You know, Miss Hannah," Clarissa said impulsively, "you are a very nice person."

Hannah blushed to the roots of her dark blond hair. "You don't know me very well," she said quietly.

Clarissa went on. "And you are probably right. The rest of this day has got to be better." Silently she added to herself: I've survived Mrs. Granville and Miss Evans. Now if I can just avoid Adam, I may make it through to evening!

Five

The rain had continued steady for days, a gray, dismal constant drip which kept everyone indoors. Its chill dampness spread through the house so deeply that Clarissa thought she would never be warm again. Even Judge Granville, his morose air more subdued then ever, went about with an old plaid shawl draped around his shoulders. The long wet days and enforced idleness that made the children almost unmanageable at the same time depressed Clarissa's spirits terribly. Irritable and sad, she couldn't seem to wrench her mind from thoughts of her lost family.

Then, just when sunshine seemed all but forgotten, it burst over the world again, turning the morning to a shimmering gold. The heavy clouds moved out over the great ocean, and the day dawned clear and newly washed.

After breakfast Hannah stopped Clarissa on the stairs. "I thought this would be a perfect day to drive into the village," she said. "By this afternoon the roads should be somewhat dried out, and I need some silks and ribbons for a hat. Would you care to come?"

Clarissa was delighted. She gave the children their lessons that morning on the veranda, so anxious were they all to be outside again. Then, after lunch, she wrapped her cloak around her shoulders, took a few coins from the small sum she had hoarded after the sale of her father's farm, and climbed into the pony cart where Hannah sat waiting.

The little cart was just the right size for two women. Hannah was a skillful driver, but her talents were almost not needed, since Straw-boy seemed to know just where to go by himself.

"He almost resents my interference," she explained.

Clarissa laughed. For the first time in days she felt almost lighthearted. "He's a lovely pony. I'm ashamed to confess it, but I feel much more comfortable with him than I would on Augusta's Sultan."

"Oh, Miss Shaw," replied Hannah with feeling. "How glad I am to hear you say that. I'm terrified of Sultan, he's so big and fast. Adam and Augusta would always ride any horse, the harder to manage the more they enjoyed it. But I could never get over my fear no matter how hard I tried. And I did try very hard once; but now I just drive my pony and let them scoff. I could never keep up with them in anything."

"Please call me Clarissa. Everyone else does now . . . except Adam, but that doesn't signify."

"What a pretty name. Clarissa it is then." Her delighted smile gave Hannah's face an unusual animation. She has some of her mother's beauty, Clarissa thought. More than her sister Augusta, whose natural beauty was obliterated by her habitual dour expression.

The pony ambled through the iron gates of Zion Hill and out onto the wide hard-packed dirt road leading north. "This is the High Road which your stage took up from town," Hannah explained. "It runs north to Bennett's Corners, then angles off toward the river." The wide road was lined with trees, huge oaks, elm, and ash, whose branches reached across the path to link hands. In the summer, the road would wear a canopy thick with leaves. To the right the ground rose steadily toward the high hills beyond. They passed patches of heavy wood at scattered intervals, but most of the land was cultivated, fenced either into small farms or grazing pastureland. At Bennett's Corners Clarissa recognized the two squat buildings where Edwards had met her on her arrival from New York. One was a grubby smithy's shop, and the other, an ancient, rundown meetinghouse.

When the road turned toward the river it grew narrower and the overhanging brush even thicker. There were no fields here, the ground being too rough and uneven, but occasionally they passed a neat little cottage with a patch of vegetables alongside. Through the trees Clarissa could glimpse the river, very wide at this point, a still, glassy blue mirroring the sky above it.

Hannah pointed to the left where the road forked down to a small cove. "That's Mr. Kemey's property. He owns a lot of land around here. Most of the small houses belong to the local fishermen. And up ahead is the Old Post Tavern. It's sometimes called 'the Jug.' We'll stop there on our way home for tea—if you're agreeable."

The tavern was built right into the hillside, a simple shingle building with rock and daub walls and at each end two chimneys rising over the sloping roof. It was built Dutch-style, with four narrow wooden posts supporting the roof and a slim porch running along the second story.

"It was once a stage stop," Hannah went on, "before the turnpike was rerouted. Now it is mostly a tavern, but Mr. Acker keeps a little room for ladies to take tea while the men have their pints in the common room. All very proper."

Three roads met on the bridge in front of the tavern. As the pony continued north Clarissa looked toward the river where one narrow trail wound its way toward a cluster of houses and the tall masts of sloops in the distance.

Hannah noticed her interest. "That is Sparta down there. It's a small place, but it has some enterprising businesses and one or two stores. I happen to prefer Mr. Carpenter's store in Sing Sing; so I don't usually trade there. Also, it is too near the state prison farm, which I find somewhat oppressive."

"I heard about the state prison farm before I came to Zion Hill. Is it as terrible a place as they say?"

70

"No. For a prison I believe it is quite modern and enlightened. But the prisoners work in the limestone quarry in Sparta, and one can't help but notice the wretched creatures in their drab gray clothes, guarded by men with long rifles. And now there is talk of bringing in women prisoners, even of constructing a special building on the grounds of the state farm to house them! It's such a—a shocking idea! I was quite unnerved at the thought of coming across such a sight and I decided then and there not to go to Sparta any more than I could help. Actually, it is too bad, because some very fine people live there and the dock is quite a busy place."

Clarissa felt her hands trembling. How close had she come to finding herself among such a group? What would Hannah think if she knew? Nervously she fidgeted with the ribbons of her hat and said in an offhand manner, "Does Sing Sing have no dock then?"

"Oh, yes. And they are both quite busy places. However, I think there was some dissension about levies on produce arriving at Sparta which had the town fathers in Sing Sing terribly upset. Since the new turnpike road is so much more convenient for Sing Sing, I fear Sparta may suffer in the long run for their greed. So Adam says, at any rate."

Clarissa was suddenly aware of Hannah's animated conversation. Gone were the quiet shyness and hesitation so prominent when she was around the other members of her family. At those times one might think her a little slow, when actually she had a keen and inquiring mind. Loosening the ribbons, Clarissa removed her hat to let the warm sun play on her face and smiled to herself. The beautiful dappled countryside and Hannah's comfortable companionship led her to feel more at peace with herself than she had for months. For the first time since she had arrived at Zion Hill she was almost happy. Without being aware of it, she was beginning to heal. Like waking up one morning, she thought, and realizing that where a painful sore had been, there was now only a dull ache.

A bend in the road brought them at length onto the main street of Sing Sing, and Clarissa hurriedly replaced her hat. Though not a large town—it was scarcely more than a small square with a long tail of a road reaching down the hill toward the river—yet it had a settled coziness. There was a small dignified hotel, several stores, and a blacksmith's shop—all interspersed by neat little houses. The grassy market square lay emerald green in the sunshine, surrounded by the brown track of the road, still thick with mud from the rain.

Hannah sat straight-backed on the seat of the cart, her gray squirrel pelerine rippled by the soft wind that also heightened her creamy complexion with its coolness. "The next time we come," she said, "we'll have to make sure it's on market day. In the summer and autumn there are wonderful fruits and vegetables, flowers and dried herbs, and all the best produce from the river—oysters, and clams, eels and crabs and bass and sturgeon. The river is estuary here, but above Sing Sing it changes to fresh water. So, we have the best of both worlds."

She guided the pony to a shaded spot under an old black oak and fastened the reins to a hitching post. Stepping carefully on the planks laid across the thick mud, they made their way toward a wooden building with a wide sign across its front: "D. Carpenter—General Store"—a low wooden building composed of two long rooms connected by a door in the center wall. The street door led into the grocery side of the store where entering customers were greeted with the wonderful pungent odors of coffe, spices, leather, and new wood from the handcrafted barrels along the wall. Clarissa wandered among the crammed aisles trying to take it all in at once—sugar, tea, chocolate, rice, and great wooden firkins of butter and cheese. Then they moved through the connecting door to the adjoining room where stacks of brightly colored woolen cloth, expertly spun and dyed by the local women, lay piled almost to the low ceiling. There were boxes of yarn and ribbon, spools of silk, bolts of guernsey, bombazine, and peau-de-soie. There were stacks of newly turned hogsheads from the copper shop in Symsville, and farm implements piled haphazardly among

72

rows of boys' and men's hats and shoes of simple black and drab.

While Hannah fussed over matching colors of silk, Clarissa browsed through the shop until she found herself at the rear, facing a table set apart for the particularly fine work done by local artisans. Beautifully patterned quilts and heavy woven coverlets in intricate designs were neatly stacked next to hand-hammered copper jewelry made of metal from the local copper mine. Delicate flowers formed of tiny shells gathered from the shore of the river, and silver filigree work vied for space with painted enamel boxes and carved wooden figures of an untutored primitiveness.

Clarissa saw an unusual lavaliere lying unobtrusively in a corner, which drew her eyes at once. It was a lovely thing, obviously done by a talented craftsman with a crude, yet delicately beautiful, hand. Staring up at her from the table was the painted face of a young girl with blue eyes and a long braid of yellow hair. Her white neck rose above a dress of deep blue, almost indigo. There was a delicacy in the faint smile on the lips and the narrow black ribbon around the throat, even though the artist was obviously untrained. It had been painted on ivory and set in a tin frame carefully encircled with dainty shell flowers in pale hues of gray, beige, and pink, and it hung on a narrow black velvet ribbon. Clarissa was enchanted with it. For a long time she had not looked at any ornament, indeed she had not cared what clothes she wore on her back. Now she remembered that her best dress was a gray silk made for her by her mother and carefully packed away. How pretty this lovely thing would look against the pearl shimmer of that dress. She was so intent on picturing the two together that she did not hear Hannah behind her until she spoke.

"That must be one of Ellie Dawson's trinkets."

"I think it is lovely," Clarissa said, holding the necklace up to the light. "Does this Ellie Dawson live in Sing Sing? Does she make these in her home? She has a talent, I should say."

"Actually it is her son who has the talent. He would

like to be a painter but, of course, has never had the opportunity to study. He takes these likenesses from prints in the chronicles and paints them up in his own way. Then his mother decorates the frames. It takes a long time altogether; so I don't suppose they realize much money from them."

"How do they live then?" Clarissa asked absently, absorbed in the brushwork and colors of the miniature.

"Oh, like most people, they have a little farm. They try to make something extra with things like this. I believe the coverlets are Ellie Dawson's work also."

"You know, Hannah, I would really love to have this lavaliere. It would cost a whole dollar, which is a lot of money, but it's been such a long time since I've really wanted anything. I'm so tempted to buy it."

Taking the pendant from Clarissa's hand, Hannah held it up against her slim neck, appraising it seriously. "Yes," she said, "I think it would look well on you. Have you anything special to wear with it?"

"A gray silk dress my mother made for me."

"Gray. Yes, the blue would look lovely with gray, especially if it is a soft, subtle tone. If you have the dollar to spare, I do think you should buy it. After all, we ladies must pamper ourselves once in a while, don't you think?"

Clarissa made her decision with a singing heart and a delicious feeling of shared camaraderie. It almost made her tremble to think of giving up a dollar from her precious horde; yet she was so delighted to have the necklace that she felt the happiness it gave her worth the loss. This money from her father's farm was the only estate she would ever have, but she had used it very sparingly and was determined to be even more careful with what was left.

"Oh, but, Hannah," she suddenly thought as she handed the lavaliere to Mr. Carpenter and rummaged in her beaded purse for the coins. "I only brought one dollar with me, and if I spend it here, I can't afford tea on the way home."

Hannah laid her little gloved hand on Clarissa's arm.

"Don't worry a minute about that," she said gently, "I'll get the tea today, and the next time you can treat me."

As the fat pony jogged along the road homeward Hannah told Clarissa a little more about Ellie Dawson and her talented son. "It was long before we moved here, of course, but the story is well known. She was the daughter of a rather prosperous farmer, very pretty and gay, who was caught 'in flagrante delicto' as they say. Everyone knew the lover was a handsome, itinerant painter who had been hanging around Sing Sing trying to earn a living by doing likenesses. He must have been a man of low character, because he ran away soon after, leaving poor Ellie a fallen woman.

"Her father was a stern Anabaptist, and he married her off just before her son was born to Caleb Dawson, a fisherman far below her, who proceeded to make poor Ellie's life misery itself before he died in a storm. They say that Ellie's father was being egged on by that horrible Matthias, the preacher who had a lot of influence around here then. He turned his religious wrath on Ellie and had her all but stoned in the marketplace, like the adulterous woman in the Gospels."

"Wasn't he the one involved in the murder at Zion Hill?" asked Clarissa.

"So the story goes." Hannah flicked the reins against the pony's back, and he took a few quick steps before settling back into his lazy ramble. "Ironic, isn't it. 'Cast the first stone' and all that. Anyway he got what he deserved later, but by that time Ellie was a widow living quietly with her little boy. They keep mostly to themselves—she never got over the public censure, and most decent folk just tolerate her. I suppose she deserves it."

"Her son must have inherited some of his father's talent. What is he called?"

"Morgan Dawson, and I think he has more talent than his father. I've seen some of the elder's work, and at best it is crude and stiff. Morgan's painting has more naturalness and delicacy."

"Yes, that is apparent in the lavaliere, isn't it? Well perhaps the dollar it cost me will mean a lot to them,"

Clarissa laughed. "Then I won't feel so bad about spending it."

Later, as they sat in the tiny parlor of the Old Post Tavern amid the shelves of blue delft and bleached linen curtains, drinking steaming cups of tea and enjoying Mrs. Acker's seedcakes, Clarissa thought of the lavaliere lying within its gray wrapping paper in her purse and of the kind new friend sitting across the table. It may not last, she thought, but for this delightful afternoon I have been truly happy again.

Before she went down to supper that evening Clarissa took her purchase from its wrapping paper and inspected it lovingly. When she heard the little bell calling the family, she laid it carefully on her dresser, not bothering to wrap it up and put it away.

As was her wont when surrounded by her flamboyant family, Hannah withdrew into herself at supper and barely spoke a word. Now and then catching Clarissa's eye across the table, she would smile gently, as though they shared a secret. And such a secret, thought Clarissa. Nothing more than a few hours of companionship and the indulgence of an extravagant purchase. Simple pleasures and simple friendships, which Augusta and Adam could never comprehend. All at once she was surprised by a question from George Clarendon who, in an unusual gesture, had seated himself next to her.

"And what did you think of our thriving little village of Sing Sing, Clarissa?" he asked, turning a blazing smile full in her direction.

Clarissa was startled by the question as well as the smile, since he had hardly seemed to notice her existence after that first night. And how did he know they had been in the village that afternoon?

As though he were reading her thoughts, he went on: "I saw you and Hannah alighting from the cart this afternoon. I have a small law office in the town—perhaps you didn't know—and I happened to be standing near the window when you arrived. I wanted to come out and welcome you properly, but I was deeply embroiled with the

76

problems of William Bishop's boundary rights. Did you have a pleasant shopping excursion?"

Before Clarissa could answer, Augusta broke in. "Really, Hannah, that disgusting pony! The least you could do is learn to drive a horse and gig. Pony carts are for children."

Hannah stared down at her plate, her face gone dark red. "I don't think I could manage a full-grown horse," she said quietly.

"Well, you might try. Or get Edwards to drive you. Imagine how the yokels must laugh behind their hands to see you driving a pony cart up High Street. Why even the simplest farmhand can manage a horse. I declare I have no patience with your fears."

Judge Granville intervened. "Now, Augusta, don't be so hard on your sister. Not everyone has your skill and daring with horses. If Hannah is more comfortable driving a pony, why should it bother you? It does her no discredit."

"On the contrary, Papa, I think it makes us all look ridiculous."

"Haven't you learned by now, Papa," said Adam, turning to his father, "that it is not within Augusta's powers to understand how anyone can have feelings different from her own? As she goes, so the world must go. Right, Augusta?"

His sister glared at Adam without deigning to answer, and George Clarendon took advantage of the silence to turn back to Clarissa.

"You still haven't answered my question, Miss Shaw, that is, you were not allowed to answer it; so I'll ask it again. What did you think of Sing Sing Village?"

Clarissa's discomfort grew under the scrutinizing gaze of the very striking man beside her. She murmured what sounded to her own ears as an inept reply describing their afternoon and the pleasure they had found in it.

With a skilled grace George Clarendon set about putting her at her ease. "I suppose you must have found Mr. Carpenter's general store rather provincial after all the glorious shops to be found in New York Town. What with all those foreign ships in her harbor, New York has access to exotic wares which no small, rustic village can begin to match."

"Oh, but you forget," said Adam in his half-amused tone of voice, "Miss Shaw comes from the rural backwoods of Manhattan Island, not from the civilized town at all. She should be quite at home in a general store. Am I not correct, Miss Shaw, that the streets of Manhattan Village are fully as crowded with yokels as High Street in the town of Mount Pleasant?"

Clarissa's self-consciousness was washed away in a surge of sheer anger. How she longed to throw something right at that irritating smirk Adam wore so proudly. In an icy voice she answered: "There are not many streets in the town of Manhattan. It's a smaller village than Sing Sing, mostly fields and orchards and small farms." She turned her warmest smile on George Clarendon beside her. "Actually I did find something of interest in Mr. Carpenter's store. Some of the artifacts made by the local people are really quite lovely."

Surprisingly, Hannah spoke up. "Clarissa was especially charmed by one of the little broach portraits made by Ellie Dawson and her son."

Augusta threw down her napkin. "That woman!"

"Yes, well . . ." said George hesitantly. "She's rather notorious, but her son does have talent, everyone agrees. If you chose one of their creations, you must have good taste."

Clarissa blushed under the compliment. How foolish, she thought angrily, to become so flustered at the polite attentions of a good-looking young man. Yet, dismiss it as she would, she could not help but feel that he was going out of his way to pay attention to her. This seemed to be confirmed later when the gentlemen joined the ladies in the parlor after supper and George pulled up a chair near Clarissa in a quiet corner, speaking to her confidentially.

"I hope you won't think my curiosity offensive, Clarissa, but I've been much struck at how such a cultured, educated young lady came out of a farming background.

78

Tell me about your father. He must have been a remarkable man."

Clarissa accepted the exquisite Staffordshire teacup George offered her as he spoke. His hands were long and artistic, with carefully manicured nails. Far from being offended, she was flattered by his pointed attentions.

"My father was a gentleman, Mr. Clarendon. His father was the squire of an estate in the fen country near Ely. He had several sons of which my father was the youngest. They all received good educations, but with the estate going to the eldest there was no future for him in England. He came to America hoping to build something he could leave to my brother and me, but his dreams were never realized. When he died, I'm afraid he considered himself a failure."

George's voice was sympathetic. "A common enough story. I've heard many such since I've been in the law. Did your brother decide to continue the farm? Why, forgive me . . . have I asked the wrong question?"

Her face had suddenly gone white against the blackness of her eyes. She murmured that her brother was also dead.

"I'm so sorry. Forgive me that I caused you this discomfort. But there is this about it. If these tragic events brought you to us, then they were of some good."

Surely he wasn't jesting. His words sounded so sincere, his smile was so genuine . . . and so attractive. She felt the color flood back into her cheeks, and her heart gave an unaccustomed flutter. What was happening to her? she thought angrily. How foolish to have her head turned because of a little kindness and attention.

"You know," he went on, "I haven't forgotten our proposed trip to Andre's Cave. Do you still think you might like to go some day?"

She remembered some mention of a riding excursion. An inept rider, she wasn't anxious to set out next to that expert equestrienne, Augusta Granville. On the other hand, the prospect of a day spent in George's company began to seem very attractive.

"The weather is improving," George continued. "In a

few weeks the flowers will be out and the trees will be blooming. The first warm sunny day we must set out. We can take a lunch and make a picnic of it. What do you say? Shall we?"

Clarissa smiled shyly up at him. "It sounds very nice. I'd love to go." Some unconscious force drew her eyes away from the warm smile on George's face. Glancing across the room, she saw Adam Granville staring at them both with a dark intensity, his face frozen in a black scowl.

Later in her room, as she removed her clothes and draped her long nightdress over her head, she smiled to herself, recalling the conversation she had shared with George Clarendon. Every detail of his face was clear in her mind—the even white teeth, the silky blond sideburns which heightened his long lean cheeks, the slight cleft in his chin barely rising out of the high snowy collar points. Brushing her hair and dreamily lingering over this picture, she wasn't conscious at first that the wide dresser looked different. Something should have been there that wasn't. With a sinking heart she realized that her lavaliere, so carefully laid there before supper, was gone. Hurriedly she searched through the drawers, on the floor under the dresser, even around the edge of her bed. The gray paper on which it had been lying was still neatly folded in its place, but the necklace was nowhere to be found. Fighting down her rising panic, she finally gave up the search and sat heavily down on the edge of her bed. A whole dollar gone and for nothing! Where could it be? Who could have taken it? The children? Nancy? Surely not!

But someone must have taken it, or it would still be here in her room. Perhaps the morning would bring an explanation.

Yet, first thing the next morning when Clarissa questioned the children about her missing necklace, it was obvious at once that they had no idea what she was talking about. She knew then that she would have to speak to Nancy about it and she felt nothing but distaste at the prospect. She had heard that since servants were the first to be suspected when something was missing, they were often inclined to be defensive. Nancy had always been pleasant and kind to her. Even if she had taken the lavaliere, she was sure to deny it, and what could Clarissa do then? Perhaps she should seek Hannah's advice before confronting the housemaid.

She was still mulling this over in her mind as she started down the stairs to the dining room for breakfast. Glancing up, she saw Miss Evans coming toward her carrying a tray. Clarissa moved to step aside out of the way of the glaring nurse when suddenly her eyes were arrested by a glimpse of indigo blue through the translucent porcelain. She stared unbelievingly at the painted face of the young girl who decorated Miss Evans' ample bosom.

"With a stiff, "Excuse me," the thin-lipped nurse stepped past Clarissa. For a few seconds she stood and watched her go by, but that necklace was rightfully hers and she found that she was unable to keep still and say nothing.

"Miss Evans . . ." she started haltingly. "That necklace you're wearing. Would you tell me where you got it?"

Miss Evans stared. "I beg your pardon!"

Horribly embarrassed, Clarissa launched into a lame explanation. "I think that lavaliere may belong to me— that is, I purchased one in the village yesterday and I cannot find it. It disappeared from my room last night and I thought . . ."

Martha Evans' pinched features took on a look of outraged disbelief. "What is this? What are you saying?"

"I mean no—if you could just explain how . . ."

"Explain! Explain to you! What are you accusing me of?" Her voice rose in spite of her efforts to keep it down. Her knuckles gripping the tray turned to chalk, and the dishes rattled ominously as the tray swayed in her hands. "How dare you, you young upstart! How dare you speak to me like that?"

"Please. Don't jump to conclusions. Let me explain."

But filled with righteous indignation, Miss Evans was in no mood to listen to anyone. She was still irked at Clarissa for disturbing Mrs. Granville and by now she had learned enough about her to add ammunition to her dislike.

"Who do you think you are," she hissed. "I know about you. You're nothing but a poor relation living on the charity of the Granvilles."

"Now just a minute . . ."

"Don't think I don't know what you're after. It's my job you want, I know it is."

Astounded, Clarissa stared at the woman whose rage gave a purplish tint to her puffy skin.

"Think to find yourself a good position, don't ya'?" she went on, not even trying now to lower her voice. "Make me look bad and then you'll step in and I'll be sent packing. Well, it won't work, dearie. I'm on to you . . ."

By now her outraged reaction was filling the stairwell, and Clarissa was not surprised to see Judge Granville peering over the railing, drawn there by the racket. Hannah's pale face was just visible over his shoulder.

"Ladies. Ladies. What's the problem here?" he started in a conciliatory voice.

Her face distorted with rage, Martha Evans turned on her employer. "She as much as called me a thief! That's the problem. I'll not have it. I am an upstanding woman with a good reputation and I've never been so insulted. Who does she think she is anyway? Where did she come from that she has the right to accuse decent folks of stealing!"

"I never said . . ." Already distressed by the developing scene, Clarissa's heart sank as she saw Adam at the foot of the stairs watching them. Soundlessly, he moved to take the tray from the angry nurse before it all fell to the floor. Setting it down on the landing, he stood back and watched objectively.

Judge Granville was using his most soothing judicial voice. "Now, now, Miss Evans. Calm down, please do. I'm sure we can get to the bottom of this without screaming. Clarissa, is there a reasonable explanation? Perhaps you could . . ."

Clarissa found herself wishing the floor would open up and swallow her. This overheated reaction was more than she had bargained for, and she wished she had never mentioned the necklace. Certainly she had no desire to force the issue in front of the whole family. But she was trapped now, and there was nothing else to do, so she explained how she had purchased the ornament and it had disappeared from her room.

"Are you quite sure this is the same necklace? Could there be two alike?"

"No, Papa," Hannah said. "I was with Clarissa, and it looks like the same necklace to me. The painting is distinctive enough to make an exact copy unlikely."

"You're all against me," Miss Evans exploded, aware only that she was losing her argument. "You all hate me. I know it . . ."

"Please be reasonable, Miss Evans," said Judge Granville, whose objectivity was beginning to give way to irritation. "No one is accusing you of thievery. Perhaps the necklace was mislaid and you found it—is that what happened? Why don't you quietly tell us where you did get it, and the matter can probably be resolved very easily."

At these words the nurse became suddenly as tight-lipped as she had been hysterical before. She stared at the judge, then back at Clarissa, a new glimmer of fright replacing the anger in her eyes.

"I believe I can guess what happened, Papa," Adam said quietly, unfolding his arms and stepping up to the unhappy nurse. "Where did you last see your lavaliere, Miss Shaw?"

"I left it lying on my dresser last night when I went down to supper."

"It was mother, wasn't it, Miss Evans? She went wandering again, didn't she? And finding this lovely trinket lying alone, she took it back to her room. Then, when you saw it, she made you a gift of it. Am I right?"

Judge Granville was on the stairs, descending toward the hapless nurse. His carefully judicial coolness evaporated as his face colored in a rising anger.

"Is this true, Miss Evans?"

Staring daggers, Miss Evans looked back and forth between the two men.

"And how did Mrs. Granville 'go wandering' when you are supposed to be watching her? You are supposed to be with her at all times—she is never to be alone. Think of the harm she could do to herself or others. It is your responsibility to prevent that, Miss Evans. That is what you were hired to do, and I should not have to point that out to you!"

Martha Evans shrank back against the stairwell, suddenly aware that her position was in jeopardy. Her face went pasty white above the stark black of her high neck as her furious employer advanced upon her down the stairs.

"How is it Amelia got away from you when you have nothing to do all day but to watch her? I think I deserve an explanation."

Tight-lipped and silent, Martha Evans huddled against the wall.

"Go ahead, Miss Evans," said Adam. "Tell Papa how you enjoy your little toddy in the evening. Only sometimes the nip is just a little too strong. Or perhaps there is just one too many and you drift off for a short nap."

Judge Granville's face went bright red. "Spirits! My employees taking spirits in my house behind my back!" He rounded on his son. "You knew this and you didn't see fit to tell me of it? You know your mother's welfare is the dearest thing in the world to me, and you said nothing!"

Quite coolly Adam laid a hand on his father's shoulder. "I'm sorry, Papa. Perhaps I should have spoken up. I planned to eventually. I have taken Mother back to her apartment several times with no harm done. And I did warn you, Miss Evans, that something like this would eventually come of it."

"I won't have it! You knew what this position was like when you accepted it, Miss Evans, and I will not accept or excuse your conduct. If you find the responsibility for Mrs. Granville too demanding, then perhaps we had better reconsider our contract."

"Sir, I don't. It won't happen no more, I promise, sir,"

Miss Evans said lamely. "It weren't no more than one or two times, really. It won't happen again . . ."

"Papa," said Hannah quietly, "I don't mean to excuse Miss Evans' conduct, but she does have a difficult position."

"No. No excuses. And I won't have spirits!"

"It's only a drop of medicine I take now and then, sir, for my heart. Just to steady it down a little. I do have this flutterin' now and then, I did tell you, sir."

"I want to see you in my study this morning after breakfast. Hannah, you stay with your mother. We'll have this cleared up once and for all, and then no more of it. I think now the best thing is for us all to go back to our rooms and calm down." He turned as if to run from the specter of giving way to his own temper.

Adam watched his father ascend the stairs. When the short, straight-backed figure disappeared down the hall, he turned back to Miss Evans and said quietly, "I'm sorry this had to come out this way, but I did warn you. It's your own fault, you know. None of us want any harm to come to Mother."

Martha Evans' tiny eyes peered at him from the folds of pink flesh. She felt sick with rage and fear; yet she was almost as afraid of Adam's wrath as she was his father's. Without answering, she turned away and started back to her apartment. Then she saw Clarissa standing white-faced at the top of the stairs.

"You . . ." She spat out the words. "You stupid creature! This is all your doin'. But for you none of this would have happened. Take your damned fool necklace!"

Tearing the lavaliere from the ribbon at her neck, she hurled it crashing down the stairs. "I'll get even with you for this," she hissed. "See if I don't. I swear before God I'll make you pay for this morning's work!"

Clarissa, her back pressed against the carved panels of the door, watched the furious woman disappear down the hall. Only then could she bring herself to look down the stairs to where the necklace was lying in pieces on the rug. She felt all at once very sick, sorry that she had ever seen the thing, sorry that she had mentioned it, sorry that she had ever come to Zion Hill.

"Ellie Dawson would not appreciate her son's work being handled so roughly," Adam was standing beside her, reaching out his hand with the broken pieces of the necklace. There was no trace in his dark eyes of malice or humor. He was watching her closely.

"Look," he said. "Don't pay any attention to her. She's a bitter, sour old crone. She's had a hard life and she likes to take it out on other people. But she can't hurt you. So forget what she said and come to breakfast."

Clarissa was too numb to respond. Taking the fragments of the portrait, she murmured some excuse and fled to her room. Wrapping them tightly in the gray paper, she stuffed them into the farthest corner of the bottom drawer. Only yesterday the thing had given her such pleasure. Now she never wanted to see it again. The old familiar blackness of soul seemed to engulf her again. Was she always to shatter the beautiful things she touched? Was there never to be any unalloyed joy, any order or comfort anywhere? The hopes she had brought with her to Zion Hill lay in shambles at her feet. Throwing herself on her bed, she gave vent to her despair in bitter tears.

Six

"You're going to ruin your eyes, working in that poor light."

Ellie Dawson frowned as she watched her son bend closer to a delicate piece of ivory. The twilight sifting through the windows above his head cast a gray pallor over the table where he was working, gilding the strands of hair which fell over his forehead to a yellow white. He held the small ivory close to his face, staring with a painful intensity as he delicately dabbed at it with his brush. Ellie sighed. If only he could paint when the sun was bright. But there was too much to be done then, too much of the never-ending struggle to wrest a bare living from the stubborn earth. Painting pictures was for the quiet times after the chores were done, and that meant working by twilight or candlelight.

"Why don't you put it up for tonight? Perhaps you can find a little spare time tomorrow when the sun is out."

"I'm almost done," the boy answered. "Look, Ma. This time I'm painting a gentleman—my first one. I used an engraving in *Blackwood's* magazine for my first sketch. Now I'm changing it a little and adding color. It's going to be nice, isn't it?"

Laying down her mending, she walked with an easy grace across the room to look over her son's shoulder. She saw a fine gentleman with long sideburns above the high points of his stock, the head tipped slightly back, and a suggestive grin on the lips as though he were about to make some ribald remark. It was part of Morgan's talent, she felt, that with a few strokes of his brush he could turn a stiff face into a person—alive, vibrant, and real. She leaned down and kissed him lightly on the top of his golden head in a familiar gesture carried over from his childhood.

"It's lovely, Morgan. I think it will be one of the best you've done. He seems about to laugh. And the look in his eye. A real rake!"

"Doesn't it remind you of someone? Look closely. Who do we know with that wicked leer?"

Ellie leaned closer. "Of course," she laughed. "Adam Granville. Well, I wouldn't exactly call Adam a rake, but the expression is certainly his. I don't think he would be flattered, however."

"Oh, he'll never know. What do you think? A brooch or just a simple frame?"

Ellie took the slim piece of ivory from his hands and studied it. "I think this should be a miniature," she said. "I doubt if any young lady would wear such a devilish character around her neck, but someone might hang him on the wall. Yes, definitely a miniature."

"I think so too. He'll probably never sell, but it's good practice to paint him. If I'm ever going to make my living at this, I'll have to paint the gentlemen as well as the ladies."

"Oh, I hope he sells, if only just to cover the cost of the ivory. It's so dear and so hard to come by."

She handed the painting back to him and returned to her sewing. Her careless comment had actually masked the cold chill which his words had sent through her. Someday he would leave. It was inevitable and right that he should; yet she could hardly bear the thought. Jabbing her needle into the rough homespun, she tried to concentrate on the mending, but her gaze kept returning to her son's youthful face bent in concentration over his work.

How like his father he was. At the thought she could see again the handsome features of Phillipe Durand. The black eyes, the patrician face, the almost feminine mouth—forever they would be etched in her mind. Morgan did not have the perfect features, the almost too handsome good looks of his father, but in countless other ways—a sudden laugh, a pensive gazing out at nothing, the way he glanced up without rasing his head—she could see again her first and only love. He had his father's artistic hands, and of course, painting was in his blood. The one difference was that his talent far surpassed the little, mostly affected gifts Phillipe Durand had possessed.

Ellie smiled grimly to herself. I should be bitter, she thought. After all these years and all that pain, to still think of Phillipe as my "only love." It's crazy. How could one still love someone who had taken everything and then carelessly moved on, never thinking of the hurt he left behind?

But love him she had, and love him she still did. Somehow she had never found it in her heart to condemn him as selfish. He was set apart, different from all others, all the people who spent their lives digging in the earth or dragging the water for fish. They never raised their eyes from dirt. But he was an artist. He looked up and out and saw beauty and pain and sought the reasons for them. "They" said she had been seduced and abandoned, left a wicked, fallen woman. It never seemed that way to her. Before Phillipe, life had been drab and lonely, as it was again after he was gone. For that brief time when he was there, the world had held love and light and beauty.

And he had given her this wonderful boy, her beautiful son. When he was born she had wanted to call him after his father, but she knew that to do so would make his life a misery. Small villages have long memories—who should know that better than she. So she named him after his grandfather, her mother's father, and one of the few people from her childhood she could remember with affection.

No, she did not blame Phillipe. She didn't really blame her father, who in his stern rush to legitimize his grandson had forced her to marry Caleb Dawson. The very name made her cringe. If anything should make me bitter, she thought, it is that Morgan has to go through life bearing the name "Dawson"; and she jabbed her needle in and out of her sewing, hearing again the drunken ravings, the cruel taunts. "Whore" was the mildest, but it was the one she heard the most, and not only in the privacy of their own home. She had taken the insults, the welts and the bruises, accepting them as her punishment. For two years she meekly accepted chastisement. Then, just when Morgan was old enough to begin to be terrified of the brutish lout he called his father, God in His mercy had sent a storm on the river and Caleb Dawson had drowned.

Ellie laid her sewing in the basket at her feet. Even now, after all these years, she could still feel the wave of blessed relief which had swept over her when they brought her news of his death. The Lord knew what He was about, she thought, for He knew that if Caleb had ever hurt Morgan in his anger, I would have killed him without blinking an eye. Thus I would have added murder to my sins.

A sudden eruption of furious barking brought her back to the present. "That's Brute," she said to the boy. "Someone must have stopped on the road. You'd better go out before he does harm."

Morgan rose to peer through the window. "Ho, it's Adam's gig." His voice betrayed his pleasure. "Brute knows him—he'll be all right. Don't tell him I took his likeness for a picture, Ma. You won't, will you?"

Ellie picked up her shawl from the back of the rocker and started for the door. "I'll see him outside. You finish up in here."

On the road, Adam looked up from the gatepost where he was fastening the reins to watch Ellie walking toward him down the overgrown walk. God, she's a handsome woman, he thought, filled as always with the comfortable glow of pleasure her coming brought. Once it had been something more—an arousal, an urgency, warmed to life

90

not merely by the honey gold hair and sculptured smile, but by the deep, throbbing femininity of her. Now it was a quiet thing. A bond of friendship and complete acceptance, each for the other, for what they were, with no demands or apologies. It was a rare relationship and one he treasured.

"It's a balmy evening and I thought you might like to walk down to the river," she said, smiling warmly.

"Better curb this monster first, before he attacks another poor unsuspecting traveler." Vainly Adam attempted to remove the heavy paws of the big yellow mastiff from his chest. Fearsome to strangers, the huge dog was ready to devour a friend with affection.

"I don't know why you keep this elephant, Ellie. He nearly sent my horse off in a panic."

"He's good protection, and there have been times when we needed that." She pulled the dog on his chain back inside the gate, while Adam stroked his horse's long, sleek neck. Gradually the animal relaxed his skittishness and began to nuzzle the branches of a nearby bush. Ellie threw the end of her heavy shawl over her head, and they started down the long sloping path toward the river which avoided the steep drop directly in front of Ellie's cottage. The calm surface of the glassy water reflected the red gold of the evening sky. Across the river the Rockland hills were tinted black against the blue gray light behind them.

"Your artist should have painted this."

"You know, you are the only person who will speak to me of Phillipe. Most of the people who knew about us are embarrassed to say his name."

"I was never one for tact," Adam replied. "Just ask my family."

"The great cynic, Adam Granville." Ellie smiled up at him. "I know better. You are the one person who never condemned me, did you know that? Besides," she added lightly, "Phillipe was only interested in painting people."

"Well, I have seen some of his work, and he should have tried scenery. Oh, don't flash your eyes at me. It's true and you know it as well as anyone. You didn't love him for his talent anyway, did you?"

They had reached a grassy bank which sloped away to the tiny shell-encrusted shoreline. Adam dropped to the grass, glad to rest his aching leg, and leaned forward, rested an elbow on his good knee. Beside him Ellie sat with her legs crossed under her billowing skirt, pulling at the grass. She stared pensively at the darkening river before she answered.

"He was the first person I ever knew who saw the beauty in the world around him. My father and his friends, all they ever thought of was their crops and their stock and how much manure they needed for the next field. I used to feel there was something wrong with me because I felt so strongly there had to be more to life than that. Sometimes seeing the river in the setting sun like this, it was so beautiful that it hurt. Then Phillipe came along and he felt that beauty too, even more than I. I suppose that was why I loved him so much." She gave a sudden little shudder. "But why talk about it. It was over long ago."

Adam lazily twirled a thin stalk of shepherd's-purse pulled from the loamy ground. "Beauty and manure. Unfortunately in this world you can't get along without either one."

"Oh, I don't know. Most of the folk I know would give beauty short shrift next to a good fertilizer. But tell me about yourself. How are things up at the Hill?"

Adam shrugged. "About as always. Augusta tyrannizes, Hannah wrings her hands, George pontificates, Mother wanders, and Papa stands over all, passing judgment in his own inimitable, judicial way. Bah! Sometimes I think I'll give it all up and head for the West. There's freedom and adventure to be found out there. And fortunes. What do you think? Would I make a good frontiersman?"

"I think you are used to much too soft a life. The first time you used your unguarded tongue in the wrong place you would get a knife in your ribs or a bullet between your eyes. None of the polite verbal rebukes you get here."

He laughed. "You are probably right. They're much too rough a bunch for me." He paused, then added lightly, "You haven't seen our new cousin yet, have you?"

She eyed him curiously. "No, but I heard she was living at the Hill. What's she like?"

It was a perfunctory question asked without much thought, but Adam was so long in answering that he caught Ellie's attention. She watched him more closely.

"Oh, she's all right," he finally said. "She's little, not really beautiful, but pretty enough, and attractive in a quiet, reserved kind of way. She has spirit, though. I've already had one or two angry ripostes from her—but overall, I think she has a kindly nature. I believe she will be very good for Jenny's children."

"Why, Adam. What a carefully thought-out description. I do believe your little cousin has caught your interest in a decidedly uncousinly way. Is it possible that cold heart of yours has been touched at last?"

A faint flush spread over Adam's lean brown cheeks. "Never! Not by a slip of a girl like that! Besides, George has already begun to stake her out. You should see him hovering around, all solicitation and sympathy. And she seems completely taken in by his charm. George always knew how to use charm—he got Jenny that way, didn't he?"

"Well, his charm eludes me, but if she likes it, why should you care?"

Adam stretched out his legs and leaned back on one elbow, his eyes deadly serious. "I'll tell you why, Ellie. There's something about Clarissa. On the surface she seems very self-contained and poised. Yet I've never seen such pain in anyone's eyes that I catch in hers in unguarded moments. She reminds me of a wounded animal, staring at the world in its agony and wondering where the next blow is going to fall. What can George do for her except to cause her more hurt? I suppose I just feel sorry for her, that's all."

He glanced up to see Ellie trying to suppress a giggle. "Oh, Adam, I might have known," she laughed. "You pretend to be so cynical; yet no one has a kinder heart."

"Now that is just not true. And don't even say such

things or you'll ruin my reputation. Come on, let's walk back. The sun is almost gone and it is getting chilly."

Extending his hand, he pulled her to her feet and linked her arm through his as they started back up the slope.

"But seriously," Ellie said, "if your little cousin has suffered some sort of trouble, Zion Hill is probably the worst place for her to be."

"I've thought of that. It's not a happy house, is it? It's shabby and depressing and seems always to have some sort of pall hanging over it. I've often wondered if that unpleasant business several years ago marked it somehow."

Ellie's hand tightened on his arm. "That dreadful Matthias! That horrible man. Calling himself a prophet of God, yet without a drop of mercy or compassion. Prophet of Satan, more like."

"Forgive me. I forgot that you had been a victim of his too. We'll drop the subject."

"No, no. It's all right. It was a long time ago, after all. I can forget most of the misery of that time, but I'll never forget that vindictive man. He would have been happy to run me out of the village. He did call for a public whipping, but sentiment was against going that far. God forgive me, but I was happy when he found himself in jail and *he* was the one facing a trial. Let him see what it feels like."

"Ellie, what did happen at Zion Hill? No one seems to have a clear version of the story. I know I've heard it three different ways at least."

"I don't think anyone knows what actually happened, except the people involved. Matthias had been living there with the Reddicks and Mr. Allen. The two men were his "disciples," but it was common knowledge that Mr. Reddick footed all the bills. It was rumored that the Reddicks had quarreled horribly over money and that Mr. Reddick had deeded everything he owned to the prophet. Then, one day he was found dead, stuffed into the old beehive oven near the fireplace in the old kitchen. Allen and Mrs. Reddick accused Matthias of murdering him for the money, and, sure enough, when the will was read, everything was left to Matthias. Only, curiously enough, there wasn't anything. Mr. Reddick had been a wealthy man. He owned a fair-sized mill, all the land of Zion Hill, and ran an iron smelting business above Sing Sing. Yet after his death he was found to be bankrupt. Everything had been sold or turned to cash and that had completely disappeared. Matthias raved that he had never seen it, but so did Mrs. Reddick and Mr. Allen. At length they had him arrested for the murder."

"But he was acquitted."

"I suppose there wasn't enough hard evidence to convict him. He didn't go to the gallows, but his reputation was ruined forever. He finally drifted away and no more was heard of him."

"What about Mrs. Reddick and Allen? Isn't it possible they did poor Reddick in and took off with the cash?"

"Yes, except that Allen died a short time later, and Mrs. Reddick lived on for a while in the area in the most extreme poverty. She finally went to stay with some relative or other, and no more was heard of her either."

Their slow walk had brought them back to the white fence on the top of the hill. Brute's large ugly head could be seen between the tall posts, whimpeing to get to them.

"Chances are that one of the three had that money hidden and only waited for the notoriety to die down before digging it up and living in high style."

"Yes, it's quite possible."

"On the other hand, if the money was hidden somewhere in the house and never found, why we may be sitting on a fortune!"

"I should say that was extremely unlikely. Before your family moved in, the house was empty for some time. The rumor has persisted that thousands of dollars were stashed away there somewhere, and believe me, everyone in the neighborhood had a try at trying to find it. No one ever found anything."

"That explains why the place was such a shambles when we moved in. It had been badly vandalized and we couldn't understand why. Ah, well, old Matthias is probably living a life of debauched pleasure in some exotic foreign port. Likely as not we'll never know."

With a quick gesture he had the tie rope unhitched. She laid her hand on his arm.

"Come in a while," she said, straining to see his blurred features through the gray dusk. "Have a hot rum against the cold. Morgan would be happy to see you."

He took her hand. Her fingers were cold. "No, thank you, Ellie. I'd better not. I have an appointment with a friend down at the Jug and I'm already late. Since I was by this way, I just wanted to stop in and see how you were. Tell Morgan I'll see him later this week."

She smiled as he squeezed her hand, then watched him climb up into the shay and back the horse away from the post. As the leather cover swayed away down the road on its big wheels she deliberately pushed down a flicker of disappointment which came unwanted and unneeded. Then she turned away and went back into the house to her son.

When Adam entered the common room at the Old Post Tavern, the thick noise and smoke was almost like a physical force. At a glance he recognized most of the men of the neighborhood who had gathered there for a clay pipe and a pint of ale interspersed with congenial talk about this year's crop or the price of wool. They were grouped informally around the round, plank tables and leaning against the fieldstone hearth—gentlemen farmers in their black tailcoats and high stocks, small landowners in cotton drab. To one side was a third group, the really poor, hard-working, hard-drinking men who worked for hire. Adam was surprised to see among them several obvious foreigners, Irishmen from the hollow, the small settlement where emigrant labor lived. They were not often to be seen at the Jug, preferring to drink together at the grog shop nearer home, a rough place, called the Drovers, where no gentleman dared show his face.

As he worked his way across the crowded room to the counter at the other end, Adam received a warm greeting from one or two acquaintances and a congenial slap on the back from his father's friend, Mr. Ashley. There were also a few black looks thrown his way, mostly from the workers who had at one time or another been on the receiving end of his sharp tongue. These he ignored.

"Master Granville, will you have a pint?" The broad form the tavern's owner, Jock Acker, materialized through the fog extending a pewter mug filled to the brim with a foamy brown liquid.

"Thanks, Jock. Have you seen Corey about? The smoke in this iniquitous hovel is so bad that I can't make out my hand in front of my face."

"Master Adam, I'll thank you to hold your tongue about my tavern. It's a decent house and one which your own good father is not above entering for a dram or two at times."

A huge, husky fellow with bulging biceps, Jock Acker was one of the few people who refused to take Adam seriously; so they got along very well. He gestured his head toward the corner behind him. "Corey's waiting for ye over there. Working on his third pint, he is."

Using his cane before him as a cudgel, Adam worked his way over to the small table and edged his body down before a plump, cherry-faced young man with a shock of carrot-colored hair which seemed to defy control. The green eyes looking up at him seemed to blink at the world with a deceptive innocence, like a country yokel ripe for picking. Actually the country bumpkin facade hid a shrewd mind and a sharp, appraising eye, as Adam well knew. Corey Arnold was his oldest and closest friend.

Right now the voice was a little slurred. "Where have you been? I've waited nigh an hour. If you'd been much longer you'd have found me too potted to talk."

"Come on, Corey. You can hold your drink better than that. I stopped off to see Ellie Dawson on my way down."

"Oh, ho!" Corey's voice was suddenly very precise and his eyes twinkled. "And how is the handsome widow? Was it a fruitful visit, or was the beloved son lurking about as usual?"

"Watch your mouth!" Adam said sharply but without anger. "Yes, the son was about, and no, it wasn't fruitful, as you so indelicately put it, and the handsome widow is as handsome as ever. For all her shabby reputation Ellie is one of the few honest people I know. I'll never understand how one mistake can brand a woman for life."

"Well, she doesn't pretend to be a pious matron—as you, above all people, should know. It's beyond me how you can get around her when nobody else can get a civil reply. You're not exactly noted for your charm, you know; yet the fair widow who lifts her skirts for you lifts her nose in the air for the rest of us. How do you manage it?"

Adam leaned back in his chair and deliberately lifted the pewter mug to his lips. "We're good friends," he finally replied.

Corey's smile was an attempt at a leer. "I bet she knows a thing or two. What's she like in the hay? Is she good?"

Adam's eyes were unsmiling. "If you weren't my best friend, you'd get my fist in your teeth for that."

Corey laughed. "I do love to get your hackles up, Adam. You're so good at doing it to everyone else. You know she sent your brother George packing, and in no uncertain terms."

"Yes, and what a shock to his conceit that must have been. As a rule he has only to raise one eyebrow and all the ladies sink into vapors. Ellie could see through him in one glance. But come now, we're not here to discuss Ellie or George. What kind of luck did you have? Did you turn up anything new?"

Dropping his carefree air, Corey leaned across the table closer to Adam. "I did find something, but not enough to put all the pieces together. The bad news first. I could find no trace of any Mrs. Reddick anywhere. That relative she was supposed to go live with never saw a hair of her head. She just dropped off the earth."

"That's too bad. She would be our best hope. Of course, she might be dead by now, but if she were still alive and we could find her . . ."

"I don't know where to look next. If she is not with that cousin in Allentown, she might be anywhere between

98

here and there. Hospitals, almshouses, workhouses, friends—it could take years."

"I know. And we're neither of us in any position to spend our lives searching. Not to mention the money it would cost."

"But hear me out. I was luckier in the other matter. I covered every old grog shop and sinkhole on the docks of New York and I did come across one old codger who remembered that about seven or eight years ago there was this crazy man hanging about who called himself 'preacher' something or other. He dressed in some kind of brown sacking, and he went about haranguing anyone he could collar about hellfire and damnation. However, when he was in his cups, he became very confidential—claimed there was a great sum of money which rightfully belonged to him but which had been spirited away by a false disciple. According to his story, it was hidden somewhere, and he was never able to find it."

"Now what do you suppose that means? Could that old story have some truth in it after all? This eccentric—did he have any money of his own? Perhaps he only gave out this story to hide the truth of his own wealth."

"I shouldn't think so. This old fellow said he was always begging for a handout to buy a nip. They all assumed that his wits were addled by the wine, and all this talk about a hidden fortune was a lot of nonsense. No one took him seriously."

"What finally happened to him?"

"Just drifted off. One day he wasn't around anymore and he never appeared again."

Adam traced a long line down the side of the mug absently, his dark eyes staring at the table. "But Corey, if it was Matthias and he knew that this fortune was hidden somewhere in Zion Hill, why didn't he come back for it? Why live like a beggar on the New York docks when he could live like a king?"

"I don't know why. There is a lot here which does not make sense. But listen, I ran into an old friend in New York who might be able to sort it all out for you. Remember Griswold Kelly?"

"Grimy Gris! My God, yes, though I haven't seen him since he was asked to leave Columbia College."

"He's tried a number of things to earn his living, but now he's settled onto something that's perfectly suited to his peculiar tastes. He's a kind of Bow Street runner— looking up lost relatives, making inquiries, that sort of thing. He's probably just the man to go on with this. I took down his address, if you want to write him."

Adam reached for the paper and glanced at it quickly. Near Canal Street. He knew the area well. "I just might do that. Old Gris always preferred learning about life from dives and bawdy houses to searching through books. He might know just where to look for our elusive Mrs. Reddick."

"And now, there's one thing more." Corey leaned closer over the table and lowered his voice. "I wasn't the first person to come along asking about old Matthias. This fellow let it drop that within the last year there had been someone else on the docks making inquiries."

"Who?"

"It didn't sound like anyone I could place. A small fellow, of no particular description. But he was ready to pay good money for any information."

Adam drummed his long fingers angrily on the table. "I knew it! I suspected it all along. Whoever that man is, you can bet George hired him! He probably knows all about this hidden money. He may even know by now where it is. He's the one who insisted we move up here, probably so he could get inside the house and search. All that loving concern for Mother, it was all a lie!"

Corey leaned back in his chair, hooking his fingers in his wide belt. "You may be right. But I don't think you should jump to conclusions until you know more. After all, that's a pretty serious accusation."

Adam glanced up, noting the concern on his friend's face. None knew better than he himself what an easy prey he was to bitterness and what pitfalls it led him into.

"I suppose you're right," he finally replied. "It could have been anyone making these inquiries. It's just that I have this feeling, and my hunches are usually correct. If only we could trace Mrs. Reddick. We need some really hard facts. Not just rumor and conjecture."

"Suppose you do find her eventually. Do you really think she can tell you any more than the records of the trial?"

"Perhaps not. But there's a good chance she could, and there's no one else left to try. So, what do we do next, Corey?"

"You could start by searching that old house. How about tearing down the newel post of digging up the cellar?"

"I suppose the money could just as well be in the newel post as anyplace. If only we had some idea where to start looking."

Catching Jock's eye at the counter, Corey hoisted his glass over his head and turned it upside down. Behind his cage, the owner waved and reached for a new mug. "Do you want another jug, Adam?"

"No, no more for me tonight." All at once he felt very weary. It had been a long day since the emotional scene on the stairs that morning. He could still see Clarissa's great haunted eyes like black holes in her stricken face. He felt again the strange sense of pity which had overwhelmed him at that moment. Pity and perhaps something more than pity. Something he had no wish to feel and which must be put down at all costs. Rubbing his fingers back and forth across his forhead, he forced the picture from his mind.

"I'd better get back," he said to Corey. "Thanks for all the work you did. I still believe that once we get enough of the pieces it will all fit together. There are still too many missing."

"Glad to be of help. I'm becoming more and more interested myself in how this thing will work out. And of course, if you do come across that fortune, I may ask for a share."

"You will have earned one." Adam started to rise, but Corey waved him back.

"One more minute and I'll go up the road part of the way with you. I have one more question, Adam, and I confess it worries me. Why are you in this so deeply anyway? Your papa doesn't need the money. He's a wealthy man with a respected reputation. You live the life of an idle gentleman because of him. I find it hard to believe that you'd get involved in an old murder with a misfit like that Matthias just to see justice done. What is your interest? I ask it as your friend."

Knowing him so well, Adam recognized the sincerity of the question. "You have a right to ask. But I just can't tell you my suspicions right now. As you said yourself, they are serious accusations. Let's just say that I'm doing it for Jenny."

"Jenny? Your sister?"

"Yes. My sister."

"But Adam. Jenny died of blood poisoning. You don't think . . ."

Adam held up his hand, cutting off the rest of Corey's sentence. "I don't think anything . . . not now. I would just like to be sure. I have these hunches and I like to follow them up."

"But that is what worries me. You may be taking an honest dislike and turning it into a hate crusade. Be careful it doesn't become an obsession to prove you're right."

Adam smiled grimly as he reached for his cane. "I'll try to remain objective. Will you stay with me in this?"

"Oh, of course. You may need my steadying influence." Corey settled back into his accustomed lighthearted manner. "And after all, I'm enjoying the adventure of the thing."

Seven

It was two days before Clarissa was able to throw off the black depression brought on by the scene with Miss Evans. On the afternoon of the second day she accidentally encountered the nurse in the hall and made an effort to speak, but the older woman cut her short. With eyes black with hate, she turned her back on Clarissa and left her standing in the hallway. This was an intolerable situation; yet Clarissa felt she was powerless to change it when the woman refused to meet her half way. After that, she tried to put Miss Evans out of her mind and concentrate on the children, who were a delightfully pleasant contrast to the embittered nurse.

Sunday morning arrived, warm and bright with the promise of spring hovering over the world. The beauty of the morning lifted Clarissa's heart, and she found herself humming an old hymn tune as she dressed for church. "Our hope for years to come," the words came back. It was true, hope always seems to return eventually. Washed out on the tide of some terrible trouble, it seems to sweep back over you when you think you've lost it forever. How resilient people are—and a good thing too," she sighed.

Downstairs she found the rest of the family gathered on

the veranda near the door. Augusta, tall and severe in black silk with a wide lace collar and a paisley shawl, hurried everyone along. Hannah, in her best finery, was a mass of ruffles, bows, and crimped curls. Her dress had the new round leg-of-mutton sleeves, and she wore the delicate fingerless mitts which were the height of fashion.

"Can't see what use they are," grumbled Adam. "They can't keep your fingers warm because they don't have fingers and they can't keep your hands warm because they're full of holes. The things you ladies wear—frills and furbelows. Nothing sensible at all."

Clarissa glanced at Judge Granville's chin completely enveloped in his high, starched stock, so stiff he must turn his whole head to look sideways. Near him George Clarendon waited in a long greatcoat reaching to his patent leather instep, cinched at the waist with wide shoulders and sweeping furred lapels. Did Adam think perhaps men's fashions more practical?

Hannah blushed and fussed with her ruffled cape. "All the ladies in town are wearing them. They're very fashionable."

"You look very pretty my dear," said her father as he handed her up into the carriage. "You wear everything well."

George spoke up dryly. "Don't pay any attention to Adam, Hannah. He wouldn't know fashion if he fell over it in the street."

Before Adam could reply, his father sent him off to the small gig in back where the remainder of the family was riding. It took both carriages to convey everyone to the Anglican church in Sing Sing. They could have walked to the Presbyterian meetinghouse at Bennett's Corners, but Judge Granville was a strict Episcopalian and wouldn't hear of it.

As Clarissa settled down next to the children she could not help but agree with the judge's comment. With her pink complexion, oval face, and soft features, Hannah was a very pretty girl. If only she didn't overdress so, she would be quite beautiful. Her frills and bows detracted

104

from her loveliness just as her retiring, insecure manner obscured a character of great sweetness and honesty.

Ah, well, she said to herself. We are what we are and there's nothing to be done about it.

St. Paul's was a small stone church set back on a hill overlooking Liberty Street. To one side there was a low shed for carriages and horses, and beyond a group of clustered chestnut and hawthorne trees, the sloping chimneys of the rectory were barely visible. The children were sent off for their own services in that building, while the rest of the family started toward the church entrance, already crowded with chattering arrivals. Judge Granville was stopped at the entrance by his friend, Mr. Ashley. "I'm having a little supper party on Friday next," he said, "and I would like you and your family to come along. Are you free?"

"I believe so. Yes, Friday seems a good day. When would you like to have us?"

"Oh, along about seven or half past. And bring your little cousin. She's quite welcome. In fact, she may enjoy seeing my house, for it has a little history of its own. I remember our conversation, you see."

"I'm sure she'd like that," Judge Granville said hurriedly, then slipped away to the sacristy to speak to the rector about the lessons he was to read.

Clarissa had overheard their quick conversation, and she felt a stirring of pleasure that she was to be included in the family's social invitations. Once inside the church, Augusta shepherded Hannah into the family pew near the front, but Clarissa deliberately slipped into a back pew where she would be free to leave early enough to collect Mary and Georgie at the end of their lessons. A young boy on a bench near the organ began to pump the bellows up and down, sending the organ into a familiar hymn tune as the rector in gown and surplice emerged from a side door and mounted the low steps to the sanctuary. Rising from her prayer cushions, her skirts rustling, Clarissa glanced quickly up at a movement beside her. To her astonishment she saw George Clarendon slip into the pew, very matter-of-fact as he searched for a hymnal. A shock

105

of pleasure engulfed her from head to toe as he opened the book and presented one side for her hand, smiling down into her upturned face. She looked quickly away, hoping that the wide brim of her bonnet would hide the embarrassment which she felt must be obvious to everyone in the church. Vainly she tried to concentrate on the printed page, but she was too conscious of the tall, black-coated figure next to her to follow the song. When his arm accidentally touched her own, she felt a flutter of delight. As the service went on she grew a little calmer; yet every time she heard George next to her making the responses in his sonorous, assured voice, a glow of pleasure would warm her entire body. The hour passed quickly, and as it neared its end and Clarissa left the pew to go to the rectory, she passed Adam standing against the wall at the back of the church, his arms crossed over his kerseymere coat. The look in his eyes startled her with its black hostility.

She did not see George again after the service. Instead she took the children and rode in the gig. Adam drove without a word to anyone, almost sulkily, but Clarissa did not care. All the way home she hugged to herself the memory of George sitting next to her during the service. It give a lift to her heart that Adam's rudeness could not touch.

The carriage arrived at the back of the house before the gig, and as they pulled up the others had already disembarked and were grouped around Nancy, who had been waiting for them. Clarissa could tell at once that something was wrong. All their voices were going at once, and the crispness of Nancy's apron lay crumpled under her twisting fingers.

"She took down early this morning. Terrible cramps in the stomach and . . . some sort of dysentery."

"Who is it?" Clarissa whispered, slipping up beside Hannah. "Is your mother ill?"

"No, not Mother."

"I never saw anyone so sick. She can't keep a morsel down."

"It's Nurse Evans," Hannah said quietly.

106

"Has Dr. Stubbs been sent for?" asked the judge, starting toward the house. "And who is with Mrs. Granville? What a nuisance this is."

Nancy followed him, explaining in disjointed sentences how she and Mrs. McCreary had spent the morning running back and forth between the sick bed and the judge's wife. Yes, a boy had been sent for the doctor, and they hoped he would arrive shortly.

Judge Granville sent Hannah off at once to stay with her mother, while Augusta marched up the stairs to have a look at the sick woman, complaining all the way that this would certainly interfere with dinner.

Dr. Stubbs arrived about twenty minutes later. After seeing his patient, he came downstairs to the parlor where the family had gathered before lunch.

"She's a very sick woman," he said, "but I believe that her condition has somewhat stabilized for the moment. She has evidently had a severe attack of colic—perhaps the result of some flyblown meat or overcooked cabbage."

Judge Granville ran his fingers nervously through his thick white hair. "I don't think so. We haven't dined on cabbage for weeks, and the rest of us are not ill, as you can see. She complains often of a heart murmur, you know."

"Perhaps her vile disposition upset her digestion," muttered Adam.

Dr. Stubbs turned back to the judge. "This has nothing to do with the heart. Look here, I hesitate to say this, but if she has not accidentally eaten some spoiled food, then she must have accidentally ingested some poisonous substance, for she has all the classic symptoms. However, she is a little better, and I think she may be all right. What she needs is complete quiet and rest. Will you see that she gets it?"

"Well, it will certainly be an inconvenience. But, yes, we'll do what we can. I am anxious to get her back on her feet. As you know, her care of my wife relieves my mind of a great burden."

"My dear sir, the woman is ill. Surely you can put up

107

with caring for your wife temporarily. You have enough family to help."

Judge Granville glared at Dr. Stubbs, who was well known in the district for his direct manner of speaking. He decided to let it pass and moved with a careful deliberation to hand him his beaver hat.

"There's not much I can do for her now. I've given Nancy instructions for her care and I'll try to look in again this evening."

"Thank you," the judge said curtly, accompanying him to the door.

"I declare," Augusta commented when the door closed behind the physician, "all this fuss over a little matter of colic. You'd think nobody ever had a stomach upset before. They're common enough to all of us, but we bear them without turning the whole house end to top!"

Her words annoyed her father who was already feeling irritable. He didn't like by half the doctor's mention of poison.

"For heaven's sake, Augusta. I don't like having Miss Evans ill, but this is certainly more than a little matter. We must all work together to get through it as quickly as possible. I don't understand why you can't be more like your mother. Before her illness she was the most gentle and even-tempered of women."

Adam put in dryly, "Augusta is very even-tempered, Papa. She's always mad."

Clarissa turned her head to hide a smile which she could not suppress. It was too bad that Miss Evans was sick, but at the same time she found it hard to feel much concern for someone she so heartily disliked. As the day wore on to a quiet afternoon she gave little thought to the sick woman upstairs. The pleasure of the morning was still too fresh in her mind.

Later in the day Augusta took the children for a ride to visit their nearest neighbors, the Kingslands; so Clarissa had several hours to herself to quietly read the book which Judge Granville had searched out for her—a journal left by a soldier who had served in General Washington's army during the American Revolution. Once during the restful afternoon she caught a glimpse of the judge ensconced in a wicker chair in the garden, dozing in the sun. Other than that she saw no one until teatime when the family gathered once again.

It was at half past eight o'clock that evening, after Clarissa had seen the children off to bed, that she started down to the parlor and heard a commotion in the hall. Nancy stood there, her face white as her starched cap, her voice high-pitched and tinged with hysteria.

"Judge Granville! It's Miss Evans! She's died. Miss Evans is dead!"

Within the space of a few moments Nancy was surrounded by Granvilles. The judge still had his spectacles on his nose and a book in his hand. He tried to calm the distraught girl by speaking to her in a voice of calm severity.

"Are you sure? I thought she was better."

"I went to take her a little broth," Nancy went on. "At first I thought she was asleep, but she looked so pale. Then, when I touched her hands—they were cold as ice. And blue. And . . . stiff . . . Oh, dear. I ain't never been near a dead body . . . Oh . . ."

"Now calm yourself, Nancy. It's all right. Clarissa, here, you see to this girl before she falls to pieces. Augusta, you come upstairs with me. We'll have to make sure. George, or Adam, one of you, go at once for Dr. Stubbs."

"I'll take the gig," Adam said at once and started from the room.

"I'll help you get it harnessed," said George, a question in his voice.

"All right then," Adam answered grudgingly.

As Clarissa led the distraught servant into the parlor she could hear Augusta's level voice as she followed her father up the stairs.

"Perhaps the girl is mistaken. Let's not upset ourselves until we know what has actually happened."

But a few moments later, when Augusta returned to the sitting room, Clarissa knew at once by the look on her

109

face that Nancy had been correct. She went straight to the side table and poured out a glass of Madeira.

"It's true," she said in a clipped voice. "She's dead. Quite dead."

Nancy burst into new sobs. "Oh, I knew it! I knew it!"

"Be still," Clarissa said sharply to the servant, then turned back to the tall figure in black silk. "Do you know what happened? I thought she was getting better."

"It looks as though her heart gave out. The wretched creature did have some kind of heart problem, and she must have strained it with all that colic. But I'm only guessing. . . . How should I know what killed her? I'm no doctor."

Clarissa took Nancy's arm and raised her to her feet. "I want you to go to the kitchen and put on some water for tea—lots of it. The doctor will be back soon and it may be wanted."

"And get rid of this flowery Madeira and put out the brandy. I think something stronger than tea will be needed."

Clarissa pushed the servant toward the door, thinking that Augusta was probably correct. Any activity would at least get the girl back on her even keel. It was not going to help any of them to have her in hysterics.

It was not long before she heard the rattle of the gig on the cobbled walk and saw Dr. Stubbs mounting the stairs, his stocky figure in the dim light of the whale-oil lamps throwing long shadows on the figured wallpaper.

As the men entered the parlor they went straight for the brandy decanter. Clarissa sat sipping her tea next to Hannah, who kept sniffing into her handkerchief. She could not help but feel that they were all somewhat unusually on edge considering the lowly position which Miss Evans held in the house.

Finally Augusta spoke testily to her sister. "For heaven's sake, Hannah, why are you carrying on? You didn't find the body or view the corpse."

"My poor Amelia, my poor wife," Judge Granville muttered. "This is going to be hard on her—breaking in someone new. It's dreadfully upsetting."

110

Strangely enough it was Adam who echoed Clarissa's thoughts. "This house is depressing enough without a body upstairs. It casts a pall over everything."

George seemed the least disturbed of them all. "It's a common enough occurrence."

"Damned smug about it all, I must say," Adam snapped back.

"Well, after all, be reasonable. We hardly ever saw the woman, and when we did she was most aloof and unpleasant. Forgive me, but it's hard to grieve for someone I didn't know well and didn't particularly like."

"But for her to die right upstairs, and nobody knowing . . ." said Hannah tearfully.

"Bosh! People die in houses all the time. Unless it's brand new you won't find one anywhere that hasn't known a death or two. It gives them character."

Augusta looked at George with admiration. "Exactly what I say. All this concern over the death of a hired woman—it's just too much. Here's Dr. Stubbs now and I'll warrant he'll agree. He must visit house after house where sickness carries people off."

The doctor's face was grim. "That is quite true, Miss Granville. I'm accustomed to having my patients die from illness. But in this case . . . well, I'm not completely certain that it was only illness."

There was a startled silence which Judge Granville was the first to break. "Now what is that supposed to mean?"

"Well, I won't say definitely until after the autopsy— oh, yes. I am going to recommend there be one."

"But why? It's clearly a case of extreme colic, isn't it? That's what you said before."

Dr. Stubbs rubbed his thick finger along the brow of his nose. "Could I perhaps have a little of that brandy? Ah, thank you, George. You see, Judge, the severity of the attack suggested a severe colic induced by a toxic substance. Just now when I examined the body I thought perhaps heart failure had been brought on as a result of the stress of that attack to the body. I had thought she might recover when I saw her last, and this seemed like

111

an unfortunate complication but not a particularly unusual one."

With a studied deliberation the doctor raised the brandy to his lips and swallowed. "Then Nancy repeated a comment the woman had made late this afternoon. Everything looked blue, she said, the entire room had a thick blue cast. That aroused my suspicions and I began to look further. I found the remains of a teacup with enough liquid to taste. It was extremely bitter."

He paused. Judge Granville's face had gone as white as his thick shock of hair. Augusta looked enquiringly from her father to the doctor. She spoke impatiently. "Well? That doesn't sound unusual."

"I very much suspect that whoever brewed up that tea was trying to mask poison with the classic symptoms of colic and heart failure."

"Poison!" Hannah cried.

"Dr. Stubbs," said Adam, "you must be out of your mind."

Augusta silenced him with a wave of her hand. "What kind of poison could do that?"

The doctor slowly turned the stem of his glass in his fingers. "Digitalin. A corrective medicine for heart palpitations—in small doses. In large amounts, a deadly poison."

"But Nurse Evans took that already. She had those—those pills she was always throwing down her throat for her heart murmur. Perhaps she took one too many."

"I might agree with that except for that teacup. I suspect that in the simplest manner the woman had an overdose of digitalin—her regular pills added to a hefty cup of tea brewed from the Scottish 'dead men's bells.' The result is heart failure."

"Scottish what?"

"Dead men's bells? What are you talking about?"

"Oh, come now. It's been around for centuries. Foxglove. The plant source for digitalin. Someone brewed up a cup of foxglove tea and somehow got her to drink it. Only she didn't quite finish it all, and I found the remains next to the bed. I might never have looked at it but for that comment about the blueness of her vision. That brought back an old memory. The woman should have recovered, I'll stake my reputation on it. That she didn't was due to someone's help."

A teacup fell to the floor and shattered on the marble hearth. All eyes turned to where Clarissa stood staring down at the jagged pieces crazily scattered next to the impassive andirons. Then she raised her head, and her eyes were like dark holes against the shrunken whiteness of her face. She gasped once, then pushed through the room and into the hall where she pulled open the front door and fled into the night.

"Well." Augusta stared after her. "I never in all my life ... What's come over her? Has everyone gone crazy?"

"I know what it is," Judge Granville said quietly. "This is a blow for her." He started to follow, but George stopped him.

"I think you should stay here. I'll see if I can help her." Adam had already moved toward the door, but at George's words he pulled back and resumed his seat.

"But why should anyone in this house want to harm Miss Evans?" Judge Granville was saying. "We more or less ignored her. It doesn't make any sense."

Dr. Stubbs face was grave, but it was clear by his manner that he had settled the matter in his own mind.

"Is Mrs. Granville capable of brewing a cup of tea?"

"I suppose so. But ... you don't think ..."

The judge's habitual dignity seemed to be tearing away at the seams. Dr. Stubbs' voice was as matter-of-fact as he could keep it. "I am very much afraid, my old friend, that you may have to face the possibility of your wife's involvement. After all, she is of unsound mind, and insane people can be quite devious. And you must admit, she had the closest connection with the deceased and the most reason to feel vindictive toward her."

"Amelia, vindictive! Never. Even ..."

The strength went out of his legs, and he sank heavily onto the nearest chair. It was what he had feared from the beginning.

"But none of us liked Miss Evans," Adam spoke up.

The thought of such an accusation leveled against his mother was almost as disturbing to him as to his father. "Why just the other day . . ."

"Yes?" Dr. Stubbs' paunchy face wavered under the flickering shadows of the lamp.

"What Adam means to say," said Augusta, "was that just the other day our cousin Clarissa had a heated argument with Mama's nurse. She called her a thief, and in turn Miss Evans threatened her. So you see, it was not only Mother who felt hostility toward the woman."

"Why, no one one liked her," Adam interjected. "It could have been any one of us. Or none of us. Perhaps you are being a little too fanciful, Doctor. You might be wrong about all this, you know."

"I might. An autopsy will tell."

"What must we do now?" Judge Granville said wearily.

"I'll take care of everything. We don't want this to get about; so I'll speak to the magistrate, if there is need. But it should be resolved. If someone did hurry Miss Evans along to her death, justice will have to be done. I should think you of all people would want that. And you would wish to know yourself who in this house is capable of such a thing."

Judge Granville had a quick impression of his lovely wife standing swathed in ivory brocade on their wedding day, her black hair a mass of ringlets and twists and artificial flowers.

"I don't want to know," he said bitterly.

As he stepped into the darkness, it took George a moment to see anything but the blackness of the night. Then, far ahead, he made out the dark shape of Clarissa's wide skirts running toward the arbor. When he found her she was sitting, tense and absorbed, on one of the stone benches. She didn't seem to know he was there until he reached out and took one of her hands, cold as the marble on which she sat.

"My dear. My dear Clarissa. What is it? You're trembling. What on earth has upset you so?"

She tried to pull her hand away, but following his intui-

114

tion, he held tightly on to her. Sitting down beside her, he took her other hand, then gradually, as he realized she was crying, he took her very gently into his arms. She went, hardly realizing where she was.

"My poor dear. Please stop your tears and be calm. Nothing can be this bad."

"It is. It is!" Clarissa gasped between sobs. He held her for a moment, then sat back and took her face between his hands.

"Now, please. Tell me what has upset you so badly. Perhaps I can help."

"You can't help. No one can." At the despair in her voice he moved away a little and waited for her to regain her composure.

After a long silence she finally began in a low voice: "No one but Judge Granville knows this. When I came here to Zion Hill I had just been through a court hearing. I was accused of killing my brother. He had suffered a terrible accident and was crippled horribly. He could only move his eyes and speak a little. He had always been an active, athletic man, and this was like a living death for him."

She stopped, searching in her dress for a handkerchief.

"Here, take mine," George said, carefully wiping her face before putting the silk into her hands.

"He begged me to let him die—he begged everyone who came to release him. It was terrible. My heart broke for him. Then, one morning, I gave him his breakfast, and a little later, he was dead. I thought his heart had failed, but it turned out that the tea I had given him was not Bohea tea at all. It had been brewed from foxglove leaves and even had the crushed powder of several digitalin pills in the teapot. I was stunned. And since I was the only one in the house, I was accused of making and giving it to him."

"Just like . . ."

"Yes, just like Miss Evans! Do you wonder I was upset?"

"You had no idea that the tea was poisoned?"

"No. Of course not. I think he knew. Perhaps he knew

who put it there. But I saw no one. And of course, no one believed me when I tried to tell them I didn't make that tea."

"Were you out of the kitchen at all before you gave it to him?"

"Yes. Several times. I had to take care of the morning chores; so I left the tea on the table to steep."

"So someone could have entered while you were in another part of the house and exchanged pots or replaced the proper brew with the poisoned one."

"That must be what happened, but I had no way to prove it. We had this old servant. She never liked me. She accused me of killing Philip so as not to be burdened with caring for him. Horrible old crone! It wouldn't surprise me if she'd brewed that tea. She knew everything about plants and herbs. In fact, there were several people who knew and loved Philip who might have been moved by his pleas to die. But I had no way of knowing who they were."

"This trial. You were acquitted?"

"Yes. There was not enough proof, I suppose. And if there had been, the circumstances might have made a difference. At any rate, they let me go. There I was with nothing, and no place to live—I couldn't bear the thought of going back to that house—and then your father-in-law's letter came. I thought that by coming here I could forget the past and make a new start. Instead . . ."

"Instead the past has caught up with you." It seemed a natural gesture of sympathy to take her hands again, and this time she did not try to pull away. Rather, looking up into his face, even in the darkness she could sense his compassion and concern, and it was like a healing balm drawing her nearer.

"You are afraid suspicion will fall on you, since you have already been accused of using this poison once before."

"It will. It's bound to. I'll be the first one they accuse, I know it!"

"My dear, calm down. *I'm* not accusing you and I seriously doubt anyone else will either. After all, Dr. Stubbs
116

might be making a mountain out of a molehill. He could be wrong and Miss Evans died from a perfectly natural malfunction of the heart. You mustn't jump to conclusions any more than he."

Clarissa could barely see him through the tears in her eyes. "Do you really think so?"

Smiling down at her, George cupped her chin in his long fingers. "Yes, I do. Poor little Clarissa. Life has treated you badly, I'm afraid."

Leaning down, he kissed her lightly. His lips were soft, gentle, warm, with a faint taste of brandy. Clarissa was so startled that for a moment she didn't realize what was happening. Then as he pulled away, she gave a quick gasp and his arms were around her, his lips not gentle now but hard and urgent. Caught in the grip of his arms, with her arms pressed against her sides, she wanted desperately to respond, but her body was like ice—brittle and unyielding.

All at once he broke away, turned from her, and ran his fingers through his hair.

"I'm so sorry! Forgive me, I quite forgot myself."

Embarrassed, Clarissa smoothed out the skirt of her dress. Her mind was a jumble of raw sensations all rubbing against one another at once. Yet high among them was the thrilling realization that she had just experienced her first real kiss.

"It's all right," she murmured. "I—I don't mind."

He gave her a sideways glance. "You didn't? Then, do I dare to think—perhaps—"

"George—Mr. Clarendon, perhaps we'd better not say anymore about it. I thank you for your . . . your comfort."

"It is true that I do want to reassure you not to worry about this dreadful business. But Clarissa, please don't think that . . . that is, comfort was not my only concern."

Unable to look at him, Clarissa stared down at the folds of her skirt. She had run out into the night without a wrap, and the cold air added to her inner turmoil was beginning to chill her body. Noticing how she was trembling, George put his arm around her and drew her to her feet.

"Come, let's go in before you catch a cold."

"But how can I face them?"

He started her back toward the house. "Does anyone else know of this business with your brother?"

"Your father, of course. But no one else in the family."

"Then hold your head up and look them in the eye and try to remember that we are all under suspicion. You are not alone in this."

Clarissa leaned gratefully against him. It was the first time since Philip's death that she felt she had someone beside herself on whom to depend. Even the memory of that disturbing kiss filled her with happiness.

"And I will be most honored," George went on, "if you will think of me as your friend . . . more than a friend. Someone who will watch over you and protect you. Depend on me Clarissa. I won't let them persecute you. I'll be behind you no matter what happens."

Yet for all George's brave words, she found that when she entered the parlor she could not look at anyone sitting there. She was overcome with the thought that they must all be able to read from her red and swollen eyes both her guilt and the fact that George had kissed her. She choked down the brandy he gave her and, as soon as possible, retreated to her bedroom. There, between her exhaustion and the strong spirits, she fell asleep almost at once, though she had feared she would never sleep again.

It was three days before they saw Dr. Stubbs again. Then he stopped by bearing the news that an autopsy had indeed verified the remains of a massive amount of digitalis in the dead woman's stomach. He was accompanied by a tall, stooping man with a drooping grayish mustache and pale blue, kindly eyes whom he introduced as Robert Peckham, the magistrate of the western townships of the county. Quietly and unobtrusively, he had each member of the household summoned to Judge Granville's little study for a private interview. As Clarissa waited for her turn the panic she had felt on Sunday began to give way

118

to a helpless anger. What was the use! Her guilt was so obvious that no one was going to believe that she had nothing to do with Miss Evans' death, just as no one had truly believed she was innocent of her brother's.

Yet her anger gave her a new strength, and when she entered the study she was able to face Magistrate Peckham with a belligerent eye. He sat back on the upholstered settee and watched her with a calm, detached scrutiny.

"Miss Shaw?"

Clarissa was not taken in by his relaxed, casual attitude. It was obvious that behind that quiet exterior the magistrate was observing every detail of her dress and manner. Well, he wasn't going to have the satisfaction of seeing her cringe.

"Won't you have a chair?"

"No, thank you. I prefer to stand."

Robert Peckham frowned at the slight figure standing resolutely beside the fireplace. Slowly he dangled his watch fob, his mind calculating.

"You know why I am here, Miss Shaw?"

Yes. Because someone poisoned Miss Evans. And I, having been accused of doing exactly that once before, am naturally your most likely suspect.

"You seem anxious to condemn yourself."

"Why not? If you have done any inquiring at all, you know that just a few days ago Miss Evans and I quarreled. She threatened me. Many people heard her. There I was with my new home in peril and with my dubious experience to draw on. What better answer than to brew up some foxglove leaves. How shrewd of me! Well, I'm ready to go to jail when you are. I came here with little and I'll leave with little."

Her face was pale, but the telltale red flush on her cheeks betrayed her helpless anger. He studied her closely, being careful not to smile.

"Yes, it all seems to fit, doesn't it. Very neatly. Only, it does seem to me that you would have to be either incredibly stupid or else a little crazy to use foxglove again so

119

obviously. Somehow, Miss Shaw, I cannot quite see you as either."

In silence she stared at him. He went on silently twirling his gold fob, relaxed against the cushions. Finally she moved and sat carefully down on the edge of a low wingchair next to the hearth.

"You're not going to arrest me?"

"Not at this moment."

She said quietly. "But I can't prove that I didn't poison her."

"I know. It would help a great deal if you had been in the company of some other person in the household that afternoon."

"How I wish that I had!"

For the first time Robert Peckham sat up and assumed a businesslike air. "Suppose you tell me what you were doing. I want to hear every detail you can remember, both of that day and of the day you quarreled with the deceased."

"The truth is I spent a good part of that afternoon enjoying the solitude. I once saw Judge Granville from a distance, but I have no idea whether or not he saw me."

She went on to describe in some detail both her activities of that Sunday afternoon and of her quarrel with Martha Evans. Robert Peckam listened with what seemed sympathy, but his shrewd questions betrayed just how much he understood human nature as well as how much he already knew of her background. Finally, as he rose to lead her to the door he said:

"Remember, Miss Shaw. If no one can speak for you on that day, neither can you speak for anyone else. It seems as though there were several people in this house who might have unobtrusively slipped into Miss Evans' room. We won't jump to conclusions too early, I can assure you."

Her anger was dissipated by her relief. "Thank you, Mr. Peckham. Thank you more than I can say."

After everyone had suffered an inquisition, Judge Granville and Dr. Stubbs sat down with the magistrate to evaluate the results. Robert Peckham's kindly manner was transformed to a steely-edged hardness as he faced the elderly judge. He came right to the point.

"We are reasonably certain that the deceased was poisoned, but almost anyone in this house could have been responsible. I intend to do a great deal more looking about, but I tell you now, Judge, the likelihood of finding enough proof to accuse anyone of murder is almost non-existent."

"Do you mean that we shall never know who prepared that tea?"

"That is quite correct. Unless I come up against a striking piece of damaging evidence. However, for the time being, I should like to keep this quiet. It would not do at all for a gentleman of your standing to have to suffer the notoriety of a scandal."

Judge Granville did not seem to be listening. "Whom do you accuse?" he said forcefully.

"Why, I don't think I should want to label anyone as a murderer at this time. It would be premature, to say the least."

Doggedly Judge Granville pushed on. "Mr. Peckham, I deeply appreciate your consideration for my reputation, but I want you to tell me honestly. How much suspicion falls upon my poor wife? Are you doing this for me or for her?"

"Well, to be truthful, Judge, she *is* my first suspect. I believe Dr. Stubbs agrees with me."

"Yes, I do, Silas," said Dr. Stubbs. "Of course, there is your cousin, Miss Shaw. Her past places her in a very suspicious light."

"I explained about Miss Shaw to Dr. Stubbs," the magistrate interrupted. "But I simply cannot believe that anyone would be so clumsy and idiotic as to turn around and commit so openly the exact crime which she had just evaded. She doesn't seem the type to me to do such a thing."

"There is this, Silas," said Dr. Stubbs. "*You* would never be held accountable for Amelia's actions."

Judge Granville sank his head into his hands. It was

the realization of his worst fears, the thing which he had uprooted his whole family to avoid. If Amelia had done this terrible thing, it would never do to keep her at home. He would have to place her in one of those terrible institutions for the insane. Those dreadful places!

"Come, come, Judge Granville," the magistrate said. "You don't wish to see your wife brought up before Judge Tompkins in White Plains do you? Accept the matter as it is, at least for the time being."

"But never knowing for certain—that's very hard. I can't have her harming people. I'll have to confine her to her room or remove her to an asylum."

"Don't do anything like that yet. But you must make sure she has a competent nurse who will watch her at all times. I'll try to help you find the right person."

"That's kind of you, Stubbs," he muttered. There were dark shadows under his eyes, and the lines etched deeply across his cheeks made his jowls more prominent than usual. He felt very old and very tired.

Later, as the carriage rolled down the drive, Dr. Stubbs settled back against the leather cushions and turned the brim of his high hat thoughtfully in his fingers.

"Are you sure we've done the right thing?" he said to the magistrate beside him. "Perhaps we should have insisted that poor woman be put away."

Peckham shook his head slowly. "No. I think this is the way to handle it, but I confess the whole business is very unsettling. Certainly she will have to be watched a good deal more carefully."

The doctor settled his beaver hat carefully on his bald head. "We may be putting compassion ahead of justice, but I do believe it would kill that old man to place her in one of those asylums. They're like prisons. The idiot, the deformed, the insane—all thrown together in a dung heap."

"Well, I'm not finished yet. I intend to keep digging away at Zion Hill myself. In the meantime, you must let me know if anything of significance comes to light. It hasn't been a lucky house, that, has it?"

Dr. Stubbs pictured what he remembered of Matthias the Prophet, arms upraised, face contorted, his tattered burlap robes billowing around him. "Unlucky! I would call that an understatement."

Eight

As the Friday evening of Mr. Ashley's diner party approached, the discussion over whether or not they should attend became the favorite topic of family debate. Though none of them really felt like facing a social affair, neither could they come up with a reasonable excuse to beg off. As Augusta so succinctly put it, how could they say they were in mourning for Mrs. Granville's nurse!

Early that Friday morning Samuel Evans arrived at Zion Hill to dispose of his sister's effects and to take her body back to Richmond for burial. Nancy ushered him into the study where Clarissa was working with Judge Granville. Adam, who had been lounging in a chair by the window, looked up curiously from the brief he had been reviewing with his father.

Samuel Evans could hardly have less resembled his dead sister Martha. He was stooped and slight, with a gray pallor that made his face look like a continuation of his threadbare suit, and the most prominent thing about him was his nose. Above it his brow sloped back toward thinning hair, while below it, thin lips and a receding chin slanted inward to a limp, dingy, four-inch-wide cravat.

He continually bowed and touched his forehead to

Judge Granville, calling him "your honor" and "sir" between every sentence, but Clarissa noted that his eyes were filled with an unsmiling malevolence. When at length the judge rose to accompany him up to his sister's old room, Adam closed the door behind them and fell laughing against it.

"My God! Did you see that? He's worse than she was, and I didn't think such a thing was possible. Such a family! What could the parents have been like? Museum specimens!"

"He did not seem to be very upset over his sister's death, did he?"

"He probably didn't like her any more than we did."

Clarissa couldn't help smiling. "It isn't kind to say so, but . . . well, he had a king of 'ferrety' appearance, didn't he?"

"Why don't you come right out and say it. He looks like a weasel! A human weasel."

"Now that is not charitable, Mr. Granville."

"No, it isn't. But he didn't look particularly charitable himself. Under all that obsequiousness, he wanted to murder us all."

Clarissa blotted the letter she had just finished and laid it on a neat stack in the box.

"It's difficult to imagine those two—Evans and his sister—as children. I wonder what they were like."

"I'm sure they were never children. They just appeared, full-bodied, in all their shallow nastiness. Like an insect crawling out of a chrysalis." He flung his long body carelessly across a small sofa. "What is that country—India, I believe—where people think that when they die they come back in the body of an animal."

"Yes, India. Are you suggesting Mr. Evans didn't completely evolve?"

"Something like that. It's the only explanation."

She couldn't help laughing, for once not taking him seriously. "Adam Granville, you are too irreverent. Mr. Evans must have the same hopes and aspirations that we all share . . . though I do sometimes wonder what kind of feelings people like that have."

"Now that is exactly what I mean. Do they have a sense of beauty in the world around them? Do they love deeply? Do they ever ask 'who am I?' and 'why was I put on this earth?' Do they have a sense of history or of destiny? I don't think so. In fact, I doubt if any of those thoughts ever occur to them."

"Yes, but you can't know. We might be doing Mr. Evans a grave injustice. He may be feeling sorry for us!"

Adam laughed, watching her reflectively under his dark brows. "Sorry for me! That scurvy creature."

Clarissa smiled up at him mischievously. "Oh, for a moment I forgot how all-knowing are the reaches of your mind and the depths of your character. Forgive me, sir."

"Well, just see that it doesn't happen again."

He was so obviously teasing her that Clarissa found herself almost liking him again. She laughed delightedly.

"Adam Granville, you are too much. I think half your pomposity is sham."

He smiled back at her. "You know, this is the first time I have been able to make you laugh."

"The first day I came here Augusta told me not to take you seriously, but it was difficult not to. And sometimes I think you deliberately try to make me angry."

"You are very pretty when you get angry. Did you know that?"

Clarissa looked quickly down at her hands, all at once terribly self-conscious.

"Even if that were true, it is no excuse for provoking people."

Reaching for his cane, Adam pulled himself to his feet. "I know. It is my fatal flaw. I hope you will not take me seriously again."

She glanced up at him from under her lashes. "I wonder sometimes if underneath that carefully cultivated, prickly exterior there is not perhaps a very nice person."

"Humph! Before my reputation is completely destroyed, I will flee to the stables. I don't think I want to run into that Evans fellow again. Tell Papa I'll be back within the hour."

From the window Clarissa watched him limping across

the grass, leaning heavily on his cane. He was a young man to be burdened with a crippled leg. Even as he walked with a cane, there was a grace and rhythm to his stride, the sinewy control of the athlete. Was it Augusta who had told her that he had loved horses and been a superb rider? It could not have been easy to give all of that up and live as half a man. It must not be easy to live with constant pain. She recalled the tiny beads of perspiration on his lip on days when the weather was particularly damp and raw. That shattered leg probably gave him a great deal of misery at times, though he would never admit it. Perhaps that accounted for some of the anger behind so many of his caustic comments.

Judge Granville did not return to his work, and after waiting almost an hour, and having accomplished all she could do alone, Clarissa decided it was time to get back to the schoolroom. She was just replacing some papers in the gilt letter-box when the door opened and George Clarendon slipped inside.

Her heart gave a flutter. It was the first time she had seen him alone since that night in the arbor, and many times since, she had relived the memory of his lips brushing her own. She expected to feel nothing but delight to be with him again, but as he moved to sit beside her, taking her hands, she felt herself pulling away from him.

"My dear Clarissa. What luck to find you alone. I've searched for this opportunity for days."

Looking into his blue gray eyes with their feathery canopy of honey-colored brows, Clarissa was engulfed in a wave of self-consciousness. He held tightly to her hands.

"Tell me about your ordeal with the law. Did that horrible magistrate give you a difficult time?"

"No, no," she stammered. "He was very considerate."

"And there was no question of his accusing you, I take it."

"Not for the moment, at least." She attempted to describe her interview with Robert Peckham, all the while conscious of how stumbling her words sounded.

His face was all relief. "I am so glad for you. Your

fears were unfounded, as I told you they would be." He raised her hands to his lips, lightly brushing her palms and fingertips. Clarissa found herself cringing. What in the world was wrong with her? She longed to move into his arms, easily and naturally, as she had done that night in the arbor, but she seemed to be walled in behind an immovable reserve.

At last George sensed her discomfort. He laid her hands in her lap and moved to stand beside the mantel.

"Forgive me, my dear. I go too fast. I am carried away in my . . . my admiration for you. I forget your delicacy, your fragility."

"Oh, no," Clarissa stammered. Good heavens, she was neither delicate nor fragile. Couldn't he see that?

"My dear, this is not the time for declarations. There is too much that is upsetting in this house right now for that. Yet, I hope I do not offend you if I dare to hope that you may come to feel some of the same . . . admiration for me that I feel for you. May I just say that much?"

"I—I already do," she said, not able to look at him. She could feel the flush on her cheeks.

"Thank you," George said quietly. "You make me very happy. Now, for the time being, we'll rest at that. Only, I do want you to remember that I am watching over you and that if you need any advice or—assurance, you must come to me. You will do that, won't you?"

"Yes. And thank you."

He moved back to the small sofa and cupped her chin in one of his long hands. "Our time will come, my dear." Leaning down, he kissed her delicately on her forehead and then was gone as quickly as he had entered.

Clarissa sat for a moment, her thoughts in turmoil. He loves me—or at least he will love me. My heart should be singing and I should be completely happy. For the first time in my life to be loved and in love . . .

Yet this feeling which obsessed her was not happiness. It was anxiety, trepidation, and yes, even fear!

She gathered the papers together and locked them in the letter box. Why on earth should she be afraid? It must

128

be because of all that has happened, she told herself. Miss Evans, reminders of Philip's death, her concern over a second accusation of murder—no love could thrive in that kind of soil. It had to be that.

Since it was a raw, blustery day, she kept the children inside playing in their room, while she sat near the fire mending a petticoat. There was a small copper kettle on the fireplace trivet whose quiet sputterings indicated the water inside had boiled away. Feeling the need for a little exercise, Clarissa took it and climbed down the stairs to the kitchen to refill it. The room was empty at that moment, although a savory stew bubbled on the old-fashioned black iron stove, filling the low-ceilinged room with the pungent odors of onions and squirrel meat.

She went into the old kitchen where a rusted iron handle stood above a wooden sink, and began working the pump up and down. Low voices seemed to come from the ceiling above her head. Someone was talking in the dining room above, quietly and indistinctly. A flue near her shoulder almost allowed her to eavesdrop, had she been so inclined; but she ignored the conversation until the speaker's loud agitated voice came through so clearly that it caught her attention. She recognized the whining voice of Samuel Evans, more brittle now with anger.

"I didn't bargain for nothin' like this!" he said distinctly. "Snoopin's one thing, but killin'! And my own sis, too. I'm not sayin' I'm cryin' over it—she was misery to live with, that one—but still! I'm just sayin' I didn't reckon on no murder."

Clarissa strained to hear the second voice, but she could only catch a quiet blur not clear enough to identify the speaker.

"The money's not worth it—" Evans broke in. All at once his voice dropped abruptly. His companion must have warned him.

Clarissa pressed her ear to the opening of the flue but could catch nothing. Then Evans' voice rang out again.

"Don't you get uppity with me! Maybe there's them as would like to know who paid me to go round the docks askin' questions. Maybe it was you that fed that tea to my sis—"

She gasped and pressed closer, but the voices seemed to be moving away. Only a few words were distinct now— "know," "tell," "them as . . ."

They must be leaving the room, she thought. If I can get upstairs, I can see who it is that was talking with that man. They won't know I heard them. This may be my only chance to find out who killed Martha Evans!

She ran through the room into the new kitchen, then toward the stairs. In her haste she caught her wide billowing skirts on a protruding nail in the baseboard and almost fell backward. She yanked at the cloth, losing precious seconds as her hurried attempts only twisted the fabric more tightly around the rusted spike. Finally yanking it loose and leaving a piece of her skirt behind, she raced up to the main floor.

The hall was empty. She moved quickly down it to the dining room, but there was no one there. Fighting down her disappointment, she retraced her steps to a bench in the hall and sat down, too absorbed to notice the unsightly rent in her skirt.

Obviously Evans was involved somehow in the death of his sister. Or, at least, someone in this house was involved, and Evans was working with that person. If only she knew who it was. If only she hadn't been too late to see them.

Voices from the front door to her right brought her to her feet. One of them was surely Evans. There he was, framed in the doorway, holding a battered carpetbag and winding a tattered scraf around his scrawny neck. And talking to someone who stood on the veranda out of her line of vision.

She could see an arm reaching out, handing something to the slight man as he buttoned his shabby greatcoat and tucked the parcel into the cloth bag. Clarissa stepped softly against the wall and peered down the hallway just as Evans moved off and a figure stepped back inside, silhouetted against the gray light of dusk. Quietly he closed

130

the big front door and turned to stride down the hall straight toward her.

She found herself looking directly into the pale, stern, fatherly blue eyes of Judge Silas Granville.

Nine

By that evening Clarissa's thoughts were still in a jumble as she went about the business of curling her hair and slipping into her gray silk. Her motions were automatic with barely a thought of what she was doing and very little care as to how she looked.

She could not believe it had been Judge Granville talking to Samuel Evans in the dining room that afternoon. How was it possible that a man of such stern integrity could be involved in the sordid and sinister business of murder and deception? Was this picture the judge presented to the world just a masquerade? Was there another person underneath, secretive and ruthless, that no one suspected was there?

Surely not. Perhaps it had been someone else in the dining room, someone who slipped away as the judge came to show Evans out. Yet the uneasy suspicion persisted that it had taken her so little time to run up the stairs, even considering the moments she lost trying to free her skirt. The man on the porch should have been the same man who was talking with Evans in the dining room, but it was unthinkable that Judge Granville was that man —the person who had poisoned Miss Evans, who had cast suspicion on her even though he knew what she had already suffered, who cast suspicion on his wife! It just wasn't possible.

Over and over it went, and finally she resolved on one conclusive step. Somehow she would discover whom she'd heard talking with Evans in that room upstairs.

Fully dressed, she sat down on the bed, mulling over what unobtrusive question she might use to trap that man into revealing himself. Across the worn Wilton carpet she saw the door to the children's room swinging quietly open.

"You look pretty!" cried Mary, running to Clarissa and climbing up beside her. Georgie followed in a long, white nightshirt, clambering up into Clarissa's lap and snuggling against her.

"Stop it, Georgie. You'll wrinkle Miss Shaw's pretty dress!" His sister tugged at the boy's thin arm, but Clarissa gently moved her away, then slipped her free arm around the girl's shoulders.

"It doesn't matter. We are just going to supper at Mr. Ashley's, and a few wrinkles won't spoil the dinner."

"Are you going to ride in the barouche?" George asked, taking his thumb out of his mouth long enough to speak the words, then darting it swiftly back.

"I imagine that we will. The whole family is going, so it will probably take that and the gig to carry us." Clarissa knew that she should remove the offending thumb, but somehow it didn't bother her as much as it did all the other adults. She had been so anxious to have the child relax with her that it seemed a mistake to nag him about something he loved, bad habit that it was. Perhaps he would grow out of it.

As though he read her mind, out came the thumb, and Georgie looked up at her, his eyes round and wide. "I hope I get to drive the barouche someday. Do you think Papa would let me?"

"You're only a baby," Mary said with scorn. "You have to be big like Papa to drive a carriage. Especially such a big one."

Clarissa smoothed back the long wavy strands that fell

over the boy's forehead. "I'm sure that someday when you are grown up and are a fine gentleman like your father, you will drive a carriage as much as you want."

"Do you like my father?" Mary's sudden question and sideways glance caught Clarissa by surprise.

"Why, yes, I do," she answered, hoping that her voice didn't betray how much.

"I don't," Georgie said matter-of-factly.

"Why, George. You mustn't say such a thing."

Mary quickly stepped in. "Oh, we love our father because we must, but he really doesn't pay much attention to us. Sometimes he is not nice to us at all. I think that is what Georgie means."

Clarissa was startled; yet on reflection she could understand how they had come to feel this way about George Clarendon. He was so often cold and aloof toward them. They had never seen the warm, affectionate man who had shown her such tender concern.

"I think you will probably come to like him better as you grow older. That is often the way it is with fathers."

"I never liked Miss Evans either," Mary said suddenly.

Georgie sat up in Clarissa's lap and tucked his thumb protectively under his arm. "Nancy said that Miss Evans went to heaven. Is that true? Did she really die?"

Oh, dear, thought Clarissa. They had all hoped to shield these children from this unpleasantness, but no telling how much of the commotion over the nurse's death had filtered up to the schoolroom. She tried to make her voice casual.

"Yes, unfortunately she did die. Very suddenly."

"Don't you know that she was murdered?" Mary said with all the air of her grandfather making a pronouncement.

Clarissa caught her breath.

"That's right—she was!" cried Georgie, his eyes alight with animation. "A man ten feet tall with a big sword and two pistols chopped off her head. Bang! Bang! Just like that."

Mary looked at him contemptuously. "No, you silly boy. That is not the way it was at all. He came through

134

the window at night and put a pillow over her head, just like the picture of the two princes in the Tower of London."

"No, no," Georgie cried angrily. "He chopped off her head. I know he did!"

By this time Clarissa had got her voice back. "I don't know where you children get such ideas," she said sternly. "Miss Evans ate some spoiled food and it made her sick."

"Oh, is that all?" Mary's disappointment was obvious.

"So sick that her body could not fight off her illness and she died."

"Just like Mama," Mary added gravely. "That is what happened to Mama. She got so sick that she died."

Georgie snuggled back up against Clarissa, crushing the ruching she had so carefully ironed. "Mama went to live with God in heaven."

"Miss Shaw," said Mary, "does that mean that Miss Evans is with Mama and God in heaven now?"

Clarissa hardly knew how to answer. The thought of that sour-faced bitter woman walking the golden streets surrounded by the blessed angels—it was ludicrous. But Mary went on, answering her own question.

"I don't think Miss Evans would go to heaven, because she was mean. Mama was kind and good. She deserved to be with God. But Miss Evans—she wasn't a nice person at all. I think she would go to that other place."

Her words brought back the conversation Clarissa had shared with Adam in Judge Granville's study. Perhaps uncle and niece had more in common than either of them suspected.

"Well, Mary," she finally answered, "Miss Evans was not a happy person, and perhaps that is why she was so often mean. I think we should leave her to God to judge. Now, you children must let me get downstairs or I'll miss the party."

She kissed them both and sent them back to their bedroom feeling better about the evening. That was the wonderful thing about children—they took your mind off your own problems.

Downstairs the family was gathered in the hall waiting for her. Augusta tapped her foot impatiently.

"I hope you realize, Clarissa, that you have very nearly made us late."

"I'm sorry. I was saying good-night to the children."

George quickly stepped up to place her cloak over her shoulders. "You must not coddle the children, Miss Shaw. I speak as their father. They cannot learn too early in life that punctuality is the hallmark of a considerate person."

"But they are so young. They will learn soon enough. I think they already know more than any of you suspect."

"Oh! And now we are to have a lecture on child-rearing from the expert governess." Augusta put extra emphasis on the last word.

"What do you mean, Clarissa?" the judge asked, ignoring his daughter's rudeness.

"Only that they have learned of Miss Evans' death and are upset and confused by it. I wanted to help them understand it better."

"Dear me. But I suppose it is only to be expected. Children have big ears and an uncanny way of knowing when a household is upset. You did the right thing, my dear, and we shall still arrive on time if we leave right away. We must try to put all this business from our minds and act as though life here is going along as usual."

"Yes, indeed," Adam said archly. "The only thing worse than a murder in the house is the neighbors talking about it. So let's put a good face on things."

And they did exactly that. In fact, the warm cheerful fire, the delicious dinner graciously served, the hearty good humor of their hosts—all gradually dispelled the gloom of Zion Hill and created a relaxed camaraderie among the Granvilles. Mr. Ashly took great delight in showing Clarissa over his charming house, pointing with pride to every ancient stone, wide plank, and antique whatnot left from the previous century. She made the expected responses, but all the while, at the back of her mind, she was watching for an opening when she might slip in a question designed to discover who Evans' companion had been in the dining room at the Hill.

Such a moment finally arrived after the gentlemen finished their port and joined the ladies in the pleasant drawing room. There was some discussion as to whether to set up the card tables or have the ladies provide a bit of musical entertainment, which burning question was at length resolved by two tables of whist. At eleven the tea table appeared, and the company regrouped itself on the sofas and chairs to enjoy their coffee and cakes.

Mrs. Ashley, a plump, affable counterpart to her husband, sat beside Clarissa on the velvet tufted sofa and attempted to draw her out.

"My husband tells me that you are from New York," she said as she offered Clarissa a delicate pink and white Staffordshire cup. "I lived in New York myself for several years and found it a most stimulating experience. So many delightful social functions to amuse one—balls, afternoon teas, the gardens, the theater, the opera. I fear our quaint country living is sadly dull after the society of the city."

"I was never a part of New York society, Mrs. Ashley. I lived very quietly on a farm above Manhattanville, almost at the end of the island. It was as much a rural life there as any here in Mount Pleasant."

Mrs. Ashley had the grace to look flustered. "But you must have taken advantage of the town, being so near. And I believe there is a railroad now . . ."

Adam spoke up before Clarissa had a chance to answer. "The railroad stops at Thirty-first Street, Mrs. Ashley, although it is extended farther every year. In not too many years it may even reach Manhattanville."

Clarissa was conscious of George leaning on the couch behind her. "In fact, I doubt that there will be any farms left on Manhattan Island in a few years," he said. "The open land now beyond Thirty-fourth Street is already being sold at unbelievable prices."

"Did you know, Robert," said Judge Granville to his host, "that there is serious talk of putting in a rail line along the river as far up as Poughkeepsie? I was approached about purchasing stock in it, but I can't make up my mind if it is a good investment or not."

"Not only do I know, but I have already committed myself to several shares. You should too, Silas. It's the coming thing, mark my words. That and the water line they are proposing from Croton. What do you say, George? You're a lawyer. Am I right?"

"Oh, I agree with you completely. Once the railroad comes—although that probably won't be for another ten years—it will signal a period of great expansion for the entire county. And you may make a tidy bit of money on it."

"I'd rather put my money in the mills," said Adam. "If I had any to invest. They are springing up all over Westchester. In a few more years there may be no more farmland up here anymore than in New York City."

"Oh, no, Adam," Mr. Ashley puffed expansively on a newly lit Havana cigar. "If such a time ever comes, it will be many, many years away. As important as industry is, it will never replace the simple yeoman farmer with his small plot and his milch-cow. Why, the backbone of this nation is the small farmer working his own little part-hundred in peace and contentment. The country could never get along without him."

Clarissa watched in amusement as the pink-cheeked, well fed, heavily paunched Mr. Ashley extoled the virtues of the simple farmer scratching for a living; Mr. Ashley, sitting in his creweled wing-chair, surrounded by his silver and antiques, who a moment before was extoling the virtues of investing in the railroads. Her thoughts were interrupted when the exquisite French clock on the mantel struck twelve.

"Dear me, I didn't realize how late it had become, the time has passed so pleasantly." Judge Granville dug at the pocket of his waistcoat for his huge, round gold watch to check it against the clock.

"Oh, I forgot. I have misplaced my watch somewhere and am quite lost without it. Such a nuisance."

Augusta stirred restlessly in her chair. "Perhaps you put it down somewhere, Papa, and forgot to pick it up. Though I must say that is certainly not like you at all."

138

He turned to Clarissa. "You haven't seen it lying about the house, have you?"

She was about to answer no when she saw her chance. Looking him straight in the eye she answered: "I believe I saw it lying on the sideboard in the dining room this afternoon."

He stared at her, his face suddenly an unreadable mask; yet, not before she caught the sudden darkening of his eyes. "Oh, no, I don't think so. I haven't been in the dining room at all today."

Clarissa was conscious that the room was very still. Yet she dared not stop now. "Oh, but I heard you. Downstairs in the old kitchen. I was filling the kettle at the pump and I heard voices through the flue . . ."

The silence in the room was oppressive. Everyone seemed to be watching her. She glanced around nervously.

"Perhaps I was mistaken . . ."

"No doubt you heard someone else. Yes, I distinctly remember now. I missed breakfast completely and had a simple lunch in my study. I never entered the dining room all day. Perhaps you saw the watch somewhere else?"

"Yes, it may have been somewhere else—" she murmured nervously, smoothing the folds of her skirt. The other voices began to cover her embarrassment. Well, that hadn't accomplished anything. And whoever had been talking to Evans now knew that she had overheard them. If only she could control her tongue! She glanced furtively around at each face; Augusta, laughing quietly at some remark of Mrs. Ashley's; Hannah, fussing with her curls, withdrawn and silent; Adam, dark and inscrutable; George, graciously agreeing with his host over the merits of the aqueduct; and Judge Granville, stony and unusually quiet. Was he avoiding her eyes? She was grateful when, a few moments later, he rose to begin their leave-taking.

The night air was crisp and cold in spite of the warmth of the day past. George Clarendon, sitting next to Clarissa in the coach, saw her pull her cloak around her shoulders and, unnoticed by the others, edged nearer her. She could feel the warmth of his body next to hers, and it awoke once again that delicious excitement which at once embarrassed and delighted her. She looked quietly over at Adam sitting across from them, but for once he was too absorbed in his reflections on the evening to notice.

"That Robert Ashley!" he exclaimed to his father. "He's a good man, but he has no more idea of the kind of life the 'simple yeoman farmer' leads than Hannah's pony! Why, give him a 'part-hundred' plot and a milch-cow and he'd starve to death. I doubt he's ever been hungry or had dirt under his fingernails in his entire life."

Judge Granville half-heartedly attempted to defend his friend. "Robert had always been inclined to take a romantic view of life. It's a strange trait in a man so shrewd in business matters."

"That's just it. He lives cleanly off the grime of poorer men. We both know he has interests in the mills both at Bedford and Owensville, and I've seen some of those places. They are downright inhuman. He's living off these people while he postures about the beauties of the 'simple life.' It turns my stomach."

"You don't understand, Adam. He just prefers to see the beauty of this world and ignore the ugliness."

"It takes both kinds," George added absently. "What is that old proverb? Two men walked through the woods, and one saw the stars, while the other saw only the mud."

"Yes, and one came home dirty!" Adam exclaimed. "Good-hearted or not, he talks like a pompous ass."

Clarissa was sorry when the gentle rocking of the carriage ended as the big blond horse pulled it up to the rear of the house. When George handed her down, she tried to ignore the affectionate pressure he gave her hand. He stood looking down at her as though there were no one there but the two of them.

"Good night, cousin Clarissa."

"Good night," she answered, her voice barely audible. She almost ran into the house, confused but at the same time exhilarated. Everyone must have seen the way he spoke to her. It must be obvious to the whole family that there was something between them. Once again she was obsessed with that strange mixture of happiness tempered by fear. She ought to feel proud and excited; yet she could not put from her mind the way Judge Granville had looked at her when she revealed that she had heard the voices in the dining room, that sudden coldness in his eyes. Still the judge was a good man. Surely it was non-sense to suspect him of doing anything evil or depraved. Surely it was ridiculous to be afraid.

But she was afraid. And no amount of concentration on George Clarendon could push that fear from her mind.

Ten

The day dawned with a full burst of warm, spring sunshine. Unusually mild weather had touched the budding trees and shrubs and nudged them to open their precious new foliage right before the eyes of the thankful populace. George came into the breakfast room with eyes shining and full of plans for the day.

"This is it," he exclaimed. "The perfect day for a ride to Andre's Cave! What do you say, Clarissa? Augusta? Hannah? Let's make a picnic of it."

Clarissa felt a cold knot of fear in her stomach. She had hoped this idea had been quietly dropped forever. The thought of a long ride on a strange horse filled her with foreboding.

Hannah spoke first. "You know I never ride, George."

"Well," said Augusta. "I'll go along. I was going to take Sultan out anyway and I haven't been that way for some time."

"Good for you!" said George. "You can be in charge of the picnic basket. Get Nancy to put some things together for a light lunch. Well, Clarissa? What do you think?"

She hoped her lack of enthusiasm wasn't too obvious.

"I don't have a riding habit, you know. And I haven't ridden in some time. I don't think . . ."

"I have one which might fit you," Hannah broke in. "Papa had it made for me, but I've never cared for riding; so it's hardly been worn. It's a beautiful dark green and would look lovely with your auburn hair. Please take it, Clarissa. It would please me so for you to have it."

Clarissa wished that Hannah's heart were not so generous, but there was nothing to do but accept her offer.

George was not to be deterred. "You can ride that old blond, Russ. He's as friendly and gentle as a big dog. Believe me, it will be like sitting in a rocking chair."

Clarissa doubted that, but before she could think of an answer George had turned to Adam. Now it was his turn to speak without enthusiasm.

"How about you, Adam? Will you join us?"

"I have things to do," Adam said with disdain. Of course, thought Clarissa, riding would be out for him, but it was thoughtful of George to ask.

"Then it's settled. We can ride across Bishop's Hill, then cut across Pocantico Creek. And we'll take Edwards along as groom so that Clarissa can feel doubly safe. Such a beautiful spring day—perfect for a ride and a picnic."

Clarissa made one last effort. "But the children. Their lessons. Their regular schedule will be upset."

"Nonsense." Nothing was going to dampen George's high spirits. "As their father I command you to give them a day's holiday. I'm sure they would much prefer being out of doors to poring over schoolbooks."

It was on the tip of Clarissa's tongue to say, "What about discipline and punctuality?" but she held back the bitter words. It must be just her fear of riding that made her so caustic about this venture. Even the most strict disciplinarian had to relax sometime.

George consulted the clock. "We'll try to be away in an hour. Clarissa, you are going to enjoy this, I know you are."

Clarissa tried to smile, wanting to share some of the delight that so animated his face, but unable to throw off her dread of the whole thing.

As it turned out, the lovely green riding habit fit her tolerably well, but old blond Russ was, as she suspected, a long way from a rocking chair. Even the most gentle and good-natured of horses knows instinctively when an inexperienced rider has climbed aloft, and Russ was no exception. Without a firm hand on the reins he found he preferred the pleasure of standing and pulling at the tender new shrubbery leaves to starting on a long walk. Clarissa kicked at the broad side, her face pink with embarrassment, while Augusta, deftly holding her spirited Sultan in check, could barely contain her contempt.

"Got to let him know who's master, miss," said Edward as he circled his mount around to give Russ a swat on the backside. The horse lurched suddenly forward, and Clarissa rocked in the saddle, pulling frantically at the reins.

What an inglorious beginning, she thought gloomily as they started down the wide riding path through the woods. As they rode however, her confidence returned by slow degrees, and she found she could manage the amiable horse well enough to feel that she would get through the day.

"Come on, Edwards," cried Augusta. "I want to let Sultan have a gallop. He's bursting to have his head." In a cloud of dust she and the groom left the others far behind, ambling sedately under the canopy of beech and ash which lined the road.

Clarissa eyed George from under the low brim of her green felt riding hat. "I am sure that you would prefer to have a run with them rather than saunter along at my slow speed."

"On the contrary," he smiled. "I was hoping they would go ahead and give us some time to be together. It's rare enough that we have these minutes alone and I treasure them."

To her dismay Clarissa felt her cheeks burning. How annoying to be tongue-tied when she ached to be charming and flirtatious.

"I treasure them too," she murmured.

"Is that true, Clarissa?" His frank gaze was disarming.

144

"I have been wondering if perhaps the idea of an elderly widower with two small children might not be unattractive to someone as fresh and young as yourself."

"Elderly! You are certainly not old. And I love your children!"

"And their father? Could you love him also?"

She tried to return his frank gaze, but her eyes fell almost against her will. He could see that she was embarrassed.

"That was an indelicate question. Please don't answer it now. Let us enjoy the day and the ride, and I will withhold my question until a more appropriate moment. But I promise you—I will ask it again."

"What was your wife like?" She could hear the quick catch of his breath and she was astounded at her own words. Yet she realized for the first time that this was a question which had been seething at the back of her mind since she first met George Clarendon.

For a long minute he didn't answer. The gentle thudding of the horses' hoofs on the packed clay kept a rhythmic accompaniment to the noises of birds and insects in the woods around them.

Had she offended him? Glancing sideways, she saw him sitting straight in the saddle, the reins caught lightly in his gloved hand, his profile like a marble statue under his smart beaver riding hat.

"So that's what's troubling you," he finally said. The debonair gaiety was gone, replaced with a chill formality. "She was a lovely girl. Very pretty and very young. She was fond of the children and especially coddled young George. I think much of his excessive shyness is the result of her overprotection." He paused. "We didn't always agree, but she was an obedient wife, a good hostess, and ran a trim household."

Not the words of a grieving lover, Clarissa thought.

He seemed to read her thoughts. "I was very sorry when she died," he went on, "but life must be lived. The children needed the care of a family, so we moved out here with my father-in-law. It hasn't been a bad life for them or me, especially since you joined us."

"They don't mention her very often at the Hill. I've often wondered how she fit in with the others."

"Oh, she was very much like Hannah but with more poise and social grace. Augusta, of course, tried to direct her life, but when she realized that Jenny was having none of that, she gave in and left her alone. I believe that she and Adam were very close as children, but after our marriage they grew apart."

Suddenly the infectious grin was back. "But come, let the dead rest. Why discuss the past on such a beautiful day. Do you think you could manage a canter if that lazy beast can be encouraged to move? Let's try."

He was right of course. The past was gone and better forgotten. The present was here to enjoy. Clarissa gave Russ a heaving kick, and he grudgingly broke into a sedate canter. At the High Road, they found Augusta and Edwards waiting for them.

On the other side of the road the path wound upward through increasingly rough, wild foliage. Occasionally they skirted a neatly plowed field and once they had to weave their way through a small flock of sheep ambling across the riding path toward the meadow on the other side. Then, as the land rose, they left behind the cultivated fields, and the path wound between thick coppices of chestnut, maple, and tulip trees, or broke out into wild open fields cluttered with great jagged rocks whose sides looked as though they had been split with a giant anvil. When they finally stopped for lunch, they were on the highest point above the river. Below them the wide expanse of the Tappan Zee narrowed down toward New York, a doorway to the Atlantic, while to the north the river twisted and wound its way between the green walls of the highlands. A thin, opaque haze hung over the edge of the Catskills, but above it the sky was a brilliant clear blue tufted with white cotton-ball clouds.

Clarissa breathed deeply of the clear, pure air and thought how beautiful the valley was when you looked down on it from above. While the horses cropped nearby, they enjoyed the sliced ham, cheese, and fruit Nancy had

146

put up for them, then lay on the grass languidly watching the changing sculpture of the clouds.

George finally got everybody back on their feet. "Come on. Just another half hour and we'll be at the cave. You can rest longer there, everyone but Clarissa. It's her first time and she has to explore."

With some good-natured grumbling they were on their way again and soon arrived at the rock formations which encircled Andre's Cave. It was a bleak spot—huge barren boulders scattered among the wild trees and thickets of barberry. The famous cave where Major Andre supposedly spent the night before his capture was not a cave at all, merely an indentation reaching far back under a stone overhang. It would afford some shelter, of course, and Clarissa could almost picture the haunted man, wrapped in a black cloak, huddling under the far recesses of the rock.

"It's not much of a cave, is it?" she commented as George helped her to dismount.

"No, but there is a real one back in there which I intend to show you as soon as the horses are tethered. There's a small grassy spot through those trees where they can graze for a bit while we look around."

As Augusta and Edwards led the horses away, George took Clarissa's hand and led her past the hollow, working his way behind its jutting sides toward a narrow slit. By turning sideways they could manage to slip between the two steep granite sides to a small entrance.

"Now this is a genuine cave," said George, amused. "If you bend down far enough, you can see inside."

Clarissa hunched over low enough to peer into the darkness of the small hole. There was just enough light to suggest that beyond the opening the cave became larger, almost big enough to stand. She thought she heard the faint murmur of running water deep inside.

"Oh, it's fascinating," she said, pulling up her skirts to crawl inside the small opening. "Does it go far back?"

"Yes, but we won't follow it very far. You have to have candles and lanterns once you're beyond the pittance of light allowed by this entrance. I'm told it leads eventually into some of the old mine shafts near the house, but that's just a rumor. I don't know anyone who has actually explored these depths to that degree."

"You mean, if you started at the old mine entrance by the river, you would go back this far? I can hardly believe it!"

"I know. It does sound far-fetched, but that's what I've been told. Here, let me help you . . ."

He had grasped her arm, but a sudden shout from the copse beyond the rocks caused him to turn back. "Oh, blast," he said, "that's Augusta. There must be something wrong with the horses."

Clarissa could just hear Augusta's voice calling George in her usual preemptory manner. How annoying, just when she was about to enter the entrancing little cave.

"I suppose I must go and see what they want, although why those two experts can't manage a few horses I can't imagine. Wait here for me."

Clarissa pulled back. "All right," she sighed.

"And don't go in until I get back," George called over his shoulder as he started toward the copse.

"Why not? Are there snakes, or bears?"

"No, but it's dangerous all the same. I'll be right back."

He disappeared around the edge of the rocks, and Clarissa sat down on a low boulder to wait for him. The sun was warm on her neck under the V-shaped collar of the riding habit, but her impatience prevented her from enjoying its comfort. She looked longingly at the darkened entrance.

"I don't see why I have to wait for him," she said to herself, her voice startlingly loud amid the quiet noises of the woods. The minutes crept sluggishly by as she waited impatiently. Finally, when he still did not appear, she gathered up her skirts and stepped to the entrance.

"It won't hurt just to step inside," she said, still talking to herself. "I won't go any farther than the opening."

Getting through the small hole turned out to be more difficult than it looked, but with a little wiggling and pulling at the confining fabric of her habit, she finally edged her way through and stood upright inside the cave.

148

She looked around, enthralled. The black sides and roof of basaltic rock were flecked with silver which the dim sunlight filtering through the opening set afire like stars in a midnight sky. The greenish black stone was alive with the shimmer of the reflected rays of sunlight, giving her the feeling of standing inside a large jewel. She turned slowly around, soaking in the beauty of it. Then she grew conscious of the dim murmur of water far back where the light faded to complete darkness and, gently resting her hand against the clammy wall, she edged her way toward the tunnel under the rocks. Looking back she saw the entrance again, shimmering in its nimbus of emerald light, different from when she stood in it, yet still beautiful, like the changing patterns of light in a revolving diamond.

She turned to go a little farther and suddenly found herself swallowed by the blackness. No light here at all. Nothing but a vast emptiness—like being blind, Clarissa supposed. She reached out and all around her the rock seemed to close in. All at once the cave, which a moment before had seemed bright and spacious became instead a small hole carved in the rock, enclosing and suffocating. She caught at her breath, panic swelling in her chest, and groped her way back along the damp granite. It was suddenly terribly important to get out of there, to get back to light and open air. She had to catch herself to keep from running like some foolish coward.

Then the light went out completely, and she was enclosed by the dark. Gasping, she stared where the entrance had been. It was as though a solid wall had descended over the entrance, a stone door slamming shut. For a horrible few seconds she saw herself buried alive, gasping for air in a black suffocating hole.

"Clarissa?"

The darkness shifted and took shape, and she could see George silhouetted against the light. "Clarissa, are you in there?"

Clarissa could feel her breath released on a wave of relief. "Yes, I'm here," she said, thinking how foolish she had been.

"I thought I told you not to go in until I got back. Shame on you, you naughty girl."

He was standing inside now, groping for her. "Where the devil are you? I can't see a thing in here."

"Over here," Clarissa moved toward him, anxious to feel his solid flesh beneath her hand. She felt his arms go around her and gladly and willingly she leaned against him. She was annoyed at herself for her foolish fears; yet it would be wrong to pretend she had not been deeply frightened.

"Hmmm," George murmured, moving his chin back and forth gently against her forehead. "Perhaps it wasn't such a bad thing you came in here alone, after all."

"It was so beautiful, at first, but then . . ."

"Then it became just a very small cave, which is what it is."

She stepped back, looking into his face. "How did you know?"

"I guessed." He lifted her chin slightly and very gently bent and kissed her lips. His lips were soft and smooth, and under them she could feel the hardness of his beautiful teeth. Then, all at once he was pressing his mouth against hers, and she felt as if she were suffocating. Pushing him away, she shrank back against the cold wall of the cave.

"Why, what is it my dear? Am I presumptive to have kissed you like that? Forgive me, I thought you wouldn't mind."

"Please, George . . . Mr. Clarendon. Could we get out of here?"

"Why, of course. Here, take my hand . . ."

"No! I mean . . ."

"For heaven's sake, Clarissa, let me help you. What ever has upset you so? Let's get back out in the daylight where things will seem right again."

He almost pushed her through the entrance. Once back outside, he quickly dropped her hands.

"There now. You're out of that suffocating place. Are you feeling better?"

Clarissa looked up at him from under her lashes. "Yes,

150

I'm sorry I made such a scene. I should have waited for you in the first place."

"And I apologize if I was too forward. I was taking advantage of the darkness and your intoxicating nearness like the worst kind of cad."

His eyes held such amiable mischief that Clarissa could not help smiling. "It was all right. I was just nervous, I guess."

"Come on then, let's find the others."

It was an hour later before they finally gathered everything together for the long ride back to Zion Hill, and Clarissa had by that time recovered from whatever dark forces had overwhelmed her in the cave. As they started toward the horses she felt George take her arm and for the first time did not shrink from his touch.

"You're not worried about the ride back?" he asked.

"No. Old Russ was so amiable on the way up that I don't see why we should have any trouble going back. He's just the right horse for someone like me."

"I'm so glad it worked out that way. And have you enjoyed the day?"

"Oh, yes. So much. I'm glad you insisted I come along."

"Good. Never mind, Edwards, I'll give Miss Shaw a leg up."

The groom stepped forward to hold the reins while George bent to cup his hands for Clarissa's boot. Over the back of her mount she could see Augusta already regally astride Sultan, the feathers in her smart cap lifting lightly in the warm breeze.

Easily she swung up and leaned her body forward to fix her leg over the pommel and take the reins from Edwards' hand. Then she settled back with her weight against the saddle rim.

Instantly, like an electric shock surging through horse and rider, she felt the animal stiffen. The blond head jerked up, his ears flattened back. Clarissa caught a glimpse of the horse's bulging white eye before she began swaying crazily on his back as he turned rapidly in a circular motion sending the trees spinning around her.

"What the ... Russ! Whoa ..."

"What the matter with that horse," she heard George exclaim; then his words were lost as the animal's back curled up, throwing her forward. She clutched wildly at the mane.

"George! Help!" she cried.

"Grab hold." It was Edwards shouting now.

"Hold on, Clarissa," George cried, "Get the bridle, Edwards. Hold him ..." They were all moving around her, even Augusta shouting directions and sprinting Sultan back and forth trying to grab at Russ's gyrating bridle. Clarissa screamed as the frightened animal bucked, throwing up his heels and heaving her against his neck. She wanted to let go but was terrified of flying through the air; so she clutched frantically at the long mane and held on for dear life. Her back shuddered as the heaving animal threw his weight up and down. The earth slammed up to meet her; then the sky drew her away. Every bone was jarred, but in her panic she clung wildly to the heaving horse leaping and bucking beneath her.

The animal, unable to shake off the weight that was like a knife in his flesh, began to run away from it in a dumb panic, taking off wildly down the path.

Frightened nearly out of her life, Clarissa saw the trees and thickets flying by her and felt her body thumping wildly against the saddle. At any moment she expected to be smashed against the rocky ground, dead and broken. Ahead of them on the narrow path another rider loomed. They were going to collide. This was the end ...

Russ's hoofs dug into the earth and he reared wildly. She gave up the fight and loosened her hold only to feel herself sliding back through the air and slammed against a wall of dirt. Then, mercifully, everything faded into blackness.

A warmth on her skin and a painful light in her eyes brought Clarissa back to consciousness. She opened them slightly and found she was looking directly into the sun. In an involuntary motion she turned her head away and recognized a familiar voice near her ear.

"Thank God, at least you haven't broken your neck!"

She could smell the fragrant grass and feel the slight wind against her cheek. Other voices were around her, all speaking incomprehensibly at once; but her only thought was for herself. I'm not dead! she thought. He didn't kill me. That damned animal didn't kill me!

She felt her shoulders being lifted gently and heard George Clarendon bending over her, his voice almost frantic.

"Clarissa! Are you all right? Can you move? Clarissa, do you hear me?"

Opening her eyes, she found the sunlight had moved away. "Yes," she whispered. "I hear you."

"She's coming round. Don't move her, she may have broken something."

"Adam's right. You'll make it worse if she has." That was Augusta's voice. Adam! Had she really seen Adam Granville sitting astride a horse before her on the path? Then Russ had reared and . . .

She groaned and turned on her side. Her body protested the sudden motion with a searing pain that seemed to pin her to the ground.

"Clarissa, dear," George said soothingly. "Here, let me help you. Try to sit up."

She could make out the other faces over his broad shoulders. Augusta's tight features, for once tinged with sympathy and concern. Edwards' anxious, homely face. And . . . surely that was Adam. It seemed strange that he should be here. How did he get here? Why?

Very cautiously she raised herself to a sitting position supported by George's arm around her shoulders. "What a terrible experience for you, my poor girl," he said. "Are you really all right?"

Clarissa thankfully laid back against him and carefully moved her legs and arms. She could already tell that she was going to be very, very sore, but nothing worse seemed to have happened.

"What on earth got into that horse," Augusta scowled. "I've never seen him behave like that."

Edwards answered her. "T'was a cocklebur. Mr. Granville found it under the saddle blanket. A beauty of one, too, I mus' say. Big as a dollar!"

"A bur? But how the devil did it get there?" George asked.

"Must have got caught on the blanket somehow. T'wouldn't be nothin' else would set old Russ in such a fright."

"Edwards, go to my saddlebags and bring my flask. I think Miss Shaw needs a swallow of something stronger than water. Hurry now."

The groom was off in a flash. Clarissa heard Adam's voice, soft but quietly harsh. "A bur can catch onto a saddle blanket, but it seems strange to me that it could work its way up under the saddle without a little help."

"Are you suggesting that one of us . . ." Augusta glared at her brother.

"I'm not suggesting anything." Clarissa could hear the heavy uneven steps of his boots limping away. When she opened her eyes again he was gone. Her mind was so clouded she wasn't even sure that she hadn't dreamed hearing and seeing him at all.

"Here, my dear," said George, lifting the flask to her lips. "Take a little of this."

Clarissa pushed it away weakly. "No, I'm all right. Really. I was . . . it was so terribly frightening, but I'm all right now."

"Well, you held on nobly, Clarissa" Augusta said. "I couldn't have managed him any better myself."

"And it's a good thing she did, or she would have been killed for sure. Do you think you can stand?"

"I'd like to try. Was that really Adam I heard? Was he here?"

"Of course he was. He found you before we did."

Augusta said, "He met you racing down the trail. When Russ reared, you slipped off. It was probably the best way you could have escaped."

Clarissa got gingerly to her feet, her legs trembling, yet relieved to see that she could stand. "I thought I saw him, but I couldn't believe it. How did he get the gig up here?"

"He didn't," George answered. "He rode up to meet

154

us." He looked around. "But he's not here now. Where did he go?"

Augusta picked up her hat and arranged it on her heavy braids. "He rode on back to the house in his usual huff."

Clarissa watched them in a daze. "But Adam can't ride. He's lame."

Augusta laughed at the same moment that George looked at her quizzically. "Whatever gave you the idea that Adam couldn't ride?"

"I just thought . . . his leg . . ." she began.

"Did you think he would let a little thing like that stop him?" Augusta said. "Why he was back on a horse before he learned to walk again properly."

"He simply worked out a way to maneuver his lame leg and he was off," George added. "You'll find that Adam can do most anything he has a mind to."

Taking her arm, he helped her to walk a few steps. Beyond the trees Clarissa could see Russ, his blond neck stretched low to the ground where he was placidly nibbling at the grass. A shudder went through her.

Edwards saw her watching the animal. "You've had a bad experience, Miss Shaw, but the best thing you can do now is get back on that horse. It would be very wrong not to. That's the only way to get over this kind of thing."

Clarissa gripped George's hands. "I'm not so sure I want to get over it."

"Edwards is right," he answered. "I could take you up with me, but it would be better all round for you to ride Russ back. We'll check the gear carefully and make sure there are no more cockleburs. You can be sure of that."

Clarissa was grateful for his solicitude; yet she felt she would almost rather crawl home on her knees than get back on that horse. Looking around at Augusta watching her for any sign of backing down, she made up her mind it had to be done, and gritting her teeth, she climbed back into the saddle. The animal was a little restive at first, almost as though he too feared a repetition of the painful pressure on his back which had sent him into a panic before. When it didn't come he settled back into his customary placidity, and Clarissa found she could amble gingerly back toward Zion Hill. Her body ached and she knew she would not be able to relax completely until they reached the stables. Yet she was proud of herself for riding back on the same horse that had thrown her just minutes earlier.

There was little conversation on the ride down, and she had plenty of time to mull over the afternoon's events. What had they meant? If Adam was right and someone had placed that bur under her saddle, it must have been with the intention of causing her harm. But who would want to harm her? And why?

Her own words came back to her: "I was filling the kettle at the pump in the old kitchen and I heard voices through the flue. . . ." Someone—whoever was in the dining room with Evans—knew she had heard them. Perhaps that same person was with her this afternoon. She looked around edgily. Augusta, Edwards, George . . . She could not imagine any of them wishing her harm. Adam? That was possible. He had ridden up there to find them, and although she had only seen him when she was running away from the cave, who was to say that he had not been there unnoticed before then?

But Adam had found the cocklebur. The trouble was that you could never tell what Adam was thinking or feeling. Was he the other man in the dining room? Had he slipped up here and placed the bur under her saddle to put her out of the way as he had Nurse Evans? Unpleasant as he was, she could hardly believe him capable of such blatant meanness.

As they crossed the High Road and started up the sun-dappled path toward the stables, George reined in beside her.

"I've been thinking, Clarissa, and I believe that we should not say anything about this afternoon to anyone here at home. We've no way of knowing that it wasn't just a freak accident and we don't want to upset the judge anymore than he already is. Why don't we just keep our eyes open and say as little about it as possible?"

"What about the others? Aren't they bound to say something?"

"Not if I ask them not to. I think that none of us wants Magistrate Peckham back snooping around the house and who knows but he might use this as an excuse to do just that."

"But George . . . do you think it was just a freak accident?"

He considered her words for a long minute. "I don't know. I can hardly believe otherwise. But I promise you I intend to keep my eyes on you. I won't let any further harm come to you. You must trust me."

She smiled up at him, too tired to argue. Through the shadows of the new yellow-green leaves, the white gables of Zion Hill gleamed in the distance.

"All right. If you think it's wise."

He reached over and lightly squeezed her hand. "And one thing more. I'm not making any accusations, but I feel I must tell you to watch out especially for Adam Granville."

Clarissa stared straight ahead. "I've been thinking about him, I admit. But I just can't believe he'd want to harm me. I just can't."

"Nor I. But I know from experience that he is a very bitter and unstable young man. Just be guarded around him, that's all. I'll be keeping a wary eye on him too."

Russ sprinted forward a little, knowing he was nearing his stall, and Clarissa let him have his head without protest. Her own relief at nearing home was just as real. What does it matter if we talk about this or not? she thought. After the imagined terrors of that cave and the all too real horrors of this runaway horse, there was nothing that could happen to her now which would frighten her as much. Nothing at all.

Eleven

Dinner that night was a morose affair where depression sat like an uninvited guest among the people gathered around the table. Now and then Clarissa would feel her throat constrict as she remembered that jolting, wild ride through the streaming woods. Then with a shudder she would find herself sitting placidly in her chair with the candlelight before her falling in pools on the white cloth, its white starkness contrasting the mysterious dark shadows that rimmed the room beyond the table. The harsh clink of silver against the china seemed to echo through the silence of the room.

Judge Granville made a listless attempt at conversation by inquiring about the ride and Clarissa's impressions of Andre's Cave. She glanced quickly at George and, reading the warning in his eyes, made an innocuous reply. Now and then she would steal a sidelong glance at Adam, but she could read nothing of the thoughts beyond that impassive countenance. He looked tired and drawn, as though the ride to the cave and back had been a strain. His black brows were like a straight line above his eyes, and his mouth was tight and unsmiling. It was actually a very attractive mouth, Clarissa thought, noting for the

158

first time how delicately the lips were shaped for a man. Hardly the face of a murderer? Next to the heavy, carved knob of his cane his arms stretched long and muscular. For all the weaness of his face, his body exuded the self-contained strength of a natural athlete.

She leaned forward on the table and rubbed her eyes lightly with her fingers. If only she could shake off these morbid suspicions.

"My poor dear. You must be tired," said Judge Granville, reading fatigue into her impulsive motion. "It was a long trip for one unaccustomed to riding. You should get to bed early and get a good night's sleep. If you feel too weary for evening prayers, we could excuse you this once."

"Why, Papa," Augusta exclaimed. "Can this be you excusing anyone from evening prayers? Fatigue never got the rest of us off that I can remember."

For once her father answered her harshly. "You make a few moments of quiet prayer sound like a form of punishment. Besides, I've never seen you tired enough to merit being excused. Clarissa doesn't have your healthy constitution, you know."

Hannah leaned across the table. "Clarissa, dear, the day after tomorrow will be market day in Sing Sing, and I thought you might enjoy riding in with me. Do you think you will feel up to it?"

This was too much for Augusta, who was still smarting from her father's reprimand. "In a pony cart? Why that's just one step below that lazy Russ. For heaven's sake, Clarissa, surely you can't be that delicate!"

Clarissa ignored her. "I'd love to Hannah, thank you. And it will give me tomorrow to catch up on the children's lessons."

She glanced at George across the table, the flickering candlelight shining on the honey-colored hair that fell across his wide brow; then at Adam at her side, stern and dark. Both men were strangely silent and reflective, absorbed in some brooding and private preoccupation.

Later, going up the stairs to her room after the uncomfortable meal was over, she was thankful that Judge

Granville had excused her from the forced companionship of the others. In the quiet and solitude of her room she fell gratefully into bed, hoping to drift off quickly into the peaceful oblivion of sleep. But her body was sore and aching and her nerves still unhinged, and sleep would not come. Tossing restlessly in the darkness, she could follow all the sounds of movement through the house as gradually the rest of the family retired to their beds. Finally she could hear only the tall clock in the hall below striking the quarter hour relentlessly, and soon she began to dread the sound as each fifteen-minute chime announced that the night was wearing away and she was still awake.

When the clock struck twelve thirty, Clarissa decided it would be better to give up the useless struggle of seeking sleep and read for a while. As she reached for her lamp she noticed for the first time the bright iridescent moonlight spilling on the carpet before her window. Throwing back the covers, she walked over and looked out on the beautiful dull-bronze world below. The stars were brilliant in the clear night sky; the moon was a great buttery orb. The river in the distance was dark pewter against the black hills.

It was then that she noticed the light. It appeared at intervals, bobbing along the path from the stables like some large firefly. As her eyes became accustomed to the dark she could make out the shadow of a man carrying a lantern. Several times he stopped and opened the shutter to spill the dim light on the path. Perhaps he didn't know the way. Or, Clarissa caught her breath, perhaps it was a signal. Was there someone else out there waiting at the arbor at the end of the path? There seemed something furtive in the way that the shadowy light slipped along the path.

Impulsively she pulled her cloak over her long nightdress and headed quietly down the stairs, excitement and fear catching at her throat. When she reached the front door she found it slightly ajar; so she opened it noiselessly on its oiled hinges and slipped outside, pulling the camlet cloak closely around her.

The world lay motionless and silent, until once again,

the elusive light appeared on the path to the arbor. She stepped quickly down, walking on the wet grass to soften her footsteps and keeping as near as possible to the shadowy protection of the elms. As the black bulk of masonry loomed up before her she barely heard a man's throaty whisper:

"Adam! Adam!"

An answering whisper came from deep within the arbor: "Over here."

Clarissa saw Adam Granville step from the protective cover of the arbor, leaning on his cane for a moment; then both men turned toward the river and disappeared in the darkness.

Clarissa strained to catch a word, but all she could hear were the quiet noises of the night. She was anxious to follow, to get closer, but she didn't dare. She waited until the cold began to seep through her cloak and under the thin flannel of her gown, and then with no further sign of the two men, she turned back toward the house. She was filled with a curious sense of distress. Though she didn't want to believe it, it seemed clear that Adam Granville was somehow involved in some shadowy intrigue. Yet, why should she care? With one or two pleasant exceptions he had hardly ever been civil to her. If, underneath that cynical exerior, there was a violent and cruel nature, what did it matter to her? The important thing was that he be exposed and prevented from hurting someone else. And yet . . .

Oh bother! she thought. I wish I had never heard of Zion Hill or my Granville relatives!

Shortly after lunch the next day, Clarissa was reading to the children when Nancy tapped lightly on the door and informed her that Judge Granville wanted to see her in the study right away. Going quickly downstairs, she knocked on the study door and could tell at once by the sound of the old man's voice that something was wrong. She found him seated behind his massive desk, his face unusually choleric. George Clarendon stood near the window, looking out, his hands clasped behind his back.

Turning slightly, he gave her a faint sidelong smile, glanced at his father-in-law, then turned back to stare out the window. Clarissa could almost feel the emotional currents in the close air of the small room.

Leading over his desk, Judge Granville glared at Clarissa over the rims of the spectacles perched near the end of his nose. She had never seen him so angry.

"Clarissa, I think we might just as well plunge directly into this matter. My son-in-law has just requested my permission to pay his address to you."

Clarissa stared at the furious little man. The words "son-in-law" echoed in her mind. It spoke volumes that he had used that formal term rather than the more familiar "George."

"I don't quite know how to answer him," the judge went on, tight-lipped, "and I do not wish to do so until I know something of your own mind first."

Clarissa looked wonderingly over at George. The tautness of his jaw, the cast of his shoulders betrayed his fury. Obviously he hadn't intended her to be brought in on this scene.

"Did you know of his intentions, or does this come as a surprise to you . . . as much as it did to me?"

"I . . . I knew something of them," Clarissa muttered.

"Am I to understand you acquiesce in this matter?" It was almost a challenge.

"Clarissa knows how I feel about her," George broke in, "but she has been too upset to sort out her own feelings as yet."

"If you think it is too soon for her, then why involve me?" Judge Granville glared at George. "However, now that you have, I must tell you that you disappoint me, both of you—you disappoint me very much!"

"But . . . why?" Clarissa stammered.

"Really, sir," George answered furiously, ignoring her, "you seem to think that I should go on grieving forever. It's now almost two years since Jenny died. Surely that is a sufficient mourning period to allow me to think of remarrying. After all, the children need a mother, and . . ."

"Their need of a mother never seemed to cause you

162

any concern before this time. Indeed, your children hardly cause you concern of any kind. Why are you suddenly now so conscientious? And with all the eligible young women almost falling at your feet, why choose Clarissa here, who, without a mother or a father, with hardly a penny to her name, comes to me as a daughter to be cared for? Now you want to take her away when she has barely learned to love her new home."

George's eyes narrowed into angry slits. "Ah, that's really the heart of the matter, isn't it? You can't bear to see me carry off another daughter. You gave the other very grudgingly, as I recall, and now you don't want to lose Clarissa too."

The skin on Judge Granville's face seemed to constrict over the throbbing of a prominent vein in his temple. He made an almost visible effort to keep his voice down, but it grated with his fury.

"How dare you, sir! How dare you mention Jenny in that way! That beautiful, gentle girl whom you drove to an early grave—No, I shall not see you take another innocent, sweet child and destroy her too. Not if I die first!"

George lost all restraint. "I resent those words . . ." he cried, his voice rising. "I resent them bitterly. I was a good husband to Jenny, with very little return, I might add, and overmuch interference from a meddlesome father-in-law! Can you deny that I always put her welfare first?"

"You always put her dowry first! Don't you think I know why you want Clarissa. Because you hope I will remember her in my will. It's my money you want, not my daughters'. It always was!"

George slapped his fist down on the desk and leaned into his father-in-law's face. For an instant Clarissa thought he was going to strike the older man.

"Stop it! Stop it!" she cried, grabbing at George's arm. "Don't I have anything to say about this? It's my future you're arguing over!"

Both men had forgotten she was there, and she took advantage of their momentary surprise to step between them.

Desperately she attempted to keep her voice calm. "Judge Granville, I'm grateful to you for giving me a home here at Zion Hill, but I have no wish ever to be remembered in your will. Indeed, this is the first time that such a thought has ever occurred to me. I came here because I had no other place to go. George knows that."

George Clarendon stepped back, and she looked straight into his eyes. "I have been through a very difficult time," she said quietly, "and I don't know my own feelings yet. I tried to tell you—it's too soon!"

She was conscious of a trembling in her knees and her hands twisting at her waist. How dare these men put her in such a position! Was this the kind of situation a real lady would face, this arguing over her as though she were some piece of livestock up for sale? All she wanted was to be left alone.

George recovered his composure first. He carefully walked over to the sofa, as far from his father-in-law as possible, and sat down wearily. "Clarissa, I deeply regret that you were called in on this. I regret that I spoke at all. You did ask me to wait, and I fully intended to. But events seemed to be moving so fast, and I was concerned for your . . . for your safety. I thought perhaps as your husband I could better protect you. Please forgive me. It was a mistake."

"What's this?" Judge Granville broke in. "What safety? What events? What are you talking about?"

Clarissa was touched by the concern in his voice. "I understand," she whispered. "Please forgive me for not being more sure of my heart."

Rising from his desk, Judge Granville stalked between them. "Will you please explain what you meant," he demanded. "Has something else happened in this house? Something I'm not aware of?"

"Not in the house," Clarissa answered. "It was on the ride yesterday. Someone put a cocklebur under my saddle, and my horse nearly killed me."

"Oh, dear God!" The old man's face crumpled like parchment. "Who would do such a thing? And you an

164

inexperienced rider! Why would anyone want to harm you?"

"I don't know. I can't imagine who or why. It might have even been a peculiar accident that the bur got under the saddle that way. But it was a terrifying experience."

"Why wasn't I told at once, George? Why did you try to keep this from me?"

George hesitated, and Clarissa, thinking he was anxious not to implicate Adam before his father, jumped in. "I asked him to keep it quiet. So much has already happened and I can't be sure that it was not simply an accident."

"You see," George said defensively. "You accuse me of motives which were far from my mind. I am not interested in Clarissa's dowry. I am interested in protecting her and I'm convinced she needs my protection."

The judge glared back at him. This put a different face on things; but all the same the bitter words he had spoken had seethed inside him for a long time, and he was not going to retract or apologize for them.

"We will all try to protect her. But right now I think that may be more comfortably done without the complications of a betrothal. Let us first identify the thing—or the person—responsible for the evil in this house, and then we can think about the ordinary business of life once again."

It was a neat way out, and Clarissa was grateful that he used it. His skin looked very gray. It was so unusual for him to break through the structured restraints of his temper that the experience had left him exhausted. He waved his hand at them listlessly.

"Go away now, both of you. We will not talk of this again. Not for a while at least."

Clarissa fled the room, not anxious to speak to George. Once upstairs she sat down on her bed to sort out the thing. What was it all really about? Why should Judge Granville react so strongly to George's interest in her? In all the time she had been in the house she had barely heard anyone mention his daughter Jenny. Yet apparently he had loved her, grieved for her, and felt that in some way George was responsible for her early death. And why the great concern with money? George Clarendon had a successful law practice. Why should he want Judge Granville's money? If he was looking for wealth, he certainly would never have turned to her, for she had nothing. He would have instead betrothed himself to one of the wealthy heiresses who gave him such interested glances. Why had he spoken to the judge anyway, when he had promised her he would wait? It had certainly been a great mistake. Things were more complicated now than ever.

Her thoughts went back to the shadows in the arbor last night. If Judge Granville distrusted George, what would he think if he knew that his son was slipping around in the shadows of a midnight meeting with strangers he could not bring into the house? Suppose he knew that Adam had been up on the hill yesterday when someone sabotaged her horse? Perhaps the accusations were more appropriately aimed at the son than at the son-in-law!

She went back to the children and tried to forget the scene in the judge's study. Yet, in spite of her efforts, it hovered over everything she did, black and turbulent, disquietingly close, like the first twinges of an illness which you know in time is going to grip you in its merciless vise.

Twelve

As the pony cart lumbered its slow way into Sing Sing the next day, Clarissa encouraged Hannah to talk about her family. It was not difficult to do so. A few questions about their childhood and she was off, happily reminiscing.

"Augusta was the eldest; so, of course, she always felt she had the God-given right to boss us all. She has never really outgrown that tendency, although she has learned that it doesn't work with the others."

"I suppose she had to take on a lot after your mother became ill?"

"Oh, yes. She completely ran the household—and I think she enjoyed doing it. She is very capable, you know. She is one of those fortunate people who does everything well. Running a busy house, she still finds time for the things she enjoys, like her riding. When we lived in town she had a very active social life and many suitors, though none of them satisfied her well enough to marry. I'm sure she has missed all that dreadfully at Zion Hill. I admit there are times when her overbearing ways annoy me, but I also realize that she is not very happy out here in the country. And I do so admire the way she does everything so well."

Hannah sighed and flicked the reins over the pony's back. Clarissa knew she was thinking of her own ineptitude in contrast to her sister's capable ways.

"At any rate," she went on, "there were two boys born next who both died in infancy. Then came Jenny and, a year later, Adam. Jenny was a bright, happy little thing who became the darling of the family. She and Adam were very close—they did everything together. There were three other babies who did not survive, and then I came along. Shortly after I was born my mother began to fail. Actually it must have been coming on for a long time."

Clarissa thought of the beautiful woman with the vacant eyes sitting on the floor of the bedroom. Did that fragile, gossamer look suggest that perhaps her body had not been built to bear so many children or that mind strong enough to handle so many early little deaths? Nine babies and five infant burials—that would be enough to unhinge any mind.

Hannah stared wistfully ahead at the dusty road. "The strange thing is," she continued, "that I have always felt close to my mother without really knowing her in her right mind. She still thinks of me as her 'baby' and she has never turned on me as she has all the others—even Papa. Sometimes in a queer way it is as though she were the baby and I the mother." She gave a brittle laugh. "Well, life is strange sometimes."

Hannah's comments seemed to sadden her without helping Clarissa to learn what she wanted to know; so she made an attempt to turn the conversation.

"Did Adam change much after his accident?" she asked lightly.

"Adam? Not that I could tell. A little more quiet, a little more jaundiced. But I never understood Adam. He and Jenny were so close there was never room for anyone else. And I was several years younger too."

"Then I don't suppose he was very happy when she married."

168

"None of us was. Papa was bitterly opposed, though I could never tell why. George was so handsome and cut such a dashing figure. Anyway, Papa finally gave in and they were married."

"Was George terribly grieved when your sister died?" Clarissa carefully asked and was relieved to see that Hannah was completely indifferent to her probing.

"He was upset, naturally, but not unbearably so. You know how George is. He always says just the right thing and presents just the proper front. But it's always on the surface. Underneath you never truly know what he is feeling."

With some astonishment Clarissa realized that Hannah had just identified a quality in George which she herself had sensed but had not recognized. All at once she knew why she was hesitant to commit herself to him. She did not really believe all his talk about love and devotion. Something about him suggested another person underneath, a person she did not know and did not really trust.

As they neared Sing Sing the road began to grow crowded with wagons and livestock, all headed toward the market square. Children darted in and out of the melee or rode on the back of the buckboards, their spindly legs dangling over the coarse wood. Young men in their best flannel shirts and sarcenet ready-made trousers strutted before stringy-haired young girls in colorful Guernsey frocks. A wagon loaded up with an entire family wobbled by, a reluctant calf tied behind. Before Hannah's cart reached the outskirts of the village they could feel the festive gaiety in the air, a thin undercurrent of excitement born of escape from the ordinary routines of the day.

"Speak of the devil and he appears," cried Hannah. "Look, there's Adam."

But Clarissa had already recognized Adam's sharp profile and straight back riding the sorrel mare from the stables. Beside him rode a large, red-haired man with thick, heavy shoulders—not unlike those of the shadow she had seen in the arbor two nights ago. As Hannah turned the cart down High Street Clarissa had a sudden thought.

169

"Hannah, how did Jenny meet George Clarendon?"

"Why, I believe Adam introduced them. They had met in some gentleman's club in the city and Adam brought him home."

"They certainly don't behave like friends now, do they?"

"No. Something changed after Jenny died. Maybe before. I remember Adam was not too keen on their marrying. Since her death, there has been a mutual hostility between them. My goodness, look at this crowd. Let's put the cart over there under that lovely hawthorne. Then we can walk around the square."

There was no more opportunity for questions. For a small square in a tiny village the Sing Sing market was remarkably jammed. The girls had to twist their way through the crowd, easing between farmers who were haggling over prices and housewives who were picking over produce. Clarissa found the stalls fascinating. It was too early in the year for harvest vegetables, but there were abundant displays of every other kind: baskets thick with colorful spring flowers, dried herbs and spices hanging from the low roofs above them; tables of pastries and dried fruits; smoked meats and jams and jellies put up in local kitchens; flats of tiny shoots for planting, and hand-sewn bags of seed; tubs of lard, and dusty cloth bags filled to bursting with ground flour, wheat or corn; tubs of butter, crocks of fresh eggs, hogsheads of pickles, and big, buttery cheeses—the sights and smells were enough to make her mouth water. Boxes of chickens; pens of bouncing, squealing pigs; sheep roped together—all vied with the people for room to move. And everywhere was fish. The heavy aroma around the stalls and barrels drowned out all competing odors. Salted herring, fresh shad, barrels of oysters and crab, and countless other varieties. She followed in Hannah's wake, absorbed in the variety and color of it all.

"Oh, my goodness, there's that terrible woman!" Hannah's sudden stop sent Clarissa colliding into her back. Peering around her, Clarissa could see that a short way ahead stood the tall figure of a woman with long blond braids wound around her head, quietly studying a basket of baby chicks. Clarissa watched her reach out and gently stroke the creamy fuzz. She had beautiful hands.

"Do you mean that lovely blond in the brown dress? She's very attractive."

"It's Ellie Dawson," Hannah whispered. "You remember. I told you about her and her son. I have nothing against her, but if we meet her we'll have to speak."

Hannah fussily turned her back and, catching Clarissa's arm, attempted to retrace her steps toward the fish stall they had just passed. But suddenly she found that her own arm was caught in the viselike grip of her brother, who had appeared beside her.

"Good day, sister dear," he said easily. "Are you showing cousin Clarissa our market day? Dear me, Miss Shaw, I hope the excitement isn't too much for your 'delicate constitution.' One should take great moments like these in small doses."

"I believe I can bear it, thank you," Clarissa replied and had the satisfaction of seeing a faint smile play about his lips.

"Oh, Adam, how you do run on. We are only here to do a little marketing, and I thought Clarissa would enjoy the change."

Adam took his sister's arm with one hand and Clarissa's with the other. She felt herself stiffen at his touch, but she went gamely along as he steered them determinedly back toward the chicken crates.

"And what shall it be today, ladies?" he went on in his ranting style. "Some excellent Hudson bass or perhaps a delectable homemade sack, strong enough to remove the top of your head. Or, here now, how about this luscious little porker. You could make a pet of him, Clarissa."

He picked up the fat, complaining baby pig and held him firmly and gently in his arms. Clarissa ran her finger down the pink nose.

"They are actually quite intelligent animals, you know," she said. "I have known them to become pets, and very nice ones too."

"Clarissa," Hannah reacted with horror. "How could you think it? A pig in the house!"

Adam smiled. "Can't you just imagine the commotion it would cause at Zion Hill? But, then, think of the consolations. He could lie at Papa's feet and accept tidbits from the table. Or, better yet, he could make the appropriate responses during evening prayer. Stretched before the fire he could protect the family hearth. And when he gets too old to be a watchpig he will still make a credible meal. I think it is a delightful idea."

Clarissa smiled in spite of herself. He was obviously making an effort to be pleasant, and she found herself liking him for it.

Adam glanced ahead. "And here now is someone I would like you to meet."

"Adam!" The color drained from Hannah's face.

He looked contemptuously down on her. "What are you afraid of, sister? Contamination? Clarissa, Mrs. Dawson is a remarkable woman and a good friend. Would you like me to introduce you?"

Clarissa met his gaze squarely. Whatever she was, she hoped she was not judgmental. And Hannah was being her silliest.

"I should like it very much."

"Good for you." His words were low, but she could tell that he was pleased.

When Adam called and Ellie Dawson turned to face them, Clarissa was struck first off with her dignity. Her dress was drab brown woolen stuff, and her shawl was faded and patched. But, fallen woman or no, she was certainly beautiful. Her soft blue eyes were honest and direct as she bobbed Clarissa a curtsy.

"I am pleased to meet you, Mrs. Dawson," Clarissa said kindly, "for I purchased one of the lavalieres painted by your son and I think it is quite beautiful. He is a talented boy."

A smile of pure pleasure lit Ellie Dawson's face. "Why, thank you, Miss Shaw. It would please him to hear you say that."

"Then I hope you will tell him so for me."

172

Ellie turned to Hannah, who was standing half-turned away, her face beet red. "Good morning, Miss Granville. I trust you are having a pleasant day."

As if to spare her further embarrassment, she smiled briefly at Adam, then disappeared into the crowd before Hannah could mutter a half-hearted reply.

Adam did not attempt to disguise the contempt in his voice. "Come, Hannah," he said, "you can look this way again. The 'terrible person' has gone, and none of the town worthies were watching your degradation. What did you think of her, Clarissa?"

"She is very lovely. Completely without pretense. I liked her."

"Oh, Clarissa. How could you?" Hannah muttered.

"Yes, dear cousin," Adam said, sauntering on his way again. "I must warn you against such charity or you may well find yourself cut dead by the good-hearted Christians of the village."

Hannah found her voice at last. "Don't be so sanctimonious, Adam. You know it isn't proper to introduce a lady to a woman like that. I should think you would have better manners."

Rage flickered for an instant in the dark eyes. "Oh, yes, propriety. I quite forgot. Forgive my gauche mistake, Clarissa. I shall henceforth leave you to the oh-so-proper ministrations of George Clarendon and Hannah Granville and such like."

Raising his hat, he gave an exaggerated bow and moved away into the crowd. Clarissa watched him go. Now what did he mean by that remark? She shrugged and turned to follow Hannah. Well, black heart or no, he was certainly not a snob.

Adam Granville took Ellie's basket on his arm as they walked along the path toward Hunter's Landing. Below, the river lay dotted with the colorful sails of the sloops that plowed their way up and down its gossamer surface. A wind from the west frothed the little whitecaps of the waves and sent the clouds scudding.

"I liked your little cousin," she finally said.

173

"Did you? Etiquette notwithstanding, she liked you too."

"I can see what attracted you. That wounded bird quality you spoke of. But I think she has spirit too. I liked the way she looked me straight in the eye."

"In contrast to Hannah's deadly embarrassment. How do you suffer it?"

"Oh, well. Your sister is simply too much a creature of her world. But Clarissa, I believe, might be able to rise above hers."

He looked down on her fondly. "As you have," he added simply.

She smiled up at him, a warm, quickly shared response, then turned her eyes back to the path.

"Do you think she will . . . interfere?"

"With what I have to do? Yes, I am very much afraid that she will. In spite of all the warnings and the dangers, she is a curious little creature and she will probably go blundering right into my carefully laid plans."

There was a long silence. The warm wind lifted Ellie's shawl like the sail on one of the river sloops.

"What will you do?"

Adam shrugged. "I don't know at this point. I just don't know. I shall simply have to see how things—develop. It shouldn't be much longer now."

They had reached the narrow gate before the Dawson cottage. Beyond the neat garden, Ellie's dog Brute ran out to meet them, filling the air with sharp wails of welcome. Adam set the basket down on the post and waved to Morgan Dawson, who was piling hay in the field behind the house. Quieting the bounding dog, Ellie turned and laid her hand on Adam's arm.

"Please, Adam. Whatever develops, be careful. These are desperate chances you are taking. Don't let the consequences ruin your life, I beg you. Promise me you will be careful."

He cupped her chin in his large hand and looked affectionately into the lustrous eyes.

"Mon amie," he said, "I will try. I don't know if I will

be able to avoid ruining my life or the lives of others, but I promise you I will try."

Back at the market Adam sought out Corey Arnold before he went to collect his horse from the livery stable. He found his friend pitching horseshoes with some of the local young bloods. Quietly he led him aside.

"You know you are ruining my game, don't you," Corey said grimly. "And just when I am about to make a killing."

"I won't keep you. I just want to know if you found it."

"There wasn't enough time. Too many people about. And then the grand duke himself walked in before he was expected. Sorry, my friend, but no luck this time."

"All right. I will just have to try the other way. It's always wise to have an alternate plan."

"Tonight?"

"Why not? It's just as good as any other."

"What about your father?"

"He's away. He left this morning to take Mother down to the Bloomingdale Asylum for another examination. He never gives up hope that they'll find a magic cure."

"Are you sure you shouldn't wait until you've had a chance to talk to our friend in New York? You may be throwing your life away for nothing at this point."

"Everyone seems to be worrying that I'll ruin my life. As if it could be any more ruined than it is! Besides, I'm afraid to wait. I'm not the only one with something at stake."

Corey studied the brooding, dark face. Up until now this whole thing had seemed to him almost a game, lighthearted and only half-serious. Suddenly it had taken on all the aspects of a potentially deadly business. He was filled with an unexplained sense of unease. Something about it just didn't sit well.

"Do you want my help?" he finally asked.

Adam hardly glanced at him. "No, not this time. I'll let you know."

"Well, watch yourself."

Adam did not answer. Preoccupied and glum, he turned away and started toward the livery stable. For a moment Corey considered following him, whether he was wanted or not. Then he shrugged. Adam Granville was not one to be coddled. Let him do things his own way. He went back to pitching horseshoes.

Both Clarissa and Hannah were unusually silent on the journey home, absorbed in their own thoughts. Clarissa did not know what to make of Adam Granville. Over and over she mentally retraced all the things she knew of him, the words he had spoken, the things he had done, and always the same conclusions rose to the surface. Everything pointed to Adam. Hadn't George himself warned her of him? The anger and hostility that was so much a part of his manner—it was not such a big step from these to overt violence. Especially when there was the bitterness and pain of a crippling accident to spur one on.

Of course, he had a different side too that he occasionally allowed people to glimpse. That was what made him so puzzling. The honest way he accepted Ellie Dawson for what she was; his courageous determination to ride again against great obstacles; his kindness to her in that terrible quarrel with Nurse Evans.

But what about the cruel way he flayed people with words; his sneaking around the house late at night meeting with mysterious strangers; his appearance on the path from Andre's Cave just after her horse and nearly killed her? Not to mention his coldness and indifference to Jenny's children, when he was supposed to have loved their mother so much.

Remembering her own experiences with her crippled brother, Clarissa knew that things were seldom as simple as they looked. People, like events, were seldom all good or all bad. Who could know when the furies would rise up to overwhelm a person, driving him to commit some act of madness which in his right mind he would never dream of bringing about? Only that person himself.

So it must be with Adam, she thought. She told herself once more that she would keep her eyes open and watch him carefully. If he was up to some evil in the house, then perhaps if she were vigilant she could corner him in it before anyone else was hurt. It would break Judge Granville's heart—Adam was, after all, his only son. But it must be done, for the sake of the others and perhaps even for her own sake.

Suddenly she was back again clinging terrified, her hands twisted into the coarse mane of the plunging, gyrating Russ. She shuddered and pulled her shawl protectively around her shoulders.

Yes, even for her own sake.

Thirteen

She looked down at the small, white square lying on the dark rug of her room. It was obvious from one mangled corner that it had been forced under her door, and somehow it did not surprise her to see it lying there. It was a single sheet of paper, folded in half with one neatly written line across its surface:

Can you meet me at dusk in the arbor? Very urgent.

Adam

Clarissa stared at it, holding it loosely in her hand. Of course it was a trap. If Adam Granville wanted to talk to her in private, there were plenty of other ways to go about it. Or was he so used to skulking around in the shadows that he could conceive of no more proper way to meet? No, more likely he wanted to lure her out there for some dark purpose of his own. Did he know that she suspected him? Perhaps she should not risk it—just ignore the note as though she had not seen it. Yet if she did not go, she would never know what he was up to. Of course, it might be wise to tell someone where she was going, but who? George? No, he and Adam hated each other too much already. Hannah would be no help. Augusta, then? She bridled at the thought! No, she would simply have to go alone and take her chances.

When Clarissa stepped cautiously from the house, the world was enveloped in an opaque mist which was fast blending into darkness. The arbor loomed before her like a gray hulk of shifting shadows. By the time she stepped under the overhanging arches of vines and new leaves, the night had already turned black. She had brought no light with her, for she felt that the darkness might be her protection as well as her nemesis.

She inched her way forward very slowly, her breath suspended in her growing fear. She could not throw off the conviction that she was walking into danger. The twisted vines and leafy sculptures of the arbor took on grotesque ghostly hues as she worked her way under their thick gloom.

There was a faint crunch on the gravel behind her. She whirled around, her hand moving instinctively out before her, but she could see and hear nothing. Nothing moved and no sound came. She could make out only the shapes of the vines and leaves; yet she knew there was someone there. Suddenly she was aware of the chill pressure of the night air on her skin. Every nerve seemed heightened.

She drew in her breath, holding herself tightly. Scarcely daring to breathe, she turned back toward the dark tunnel of the branching vines. Far ahead at its end she could barely make out the lighter gray of the open fields.

Suddenly a man stepped into the framed archway of the arbor. Against the lighter shades of the night Clarissa recognized the tall figure, leaning on the heavy oak cane. Like someone in a dream, she saw him look up to see her standing at the other end, then come limping toward her, quickening his speed as he neared close enough for her to catch the strong odor of cigars on his frock coat.

"Adam?" she cried and watched with growing horror as in the dim light she saw him lifting the cane high over his head. Clarissa gasped, throwing up her arms as the cane came swishing through the air to strike the tough vines beside her head. With a cry, she attempted to scramble out of its way. Her first shock of surprise quickly became terror as the cudgel came thrashing down again beside her. Springing to one side, she struggled to break free, but the vines were like leathery fingers clutching at her dress and feet. She felt a painful, glancing blow against her shoulder at the same time that a choking scream tore from her throat. The stick came crashing against the trellis beside her and caught there momentarily as she bolted underneath it. Then his arm was catching at her, clutching her with an iron grip. A heavy weight pressed her against the vines, which dug their knobby fingers into her back. She felt her feet slipping and she heard the angry swish of the cane over her head. Terrified now, she threw her body wildly to the side and crawled, tugging at her skirts, as she felt the club come crashing down again, splintering against a marble bench near her shoulder.

The sound of screams seemed to come from far away; yet she knew dimly it was her own voice. In terror she yanked at her skirts caught under her and tangled in the grapevines. Then she felt tearing hands boring into her arms and shoulders, forcing her against the gravel and clawing at her throat. The pressure on her throat was horrible, and gasping for breath, she fought with all her strength, shoving against the heavy weight on her body. Like someone detached, she twisted her head and recognized lying next to her the familiar shattered knob of Adam's heavy cane. Then the thick fingers around her throat closed tighter, pushing her into even deeper blackness. She clawed at the hands, desperate for air, but they were locked like iron. No, no. She tried to speak. Please God . . . not like this, Adam . . . not like this . . .

With a last conscious effort she pulled her arm back and, calling up her last reserves of strength, sent it crashing into his body. She got him straight in the stomach. With a loud "oomph" the air went out of him, the deadly grip on her throat loosened, the suffocating weight went slack just enough to allow her to throw him off balance and roll from under him.

180

There wasn't time to gasp, to enjoy the luxury of breathing. Clutching her skirts high above her knees, Clarissa started running for her life, down the length of the arbor and wildly out across the fields toward the stables. Almost at once she could hear the thudding footsteps behind her. With some dim idea that she could escape if she could only make it to the shelter of the shadowed building, she raced down the path and inside. Only then did it dawn that she had boxed herself in. Glancing wildly around, she forced her gasping body into the darkest corner and threw herself down on the damp hay, her lungs screaming. Almost at once she could make out the huge figure looming up in the doorway and she clamped her hand over her mouth trying desperately to cover her stricken breathing.

He paused, looking around, waiting for some telltale movement or sound. One of the horses, disturbed by the intruders, flicked up his head and snorted. In the blackness Clarissa could see his white eye standing out in the darkness like a lantern. The man in the doorway hesitated a moment, then darted into his stall.

Then Clarissa remembered the doorway at the other end of the building. If she could just reach it, she might be able to get up the path to the house. It was her only hope, the only place where he might not dare to follow and harm her. She began to slide silently along the wall, sucking in her breath. The splinters of the wood caught at the soft fabric of her dress. A pool of moonlight circled the entrance, but she kept carefully to the deep shadows of the center aisle. Near the open doorway she could hear him searching the stalls methodically, moving lightly without speaking. The horses knew him. Of course, they would.

She was very near the door. With an almost detached coolness she calculated how she would be able to raise the bar without drawing his attention. If she could get it up silently, it wouldn't matter whether he saw her lunge through the door. With enough of a start she felt sure she could make it to the house.

She rose slowly from her crouching position, her hand found the bar, and slowly, noiselessly she lifted it from its socket. Just a little more . . .

Then her head struck a bridle hanging on the wall by the door, and the clink of the metal resounded through the stable. Clarissa gasped, a horse neighed, and the shadow at the other end turned and raced triumphantly toward her.

The bar fell back into its sockets, and in an unthinking wave of terror she fled for the nearest cover of an open stall behind her. Slipping on the matted straw, she clawed at the splintered wall, cringing, trapped and helpless in the corner of the stall.

There was that voice again—her voice—screaming hysterically, hopelessly. He was on her again, smashing her against the wall, the fingers closing around her throat. She had no more strength or will to fight him. She felt herself falling, back down into some beautiful oblivion.

The mist faded. With a strange feeling of irritation she began to come back. Remembering where she was, terror washed over her. Her throat throbbed with a searing pain; yet dimly she was aware that the iron grip around it was gone. Before her on the straw of the stall there was a thrashing of bodies, two people grappling and rolling on the stable floor. Surely one of them was George. Thank God! He had heard her screams and come to help her. Saved! Without the strength to move, she pressed her body against the corner, conscious only of the blessed knowledge that help had come.

With a crunching blow one of the men sent the other sprawling. Clarissa could make out his body rolling over in the dirt and grasping the handle of a bucket which he threw with all his force at the man standing over him. It knocked him off balance, just giving the other one an instant to be up and toward the doorway, fleeing the stable with a familiar lurching run.

Clarissa drew in her breath as the other man turned and started toward her. Then, there he was, his face looming over her, the black brows and dark hair thrown into grotesque relief by the shadows of the moonlight.

Adam Granville!

No, not again! Just when she thought she was saved from him. She shrank against the wall, her voice rising in terror.

"No! Go away! Don't kill me . . ."

His hands clutched at her arms, and she jerked them violently up and down, flaying at him with her fists. Her screams were sobs, and she could hear through them his voice, yelling and threatening. She began to slip on the straw, sliding downward, twisting and fighting against his hard hands.

"Clarissa! Clarissa!"

Her arms were stilled suddenly in the iron grip of his hands. His words were beginning to filter through her clouded mind.

"For God's sake, Clarissa. Stop it!"

"Leave me alone," she screamed. "Don't kill me. Don't!"

"Damn it, Clarissa. Stop this yowling and listen to me!"

Very slowly she became aware that the hands on her shoulders were supporting her, not searching for her throat. He was kneeling before her, forcing her into stillness, forcing her to face him.

"Listen to me! I'm not trying to kill you. What's the matter with you? I don't want to hurt you!"

Her hands fluttered between them, hiding her face. "It *was* you. I recognized you running toward me in the arbor . . ."

He shook her roughly; then seeing the terror in her eyes, his hands became more gentle. "It wasn't. I never tried to harm you. I want to help you. Can't you believe me?"

All the strength went out of her legs, and she fell against him. His arms went around her, supporting and comforting. His hands were gentle as he pushed back the disheveled hair from her forehead. She could not stop trembling.

His voice was quiet and calm, as it would be for a terrified horse. Finally he stopped speaking and simply held her, letting the comfort of his embrace speak for him.

Clarissa could not sort out her confused emotions. This was Adam, but he was helping her, not hurting her.

"But . . . but who?" It was all she could manage to say.

He stood back from her, looking into her blotched face with narrowed eyes.

"Who else? George Clarendon, of course."

"No . . . no . . ."

She tried to speak, but the right words would not come. She felt him gently let her down on the straw where she leaned back thankfully against the wall, closing her eyes. She didn't understand any of this.

"I don't believe it. Not George. He loves me." Her voice was only a hoarse squeak.

Adam sighed and fell back against the wall beside her, his arms resting on his drawn-up knees.

"No, I don't suppose you can believe it. Give yourself a little time to get used to the idea."

"I . . . I thought it was you."

"You were meant to."

"It looked like you. The limp, the cane . . ."

"I think he wanted you to think it was I. It was only by luck that I heard you scream. I was coming down here to take out the gig, and I found him trying to strangle you. I pulled him off."

Her voice was getting back its normal resonance. "But there was a note under my door from you, asking me to meet you in the arbor."

"I never left you any note. He must have put it there to lure you out here after dark. The bastard! I wonder how he thought he would explain your 'accident' this time!"

Clarissa suddenly remembered the ebony knob lying on the gravel floor of the arbor beside her head. "It was your cane. He tried to hit me with your cane, but it broke."

He stared at her. "He tried to kill you with my cane?"

"Yes, in the arbor. It missed and I managed to get away. Then he chased me down here and . . ."

He touched her hand lightly. "I know. Poor Clarissa. You came to Zion Hill for peace, and this is what you get. I think he must have used one of my sticks to make you

184

think it was I who was trying to kill you. If he had been successful, I guess I would have gotten the blame. Two nuisances removed in one blow. Very clever."

"But Adam. Not George. He said . . ."

"I know. He told you he loved you, and you believed him, the more fool you. Well, you'll have to readjust your thinking. Meanwhile the important thing is to get you someplace where you'll be safe. And I know where that place is." He rose easily from the floor. "And incidentally, you may also find there some corroboration for the things I've been saying."

He was suddenly very busy, dragging out the gig and harnessing an outraged Russ between the poles. Clarissa was too exhausted to do more than lean against the wall and watch. He almost had to lift her into the carriage before they started off down the drive. She watched the dark shape of the trees pass by, oblivious to where she was until at length she recognized the Old Post Road.

A little later they pulled up before Ellie's stone cottage where a barking Brute ran out to challenge them, nearly causing the gig to spill before Adam could shout him down. Although Clarissa did not know the house, she recognized at once the vibrant woman with the long yellow hair streaming down her back who opened the door.

A mug of steaming cider which Ellie thrust into her hands revived her. They were sitting at a wooden plank table, Adam's dark face across from her and a tall boy with a sensitive face hovering in the shadows beyond. This must be the son, she thought vaguely and tried not to notice how his mother moved unconcernedly about the room in her long nightdress loosely covered by the faded paisley shawl.

She heard Adam saying, "You can stay here tonight," and made a conscious effort to pull her disordered thoughts together.

"But, Adam, I can't stay here. What about tomorrow? What will everyone think when I don't appear? The children . . ."

"Don't worry about it. I'll think of some excuse. The

185

'important thing is to keep you safe and away from George until I can come up with some way to stop him."

Clarissa looked down at the trailing spiral of smoke rising from the mug between her fingers. "Are you so sure it's George? It's so hard to believe. He always seemed so kind . . . so pleasant . . ."

"Oh, Clarissa, haven't you realized yet how phony all that charm is? No, I suppose he blinded you with it as he did Jenny and the others. Even you, Ellie."

He smiled quizzically at Ellie Dawson as she bent over the table, but there was no answering grin. Her lips were tight, her face frozen.

"He didn't bother to use his famous charm with me."

She could see the unspoken question in Clarissa's eyes and she went on. "You know my—reputation from Hannah, I'm sure. Well, soon after the Granvilles moved here, George must have decided that I was merely a higher breed of lady of the river. He was extremely offensive and persistent. I tried every way to discourage him. I insulted him, I avoided him—nothing got through that conceit of his. He can be very stubborn . . ."

She paused and glanced up at Adam. "One night he just showed up here. Just walked in as brazen as you please and ordered Morgan out as though he were a servant. When my son refused to go, George threw him out. Right out of his own house. George thought Morgan had run away, but instead he had gone round to the shed and got the axe. When he came back with it George turned very meek. Lost his passion in a hurry, he did. He's arrogant with people like us. Thinks he can walk all over us and we'll just lie back and take it. But he found out different."

"So you see," Adam said, "your cultured gentleman can be very boorish when he wants something badly enough."

"But what does he want? Why should he turn against me? Against his own family?"

Adam shoved his chair back and stood near the fireplace. "What does he want? That is what I've been moving heaven and earth to learn . . . even to making thieves of my best friends. I'm fairly certain that it has to be money he's after. Greed is the one motive strong enough in George to force him to murder. For money he'll do anything. That was the reason he married Jenny."

Clarissa ran her hands through her disheveled hair, smoothing it back from her throbbing forehead. "I thought he had money."

"No, nothing of his own except what his practice brings in. And if he wanted a rich practice, he certainly wouldn't have come to a country village like Sing Sing. No, he wants a lot of money quickly, in a bundle. It didn't work with Jenny because Papa distrusted him right from the start and insisted on a marriage contract which would return her dowry in the event of her death. Very providential as it turned out."

She made one last effort to defend him. "If he is so greedy, I don't see why he came to Sing Sing at all. There was nothing to gain by it."

The silence seemed to echo in the room. Clarissa gave up trying to reason the thing out. Adam rested his arm on the mantel above the stone hearth and absently fingered a delicate shell from the riverbank in his large hands. Ellie sat down on Adam's vacant chair and turned her china blue eyes on Clarissa.

"Don't you know that there is a fortune hidden somewhere in that house?" She glanced up at Adam. "At least . . . that's the rumor. Mr. Reddick was supposed to have converted all his assets into cash before he died. The money was never found, and a lot of people still believe that it's hidden somewhere in or around Zion Hill."

"But that's just a story . . . isn't it?" It seemed incredible to her that the George Clarendon she knew—the graceful figure handing her down from a carriage, the comforting friend in the arbor, the ardent suitor of Judge Granville's study—that this man could be so obsessed with gold as to try to murder her.

But obviously it was not difficult for Adam to see both men in the same person. "How it must have driven George nearly out of his mind to know that he was sitting on all that money and unable to touch it."

Ellie gave a brittle laugh. "He won't find it so easily. Plenty of others have tried and come up empty-handed."

"Ah, but George is not the type to go at the thing with hammer and tongs. You won't find him skulking about in the dark looking under beds or taking apart hearth bricks. He's much more methodical. He'd go right to the source. I'll wager he's moved heaven and earth to discover the whereabouts of Mrs. Reddick or that preacher fellow. What's more, I think he's found one of them, but I haven't been able to discover which one. Corey tried twice to search his office, but there were too many people about." He turned to Clarissa. "That's where I was going tonight when I surprised you in the stables."

But Clarissa wasn't listening. She kept turning over Adam's words: "methodical," "found one of them," "discover which one." Suddenly it all fitted together.

"So George was the one in the dining room."

She was speaking to herself, but instantly Adam was alert. He moved over to sit near her on the corner of the table and watched her closely.

"I was in the old kitchen," she explained, "and I heard voices from the dining room above. It was that horrible man, Evans—you remember. He was talking to someone, but I couldn't tell who it was. He claimed this person had paid him to find something for him and that somehow it involved the death of his sister. He said something like, 'I didn't count on her dying . . .' —something like that."

"You overheard this? By God, I wish I had. What did you do?"

"I heard them leaving; so I ran upstairs to see if I could catch them in the hall. By the time I got there, there was only Judge Granville talking with Evans on the veranda. I thought perhaps it had been he."

"Papa! With all his faults Papa would never consciously hurt anyone. However, it may have been convenient for George to have you think that." Adam rubbed his forefinger back and forth across his lower lip. A few things were falling into place for him as well as for Clarissa. "Did you ever let on to George that you had overheard this conversation?" he asked.

"Well, I tried to draw your father out that evening at Mr. Ashley's just to see if he had been in the dining room that afternoon. He claimed he had never entered it."

"Did George actually hear you mention the dining room?"

"Yes, but so did you. Everyone did."

"Yes, but only George would have known what you meant by it. That would explain why he thought you were getting to be an inconvenience. First he tried to marry you . . ."

Clarissa looked up sharply. "How did you know about that?"

Adam smiled his enigmatic smile and went on. ". . . then he tried to put you out of the way. He must be getting close to all that money if he's that desperate."

Watching them from across the table, Ellie was struck by the way the flickering light from the fire accentuated the dark shadows on Clarissa's strained face. The poor girl was about to drop from exhaustion.

"I think we should let Clarissa rest for now, Adam," she said sympathetically. "There isn't much more about all this you can do tonight, and she looks as though she needs her bed. She'll be safe enough here for now."

Adam reached over and squeezed Clarissa's hand. "Forgive me, I was so absorbed in bringing George to bay that I forgot what you've been through tonight. Get some rest, of course." He rose from the table and took his cane from where he had propped it against the bricks. "I'm going to tell the family tomorrow that you left early to go into New York."

"New York?"

"It won't be a lie. You are going into New York. You and I are going to take the boat down together early tomorrow morning. I've got some checking of my own to do and as long as you are with me I'll know that you're safe."

He set his hat on his head and tapped it lightly with his cane. "If this trip turns up nothing, I don't know what we'll do. There is no place left to go. If only we knew of

189

some hiding place in that house. Well, you get some sleep."

He took Clarissa's hand and raised it lightly to his lips. "Adam," she said, "thank you. Thank you for helping me tonight."

He smiled down at her. "You rest," he said gruffly and started for the door.

He had his hand on the latch when suddenly she remembered. "Adam, wait," she called. "There is a hiding place in Zion Hill. The children have one in their room. They keep things there—birds' nests and rocks, things like that. But Mary told me once that they had found other things there too."

He turned back to the table at once, "You've seen this?" he asked, his hopes rising again. "Tell me about it. What did they find? Where exactly is it?"

"But I can't," Clarissa answered. "The one time they talked about it Mary wouldn't allow me to see where it was. I only know that it's in their room and near the fireplace."

"Are you sure it's an old one?" he said, his eyes searching her face. "Not one they made themselves?"

"Yes. They told me they had discovered it. Do you think it could be important?"

Try as he might to be cautious, Adam could feel his excitement growing. "In the nursery, of all places! Do you think you could talk them into showing it to us?"

Clarissa thought for a moment. "I think so. This happened right after I came to Zion Hill, and at that time they didn't know me very well. I believe they would trust me now."

"All right, here's what we'll do. Tomorrow we'll take the early steamer into town, see my friend, then come back to Zion Hill and try to discover what's in that hiding place. If, between these two things we are still unable to corner George, then, well, you are simply going to pack your boxes and move out of there. I don't know where to, but it will be a long way from Zion Hill. Agreed?"

Clarissa felt that this enigmatic man was all of a sudden structuring her life for her. Her first tinge of irritation gave way to a strange feeling of pleasure. It was rather nice to be protected.

"Agreed," she smiled back at him.

Fourteen

True to his word, Adam was at Ellie's door early the next morning with Clarissa's lightweight pelisse over his arm and her Dunstable straw cabriolet hat in his hand.

"I purloined these from your room while Nancy wasn't looking," he said, smiling mischievously.

Clarissa had braided her hair into two dignified coils, and as she carefully placed the straw hat around them she reflected that Adam was not quite as gauche about fashion as George had claimed. The hat was trimmed in pink satin with wide brown ribbons shot with white, and it perfectly matched the brown satin dress she still wore from the night before. And, thank heaven, she also still wore her stout buttoned boots. The thin, kid house-slippers which were her usual fare in the evening would never have held up for a trip to the city.

By the time they reached the pier below Ellie's house, the trumpet was announcing that the Great Northern Steamer had drawn up in the middle of the river, a black column of smoke drifting away above it. The dock was already crowded with a colorful assortment of waiting passengers: merchants going to town on business; ladies excitedly looking forward to a shopping excursion; rough farmers in round hats keeping a watchful eye on their goods which waited for transportation out to the steamer; and laborers in checked shirts ready to pay their twenty-five cents for the trip downriver.

Guiding Clarissa's arm, Adam worked their way through the noisy crowd and managed to be among the first passengers who stepped aboard the ferry which carried them out to the steamer. Once aboard the larger boat, he led her to the upper deck where a small breathing space allowed them a view of the river swelling away between the sloping hills. The wind blew against their faces, while spray from the clacking paddles covered them with a fine mist. Yet Clarissa felt her heart lift as she saw the green slopes of Zion Hill fade into the distance.

By the time the boat lumbered past Spuyten Duyvil Creek, the crowds in the enclosed cabins had thinned out enough to allow them to find a place at the end of a long table where a hot cup of chocolate revived their chilled bones. Conversation on the deck had been difficult because of the noise of the crowd and the paddles. Now, in the comparative quiet of the saloon, a strained silence seemed to fall between them. Clarissa glanced up once to find him watching her, his long mouth turned up quizzically at the corners. Under the constant drench of the paddle spray her hat had wilted, and she knew that the ribbons under her chin were limp and soggy. Tiny drops glistened like silver on her braids, and she could feel the two deep waves of her hair over her forehead clinging like plaster to her skin.

Adam chuckled. "I'm afraid you got a little drowned out there. I'm sorry."

"No matter," she smiled. "I prefer the spray to the crowds. Where are we going, anyway?"

"In New York? To an old friend of questionable reputation who may be able to tell us something about the elusive Mrs. Reddick. His name is Griswold Kelly of Canal Street, and he runs a small inquiry business which might be dubbed Columbia's answer to the London Bow Street Runners. It's a grubby little place. Will you mind?"

"I have not always lived in fancy country houses. You know that."

"Oh, yes, I forgot you were a farm girl once. But that is because you are a very elegant creature to have come straight from the farm."

Clarissa could feel the color rising in her cheeks.

"Forgive me," Adam said gently. "I didn't mean to embarrass you."

She forced herself to smile at him. "It's all right. My parents were cultured people who . . ."

"Fell on hard times. I remember. That happens in the best of families." He hesitated, uncertain of his words. "But, Clarissa, if we are to be friends, you must learn to take no notice of my unruly tongue. I've used it as a rapier for so long that sometimes I lose control over it. Truly I don't mean to hurt you."

'If we are to be friends.' She turned the words over in her mind, savoring them. "I know," she finally answered. "I have suspected at times that there was a considerate person somewhere under all that caustic wit."

He laughed. "Now it's my turn to blush!"

The quay at Barclay Street was jammed with people as the steamer made its way though a sea of masts to tie up. Once again Adam maneuvered her through the crowds to the corner of Wall Street where they were able to catch a passing omnibus rattling toward Canal. They sat beside a large square window, and Clarissa watched in fascination as the bustling city swept by.

To one accustomed to the quiet of the country, the noises of New York were like waves of heat from a blast furnace. Omnibuses were everywhere—"The City of Omnibuses," Adam had called New York and rightly so. The streets were absolutely covered from curb to curb with the horse-drawn vehicles crowding private carriages and cabs, street vendors with their loaded carts, and private gentlemen on horseback. The clatter of the horses' shod hoofs and the iron wheels of the cabs against the cobbled brick pavement was ear-splitting. Above it the cries of the vendors could barely be heard. A pervasive smell was everywhere—a mixture of packed humanity, horseflesh, and manure. They passed great piles of horse dung blanketed with flies, and once, before they left the wharf area, she spotted a dead horse pulled off to the side of the street, waiting in oblivious indignity to be carted off.

As they turned up Broadway the street widened to reveal neat rows of brick houses interspersed with shops, their colorful awnings reaching out over the sidewalk like booths at a medieval fair. Above them the tall spires of Trinity and St. Paul's rose out of a sea of leafy green trees and looked down in benediction on the lesser roofs of the town.

As they moved along slowly toward Canal Street the buildings began to change. Though still only three or four stories high, they began to be heavier, more utilitarian. These were the warehouses and depots, marts and trading centers, which were the heart and life's blood of the business world. Adam, responding to the contagious excitement of the busy, active streetlife, began to point out to Clarissa some of the places he had known so well when his family lived in the city.

"There is Tattersal's," he said, directing her eyes toward a dingy barnlike structure with a white half-arch over the door. It's just like the one in London, the biggest horse mart in the country. I got a beautiful mare there once—the one who broke my leg. God, she was gorgeous!

"Down that street a little farther on is Niblo's Gardens. Did you ever go there, Clarissa?"

"No. What is it? A beer garden?"

"Oh, that and much more besides. The best entertainment in town. Plays with Charles Kemble or songs by Italian tenors. You'd love it. I'll take you there someday."

His offhand comment brought a flush of pleasure to Clarissa's cheeks. She looked up and caught him doffing his hat to a young lady in a mauve silk dress with a wide blond lace collar who was watching the traffic from a window above. Clarissa could see that she held a small book in her hand and was smiling innocently at the omnibus passengers whose upward gaze met her own. Adam gave her a dazzling grin to match the polite lifting of his hat, and Clarissa noticed that the girl's eyes followed them until their horse carried them out of her sight.

"Do you always flirt with ladies in windows?" she asked playfully.

"Of course. She is probably never allowed out on the street without her aged abigail; so she sits at her window and throws smiles like the Spanish ladies throw roses. Oh, here we are."

Pulling her abruptly to her feet, he ushered her quickly down the steps to stand in the street in front of a bulky building with a long sign all the way across its front: MORISON'S HYGIENE MEDICINE DEPOT. Before they could safely reach the walkway, they were nearly run down by a passing ice wagon and entangled in a brief snarling quarrel between two stray dogs. They had only gone a few steps when Adam, intent on guiding her through the crowds on the sidewalk, suddenly stopped short, flinging out his arm and crying, "Look out!"

Clarissa watched in amazement as a long narrow plank began to extend from a shop door under a faded green and white antique sign which read: C. GREEN—BOOT-MAKER. As the board spread across the walk, heedless of consequences to passing pedestrians, she could see hanging from it nearly twenty pairs of newly finished men's and women's stout shoes, their polished leather gleaming in the sunlight. Balancing the pole on his shoulder was a wizened little man who looked neither right nor left as he swung the long plank and started up the street, blissfully ignoring the curses of the outraged injured he left behind. Adam ducked with what looked to Clarissa like skillful practice, but one of the swinging boots knocked off his hat anyway.

She could not suppress a laugh as he retrieved his beaver from the garbage-strewn gutter where a pig was already hopefully nosing it.

"The dangers of city streets," he exclaimed, brushing the dust and litter from the fur. "It is not always cutpurses and rowdies you must watch for. Imagine being done to death by a blow from a bootmaker's rack! Here we are at last, thank heaven."

Grabbing her arm he pulled her into a narrow doorway flanked on one side by a dingy little store with the word *SEGARS* inscribed in white letters on the window, and on the other by a neat curl and wig salon. As Clarissa followed Adam up the dark stairwell she felt her pleasure in the sights of the city fading under the depressing milieu of dirty wallpaper and chipped plaster. Once at the top of three flights of stairs, Adam tapped lightly with his cane at a worm-eaten door and stepped in without waiting for an answer. A man looked up from a cluttered desk where he was writing and, smiling broadly, reached for his coat hanging on a peg behind him. Clarissa had a brief impression of a small room in which the desk took up nearly half the cramped space, while to one side, a curtain stretched over a rope barely hid an unmade bed on the other side. Griswold Kelly seemed to fit his surroundings. His clothes were stained and crumpled, his long hair looked as though it hadn't seen a brush in days, and his fingernails were encrusted with black half-moons. Yet he had a brisk, matter-of-fact air about him and seemed blissfully unconcerned with the squalor around him. He greeted Adam warmly, and politely ushered Clarissa to the one uncluttered chair. Sweeping out a puce-colored handkerchief, he gave the seat one or two swipes that only served to rearrange the dust, then with one graceful swoop, swept to the floor the assorted piles of books and papers that lay on the only other chair, pulling it up for Adam. Clarissa sat down gingerly and rearranged her skirts around her, trying to pretend that the dirty, cluttered room was no different from those she frequented every day.

Adam had no such scruples. "By God, Griswold, I see you still live like a pig!"

Though Clarissa had promised herself she would sit quietly in the background, she soon found that she was leaning forward in her chair, completely oblivious to the disorder around her.

"You should have come to me in the first place," Gris Kelly started. "Imagine sending that good-natured oaf,

197

Corey Arnold, to go lumbering around ferreting out information. Why he couldn't find his elbow with his hand."

"He did it as a favor to me, Gris. He's a good friend, and frankly, I had forgotten about your new—new profession."

"Well, I'm a friend too." He poked Adam's shoulder with his ink-stained finger. "Remember our days at Columbia College? We had some good times, didn't we? Of course you and Corey made it through and I didn't, but a friend once is a friend always to Griswold Kelly. And, after all, I *am* a professional in these matters."

"Are you making a living with this?" Adam waved his hand, sardonically taking in the grubby office.

"Don't be so fastidious. It's growing at a rate that would surprise you. In any case, I traced down your Mrs. Reddick."

Adam's carefully studied detachment faded swiftly as he sat forward in his chair, his eyes eager. "You didn't! My God, Griswold, that's more than anyone else has been able to do. You *are* a professional. Where is she?"

"Probably walking the Elysian Fields by now. She's dead. Has been for two years."

He opened the drawer of his massive desk and pulled out a wad of papers tied with a red string. "It's all here. You'll find a certificate of death from the Queen's County Alms House, a statement from the superintendent, and a few comments from one of the inmates who remembered her. A lady with whom I spent a most enlightening afternoon."

Adam pulled off the string and hastily scanned the three papers. "Gris, I'm very impressed. I'll go over these more carefully later, but for now just tell me briefly what you learned."

Grisworld sat back in his chair and absently brushed at a gravy stain on his waistcoat. "The first thing I learned was to cut my own throat before I ever let anyone put me in a workhouse. Never become a pauper, Adam, especially an aged pauper. God, what a place! Dark, dank, and crowded with over a hundred dejected souls who sit around all day and pick at their chins. The only difference between that place and the Home for Imbeciles nearby is that supposedly these people are in their right minds. At least they were when they came there. A few days in that place and I'd be a lunatic myself."

"I wonder how Mrs. Reddick came to be there? She was supposed to be left in the care of relatives."

"They probably shunted her off when they discovered she had no money."

"But she—that is, her husband was supposed to have left her a great deal of money. Quite a fortune, in fact."

"Well, she must not have ever seen it or she certainly would not have ended up in the almshouse. Nobody would go there unless they were absolutely desperate."

Adam glanced over at Clarissa. She knew what he was thinking. That money still had to be at Zion Hill, or certainly Mrs. Reddick would have taken it and used it. He handed her the roll of papers, which she smoothed out on her lap to look over.

"Tell me what this friend said of her. Did she know her well?"

"As well as anyone there. But I couldn't make much sense of any of it, nor could her friend. She said Mrs. Reddick raved a lot and talked a lot of nonsense about religion and the wrath of God, the fires of hell—all that sort of muck. There was a lot of bitterness in her. She claimed she'd been betrayed and abandoned and God would avenge her, etc. Oh, yes, and there was a phrase she would repeat over and over: 'Bring up a child and he'll never depart from the way he should go'—something like that. She was obsessed with these words. But I got the impression that her poverty had unhinged her mind. Either that or she was just plain senile."

"She had good reason to be disturbed. She found her husband's body stuffed into an old oven beside the fireplace in the original section of the house. That may explain her fixation with fire. Perhaps she even witnessed the murder. Lesser things than that have sent people off."

Kelly remembered Adam's mother and coughed politely. "It's all there on that paper. I hope it will mean something to you."

Clarissa spoke up for the first time. "But Adam, if Mrs. Reddick witnessed the murder, why wouldn't she come forward and say so at the trial? Or if that prophet fellow knew that she had seen him kill Mr. Reddick, she would be a threat to him, wouldn't she? He would have tried to get rid of her some way, surely."

"Yes, and as it is, we know he did nothing. He stood trial and was acquitted and then faded away. From what I've learned about him it is obvious that he had no fortune either. And the other man, Mr. Allen, died shortly afterward in very modest circumstances. None of them got that money, it seems clear. Perhaps Matthias didn't murder Reddick after all. But then, who did? It certainly is confusing."

Kelly tipped his chair back against the wall, studying Adam with veiled eyes. "Now here is the most interesting thing of all. I had to do a lot of asking and searching to locate this lady and everywhere I went I found that someone had been there before me, asking the same questions and looking for the same people."

Adam looked up quickly, his eyes narrowing. "George Clarendon."

"Not unless he's suffered a dramatic change in appearance. I remember your brother-in-law as a rather gorgeous man of fashion. This fellow was a dried-up, wizened little weasel of a man."

"Evans!" The name escaped both their lips at the same time.

"That's it. Evans was his name. I ran him to earth, and with a little persuasion on the part of yours truly he admitted that George had paid him for three years to track down Mrs. Reddick and that prophet fellow. George has known about that murder for some time. Even before you moved up there to that house."

Adam tapped the letters in the palm of his hand. "Three years. And he must have also then known about the money hidden there. No wonder he was so insistent that we move to the country. Good for Mama, good for the children, and most of all, good for George!" He glanced up at Kelly. "Did you get any proof of all this?"

"Right there in writing. Signed by Evans—his mark. Are you satisfied?"

"More than satisfied. You did a splendid job, Gris, and I'm grateful."

Kelly grinned. "Don't applaud, just throw money!"

Rising, Adam drew a leather purse from his coat. "Speaking of money, what do I owe you?"

"If you look closely, you'll see that the last paper there is my bill."

Without glancing at the paper, Adam handed Kelly several large bills. The man's eyes grew wider as he took the money, protesting half-heartedly that it was too much.

"You've earned it, Gris," Adam said as he slipped the letters into the inside pocket of his coat. "Buy yourself a new waist with the extra. That one looks a little the worse for wear."

The air of the street seemed fresh and clean after Griswold Kelly's stuffy office. Taking Clarissa's arm, Adam led her without speaking to the nearby Bank Coffee House where he selected a discreet table near the rear of the building. Next to her a window looked out on a small garden, brilliantly green in the pleasant afternoon sunshine. Over coffee and sandwiches they examined Kelly's papers more closely and found that they were pretty much as he had described them.

Adam studied the letter of reminiscences, rubbing his long finger across his lower lip. "The fires of hell recur over and over. She was certainly obsessed with fire, wasn't she? I wonder what it means?"

Clarissa rested her chin on her hand and watched him thoughtfully. "I hesitate to say this, but perhaps it doesn't mean anything."

"I thought of that too. Just the wild ravings of a crazy old woman. And yet—— Well, at least we know for sure now that George was trying to find her too and that he knew about this whole business of the murder and the hidden money when he talked Papa into moving into that house."

"There's not much doubt now either that it was George

I overheard talking to Evans in the dining room. Yet that still doesn't tell us who poisoned Miss Evans or tried to kill me."

Adam watched her quizzically. "You just don't want to believe how culpable he is, do you?"

Clarissa blushed and looked down at her plate. "You mean, it was George?"

"Of course it was George, Clarissa. I know what he's capable of. I still suspect he had something to do with Jenny's death. If I ever find out for sure, I'll kill him with my bare hands."

At the look on his face Clarissa made a frantic effort to change the subject. "That phrase, Adam. The one Mrs. Reddick kept repeating. 'Bring up a child, etc.' "

He looked quickly back at her. "It meant nothing to me."

"It's in the house. I've seen it many times. It's written over the mantel in the children's room."

He looked at her blankly for a moment, then leaned forward, almost thumping the table.

"Didn't you say there was a hole in the wall somewhere in the children's room?"

"Yes. Near the—the fireplace."

They both spoke at once. "Fireplace!"

"Fire again—fires of hell! By God, Clarissa, that must be it. It's the first time anything in this puzzling business has fit together."

Quickly he dragged out his watch to check the time. "Grab your hat, my girl. We can just make the last boat back upriver."

As he was pulling her pelisse around her shoulders he stopped suddenly. "This means you will have to go back to the house and face the family again, Clarissa. Do you think you can manage it?"

Clarissa thought of George Clarendon—handsome, virile, exuding charm. How was she going to be able to play this game with him? How could she pretend that last night never happened? She would simply have to find the courage to brazen it out and hope that it would not be for long.

"I'll do my best," she replied, briskly tying the ribbons of her hat under her chin. "But I don't know how I shall be able to make small talk at supper after all that's happened."

"You won't have to," he said, pulling her toward the door with his free hand. "The boat will make us too late for supper, and with Papa away there'll be no evening prayers. I'll leave the gig tied near the stables, and we'll go straight to the nursery. With any luck we'll be back at Ellie's without anyone's knowing we were ever in the house at all."

She stumbled after him, dodging between the tables in the crowded restaurant. "But, Adam, won't Augusta wonder where we are? Or George?"

"I'll leave word with Nancy that you've gone off to bed or something." He stopped with his hand ready to push open the door and looked down on her upturned face. "Remember, if you do accidentally meet one of them, you must act as though nothing is wrong. Can you do that?"

"I think so," she said, raising her voice against the noisy traffic of the street.

"Good girl! Now come along. We've got to catch that last steamer."

Fifteen

"*You told!*"

Mary's voice betrayed her hurt. "You promised you wouldn't and then you told!"

Clarissa attempted to take Mary's hand, but it was jerked angrily away. "Mary, please believe me," she said kindly, "I'm sorry that I had to reveal your secret. But please try to understand. It's terribly important that we have a look at this hiding place. There may be something there left from a long time ago. Something that may even save someone's life!"

"You told *him*!" The child glared at Adam.

"Ahem," he discreetly coughed. "I don't think it matters so much *that* you told as *who* you told. The reward of my neglect."

Clarissa tried again. "Your uncle wants to help us— you and me—to stop something very bad which is happening in this house. You can help too, if you will show us where this place is."

Mary stared angrily down at the table in front of her. Next to her, his large liquid eyes moving back and forth between the three of them, stood Georgie. He wanted

204

very much to show Clarissa the hiding place, but Mary had already threatened him into silence.

Adam knelt swiftly beside Mary, careful not to touch her. His voice was deliberately gentle. "Your mother, Mary, was my friend as well as my sister. I loved her very dearly and she loved me too. If she were here now, I think she would want you to help us, in spite of what you feel, because we are trying to do what is right. Even if you are hurt and you don't like me, I think she would want you to help us."

Mary was silent so long that Clarissa began to despair of ever bringing her around voluntarily. They could force her, of course, or try to bribe her. Or, as a last resort, they could turn the children out and search the room themselves. Yet, any of these Clarissa felt would destroy the tenuous bond she had so patiently worked to build with these two children. She did not want to risk losing the affection which had grown up between them.

The light from a pressed glass camphine lamp on the table cast deep shadows on the child's small face. Behind the downcast long lashes, the youthful curve of cheek and the pursed lips, the struggle was almost visible—a mental weighing of countless kindnesses and loving interest against years of indifference and neglect. Finally, resigned, but still unwilling, she rose from the table and walked to the fireplace. In an instant Adam was behind her.

The fluttering light from the lamp caught the glitter of the gold letters above the hearth, touching their gilt with fire. With probing fingers, Mary dislodged three ragged bars of hardened plaster, laying bare a white brick underneath. She carefully worked the brick loose, exposing a black hole nearly a foot wide that extended back under the oak beams which formed the mantel. Then she moved back to the table, watching sullenly.

Adam reached into the hole and, with a carefully studied respect, drew out the first objects which came to hand—obviously the assorted paraphernalia placed there by the children. After the nest, some miscellaneous sticks and rocks, and a chunk of polished wood primitively carved to resemble a horse, he found he could extend his

205

arm full length under the mantel. The next thing he drew out was a tattered rag doll, very old and faintly familiar. It gave him a queer feeling to recognize it as one his sister Jenny had treasured long ago, and he very carefully placed it in Mary's hands. With these objects out of the way he found he could touch the end of the hole with his long probing fingers. There seemed to be nothing more hidden there, and for a moment he fought down his disappointment. Then he felt something move and by working away at it carefully he dislodged a small, thin, solid object which he carefully drew out and hurriedly placed under the lamp.

It was an old book of pressed paper, dry and black with age, and small enough for Adam to hold in his palm. He held it to the light, then carefully opened it to the flyleaf.

"Is it anything helpful?" Clarissa leaned over his shoulder.

Holding it up to the light, he read the title: *"The Sin and Danger of Despising a Preached Gospel.* That doesn't sound too hopeful, does it? I wonder if this was one of Prophet Matthias' tracts."

Clarissa looked longingly at the hole near the hearth. "Wasn't there anything else there? No purse or bag? No notes?"

"Nothing. Only this. But look here at the name on the inside cover—Josiah Reddick! At least it was the right connection. Perhaps Mrs. Reddick knew it was there, and that is why she kept repeating the motto over the mantel."

Clarissa pulled up a chair and examined the small book more closely. "Heavens, what a subject. Do you suppose anyone ever read it?"

"Maybe Matthias gave it to his friend, Josiah. But why would it be hidden away here?"

"Go through it carefully, Adam. It's our only clue."

"Look here, there is some faded writing on the flyleaf, but it's hard to make out. Reddick didn't have a very neat hand, did he? Is this word 'kill?' By God, I think it is!"

Clarissa read, inching her finger along the faded ink

stains: " 'They are . . . gone to,' no, 'going to, going to kill me! Everything is yours.' Look . . . Can you make that out?"

" 'Mine . . . mine here.' Now what could that mean?"

Clarissa went on. " 'In name of,' no, 'In the name of God, Robert, Hel . . .' "

"Then it just stops as though he broke it off." Clarissa sat back in her chair and looked at Adam, her large eyes luminous in the lamplight. "It's important, Adam, I know it is. But what could it mean?"

"Only one name—Robert. He isn't the one Reddick is afraid of—assuming Reddick is doing the writing—for he's asking him for help. That last part—surely he meant to write 'help me.' "

"And 'they.' Whoever he was afraid of it was more than one. Who could 'they' have been?"

"Well, as far as we know there were only four people involved. Mr. and Mrs. Reddick, Jonathan Allen and Matthias the Prophet. Not a Robert among them."

"Wait a moment! Yes, there was. Your father told me the day I came here that this Matthias' actual name was Matthews. Robert Matthews."

"But would Reddick be asking him for help? I thought he was the villain who murdered him."

"It was never proved. Just suppose this book, which is the kind of book he might give to the prophet, was his last chance to write some kind of desperate note. He was trying to ask him for help but was caught at it before he finished."

"Then who would be the 'they' who were trying to do him in? Mrs. Reddick and Allen? Why, yes it could be. Of course. They caught him in the act and took the book away. Then Mrs. Reddick hid it here where it was likely no one would ever see it. That might explain why she was so obsessed with the motto in this room."

"I'll wager that is exactly what happened. Reddick was killed by his wife and Allen for his money which he intended to turn over to Robert Matthews, alias Matthias the Prophet. Matthias must have caught them at it very

207

quickly because they hid the body so clumsily. Then they turned the tables on him and accused him of murder."

"But, Clarissa, the only thing wrong with that idea is that no one seems to have ever *got* the money. We know Mrs. Reddick and Matthias never did. And we can presume Allen didn't either since he died in poverty. Reddick must have hidden it well."

"Too well. Nobody ever found it." She took the book from his hand and leafed through its brittle pages. Standing at her shoulder, Mary studied them with her.

Adam sat for a moment rubbing his finger across his lip. "Clarissa," he said suddenly, "read me that note again. What does it say . . . 'all belongs to you?' "

" 'Everything is yours,' " Clarissa read. "Then, 'look'; then I think the next word is 'mine'; then 'here.' 'Look . . . mine here.' What in the world could he have meant by that?"

"Maybe he was saying to look in the old mine down by the river," Mary said hesitantly.

They both stared at her. "Out of the mouths of babes!" Adam exclaimed and startled Mary by giving her a sudden warm hug.

"Of course," cried Clarissa. "He has just said 'everything is yours . . .'; then, 'look'; then, 'minehere' or rather, 'mine here.' It must be that the money is in that old mine."

"Get a lantern, Clarissa. We're going to have a look inside that mine."

"Now? Tonight? Shouldn't we wait until daylight?"

"It will be just as dark inside that mine tomorrow as it is tonight. You're not afraid, are you? If it worries you, why don't you stay here and I'll go have a look at it."

"Oh, no! I'll stay with you. But, Adam, we don't even know what to look for."

"There must be a sign of some sort. He wouldn't just leave it there without marking it in some way either for himself or Matthias. If it was for Matthias it might well be some kind of religious symbol—a fish or a cross, something like that."

"There is a cross in that old mine," Mary spoke up.

"Georgie and I have seen it lots of times, haven't we, Georgie?"

Adam knelt before her. "You've explored that shaft, have you? Tell us what it's like, Mary. You may be able to save us some time."

"It's dark," said Georgie.

"Yes, and it's low, like a box. You can't go very far inside."

"And there's bats!" Georgie added.

"Oh, dear. Adam? . . ."

"Courage, Clarissa. What do you mean, Mary, that you can't go very far?"

"Well, it goes straight for a while; then it turns, like this, and then it turns again, and it's too small to go any farther."

"How long is it? As long as . . . this room? Or this house?"

Mary thought for a moment. "As long as from the porch to the road."

"Hmm. About eighty feet it sounds like. All right. And where is the cross? Do you remember? What does it look like?"

"It's scratched on a rock, on the second turn, and it's big. It starts on the ground; then it goes all the way up to the top. But the top is very low there."

"What's the ground like?"

"Just dirt."

Adam sat back on his haunches. "When I think of the time and effort we could have saved by talking to these children! I suppose it's no more than any of us deserves for ignoring them."

"Are you really going down there tonight?" Mary asked tentatively.

Adam looked a question up at Clarissa. She shrugged. "If its what you want, I'll help you."

"I don't think I could wait until morning if I wanted to. Come on. We'll find a lantern and a shovel then get to it."

He was already heading for the door. Clarissa started after him, but on impulse turned back to throw her arms around Mary, still standing silently by the table. "Oh, thank you, darling. Thank you for trusting us."

The rigid little body softened under her embrace. "Did it help?" she asked. "I couldn't tell."

"Yes, I think it was very important. We'll know soon." She laid her palm against Mary's soft cheek for a moment, then rose and hurried after Adam.

Pausing long enough to collect a lantern and a stout shovel, they made their way down the long walk past the arbor to the hill overlooking the river where the black cavelike entrance had been cut into the rock. This was Clarissa's first trip inside the old mine, and had she been given a choice, it was not the way she would have wanted to explore the place. As Mary had warned them, they had not gone far before the walls closed over their heads and they could barely stand upright. The dim lantern threw grotesque shadows on the clammy walls, it was damp and musty, and Clarissa, too conscious of her feelings that day at Andre's Cave, kept as close to Adam as possible and tried to ignore the rustlings now and then in the shadows.

"There's the cross," Adam said, holding the lantern up to illuminate a crude scratch on the stones that had been used to shore up the wall. "I think I'll start digging right here at its base. It may mean nothing, but it's the only clue we have."

"The floor is so hard packed you are going to have a difficult time of it."

He knelt to run his hand over the uneven earth. "I don't think so, Clarissa. In fact, look how loose this is. I think someone may have already found the money."

Reaching down, Clarissa picked up a handful of brown soil which ran through her fingers. "This looks as though it had been recently dug up and replaced. Could we be too late?"

Adam started removing his coat. "Well, we won't know until we look. Let's get at it."

Within minutes the hard edge of the shovel struck with a resounding clink some equally hard buried object. Adam knelt quickly and prodded under the loose dirt, feeling for a handle or a string. Instead, the long thin object he drew out of the earth caught the white lamplight, and Clarissa drew back, shrinking. It was a bone, and a large one. They looked at each other for a silent moment; then Adam picked up the shovel again.

The hole was shallow, but because it had been so recently turned over, it was not difficult to get down to what lay buried there. When all the loose dirt was lifted aside, the faltering light of the lantern fell not on a box or a purse but on the gray frozen limbs of a large skeleton, half-petrified into the hard-packed earth of the mine floor.

"Oh, Adam. How horrible!" Clarissa muttered.

"Whoever dug here before us only partly uncovered it. Look how it's still half-buried in the solid earth. It's been here a long time."

"Cover it back up, please. It's terrible."

"I wonder who this poor devil was. Instead of an answer, all we've got is another mystery."

With the edge of the shovel he scraped the loose soil back over the calcified bones. "No need to bury it completely," he said. "We'll have to tell Peckham about it—when we get the chance. Here, are you all right?"

She leaned against the cold wall, feeling sick inside. "Yes, but I'd like to get out of here. It's too close and depressing."

Draping his coat around her shoulders, Adam picked up the lamp and led her back to the entrance. The night air felt cool and clean after the mustiness of the mine, and Clarissa breathed deeply of it as she sank on one of the posts lying in the grass where it had fallen away from the entrance.

Adam sat down beside her resting his arms on his knees. "Well, so much for 'look in minehere,'" he remarked absently. "I just can't help but feel that we're missing something," he said, taking the little book out of his coat pocket and leaning over to inspect it again by the dim lantern light.

"'Everything is yours,'" he read. "That has to mean the money. "'Look in minehere.' That is certainly what it says."

"Minehere," Clarissa said quietly.

" 'Look in minehere.' That has to mean look in the mine."

"But why not say 'Look in the mine.'? Doesn't it strike you as a strange way to write directions?"

"Not if he was trying to disguise it. After all, he wouldn't want to be telling the others where the money was if they were trying to murder him for it. Perhaps it's some kind of code."

"But 'mine here'? It doesn't make any sense. Unless . . ."

Adam looked up at her sharply. "Unless?"

"Suppose he meant another word completely. He doesn't write the two words separately as we would, did you notice?" Suppose he meant them to be one word. Minehere. The spelling would be wrong, but it's the only other word that makes sense."

"What word is that? I don't know it."

"It's Dutch. Mynheer. It means 'mister,' I think."

"But, Clarissa, none of these people were Dutch. It wouldn't mean any more to them than it does to me."

"I've heard it somewhere and recently too. No . . ." she turned to him, her voice growing with excitement. "I read it. In that book your father gave me—the diary of the revolutionary soldier. Adam! I remember now. 'Mynheer' was a kind of slang name the Americans used for the German mercenaries brought over by the British. The Hessians. They called them 'mynheers'!"

He looked at her blankly for a moment, then suddenly gripped her arms. "The Hessians! The andirons in the parlor. Clarissa, by God, you're brilliant! That must be it."

"Oh, do you really suppose so?"

"Of course. Reddick had a foundry and he cast iron like other men would whittle sticks. He could have done anything with those andirons and no one would ever give them a second glance—they are such functional things."

"But I thought they were antiques."

He was on his feet, pulling her up beside him. "Perhaps they were originally. Or perhaps that was what people were meant to think. Come on. Let's get back to the house. Surely we're on the right track this time."

Pulling her along the path, the lamp bobbing in his hand, they started up the narrow track toward the arbor. So certain were they that they had finally discovered Reddick's secret that they never noticed the quiet figure which detached itself from the shadows of the arching trees and followed silently behind them.

By the time Clarissa reached the parlor he was already inspecting the fireplace. Leaning on one knee, he ran his fingers delicately, probing up and down the Dutch tiles.

"It's those andirons I'd explore," said Clarissa, kneeling beside him.

"I did, but they don't look too promising up close. I thought perhaps they might be a code of some kind."

It had been a warm day and the hearth was cold. The camphine lamp on the round table in the center of the room spread its copper glow in a mellow arc that left the corners lost in shadow. The light fell softly on the white paint of the Hessian soldiers, feet frozen forever in their mute tread, arms arrested in breasting their long rifles, black painted eyes staring unseeing across the lamplit room. Clarissa tried to lift one and was surprised at how heavy it seemed.

"They're cast in one piece," Adam commented, still probing the tiles. "Do you think there could be anything hidden inside?"

"If they are in one piece, I don't see how. Perhaps that's too obvious. Could they have another meaning, do you think? Here—put them back in place and see if they suggest anything."

"Well, the rifles are both pointing toward the top left side of the hearth. Perhaps there is a place there . . ."

Adam traced a direct line with his hand from the rifle's tip to the tiles under the mantel, probing around the tiles to attempt to wrench away any loose plaster, then tapping to ascertain if there was a hollow space behind.

"Damn! Nothing. Got any more ideas?"

Clarissa sighed. "What about directly in back, or directly in to the side, or in line with the feet?"

Adam sat back on his haunches. "I doubt it because in the normal course of use and cleaning they would have been moved so often. But we'll try anything."

Very carefully and thoroughly he went over every possible place around the hearth which might be in line with a portion of the andirons. "I've nothing to show for that," he said in disgust, "except a hand covered with soot. There must be another answer. There must!" Pulling out a square of mauve silk he wiped at his hands, then went back to inspecting the firedogs.

"Let's see that book again," said Clarissa. "The answer has got to be there and we're just not seeing it."

"Perhaps it's time I had a look at that!" came a voice from the doorway. Clarissa swiveled around to see George Clarendon leaning against the frame, his arms crossed before his chest. She could hardly believe her eyes, but surely on one arm rested the long silver-mounted barrel of one of Judge Granville's dueling pistols, and it was pointing at them.

"Surprised you, didn't I?" A second pistol caught the light, dangling carelessly in his other hand, both of them at half-cock. "As conspirators you're not exactly the most discreet. I knew you went in to New York today and I knew why. Evans had informed me about the bruising your detective friend gave him."

Adam recovered his voice first. "For God's sake, George. Put down that ridiculous pistol."

George went on ignoring him. "I was listening upstairs and I followed you to the mine. In fact, I have been there many times before. It was I who first dug up that poor skeleton. However, I never had a handy little book to guide me. I suspect that within it lies the answer to where Reddick's money is hidden; so now I think it's time I had a look at it."

"I always knew you had few scruples," said Adam angrily, "but listening at keyholes—"

"Careful. Don't move too fast, dear brother-in-law, or you'll find I have no scruples at all against shooting you. In fact, after all this time I might enjoy it."

Clarissa could not believe this was happening. "You

hypocrite!" she said, throwing caution to the wind. "Talking about love and promises and all the time—"

Angrily she jumped up, leaning forward over the round table. George merely turned the pistol on her, balancing it on his arm.

"Yes, well, I do apologize for that, but it was necessary. Someday you'll know why. Meanwhile, admit that it was quite an honor for a plain little cousin from the country to receive my attentions."

"Oh," Clarissa sputtered in indignation. "You monster of conceit! You tried to kill me!"

George looked at her obliquely.

"You're wasting your breath on him," Adam sneered. "You'll never get through his self-centered hide."

George gave a quick laugh. "I will admit to one stupidity. It never crossed my mind that the key to all this would lie in the room my own children occupied. I should have cultivated their trust a little more."

"Venal to the last!" Adam rose beside Clarissa, but George stopped him with a sudden move of the pistol.

"Careful there. One quick move and I promise you you'll not live to regret it."

"You swine." Adam glared but kept very still. "This is how you'd repay my father for giving you a home, for giving you his daughter. I always suspected it was you behind all the troubles we've had. Did you poison Jenny too? Is that how she died, by our own despicable hand?"

The mocking smile disappeared from George's face, replaced by a fluid bitterness. "Thief, forgerer, and cynic I readily admit. But I never harmed Jenny. I have never murdered anyone—though I don't expect you to believe it."

"You're right. I don't!" In a sudden lunge Adam threw himself across the room at George, sending the table flying. Clarissa heard the sharp report of the pistol and scrambled down to the floor. The lamp landed almost in her lap, and she could see the upended bottom of the table split from the shock of the bullet which struck it. Straightening the lamp, she scrambled around the side of the room as the two men crashed grappling to the floor.

She could see Adam rolling over on the rug as George managed to get astride him, pummeling his fists into his face. Then over they both rolled, knocking a whatnot crashing in a mass of broken china figurines to the floor. George reached wildly for the other pistol lying near his head, but Adam kicked it and sent it flying straight at Clarissa's corner. Clarissa grabbed it swiftly, appalled to find herself holding the thing, then turned and heaved it out the window into the bushes bordering the veranda. Just to be safe, she reached for the used gun on the floor and sent it flying after the first one. With a growing coolness she inched her way around the two men grappling on the floor, looking for an opportunity to slam her foot into George. Their constant movement made her afraid she'd get Adam instead.

Once again George rolled over on top of his brother-in-law, striking his fists at Adam's face. Clarissa hurled herself on his back, clawing at the wide cravat. Her bantam weight could do no more than annoy him, but at length the annoyance caused him to slacken his grip on Adam's throat just long enough for him to swivel over and send the slighter man crashing against an elbow chair in the corner. Throwing his body forward, Adam wildly grabbed for the brass firetongs just as George lunged for his legs. He scrambled to the side, got enough leverage to rise up on his feet, then sent the heavy poker crashing down with all his considerable strength behind it.

The blow carried with it years of distrust and dislike, traded insults, and mutual contempt. It missed George completely and smashed down against one of the iron Hessian soldiers, crashing it against the marble hearth. The head broke completely away and rolled off, but the hole that it left caught the light from the lamp standing on the floor nearby. A silver prism spilled tiny living icicles of light on the black marble before the fire.

Both men stopped dead, arrested in motion like birds frozen in flight.

"God almighty!" George stammered, his eyes almost doubling in size. With something near to awe both men leaned down to stare at, then gingerly touch, the tiny sparkling pile spilling from the andiron.

"Diamonds!" George had forgotten both Adam and Clarissa. He scooped up a few of the small jewels, holding them against the electrifying light. "Diamonds, by God. How on earth did Reddick manage? All this time, here they were, and we never knew."

Adam edged over near Clarissa, hissing through his teeth. "The pistol—the pistol? Where is it?"

"I—I threw them both out the window!"

He swerved around staring at her. "You what! Clarissa! You ninny!"

"I was afraid you would get shot."

"At least it evens up the odds, when he finally gets around to remembering us."

Adam edged his way nearer to the lean figure kneeling intently by the broken andiron. George hardly noticed him, so absorbed was he in trying to determine the value of the sparkling horde. Grabbing up the andiron, he up-ended it and shook it violently. A few tattered remnants of a small cloth bag clogged up the opening and a scattering of several loose jewels fell on the black marble. Kneeling beside him, Adam pretended to inspect the diamonds, while he quietly and slowly slipped his hand toward the brass poker lying to one side of the hearth.

A hand shot out, closing his wrist in an iron grip. "Oh, no, brother-in-law dear. No tricks now," George snarled, "Not when I'm so close to having my fortune made."

"What makes you think you can get away with all these? If they belong to anyone in this house—which I very much doubt—they belong to Papa, not you."

"Strictly speaking, you may be right. But not if I get away with them first."

"But you won't. I might be tempted to let a thief escape just to be rid of you, but a murderer—never!"

"You won't have much choice." With a sudden move he was on his feet, snatching the poker away from Adam's reach. With flexed knees he circled around Adam, who stood poised and ready to spring back. Then in a totally unexpected move, George grabbed at Clarissa, thrusting her body between them and twisting her arm behind her.

Adam straightened and stepped back as George spoke. "Now, Adam, let us see just how chivalrous you really are. Either you collect those diamonds for me and tie them up in your handsome cravat or I'll use this poker on our fair cousin's head. And I'm not joking."

Adam stood frozen, struggling between his fear for Clarissa and his hatred for this man. "You won't get away with it," he hissed. "How far do you think you will get before I'll be after you?"

"Far enough, if I take her along for company. Since you are convinced of my disregard for human life, you'd better start worrying about hers. The cloth, please."

Clarissa struggled against the grip on her waist and arm, but she could not budge it. Carefully spreading the mauve rectangle on the rug, Adam filled the center with the loose diamonds, then folded it over several times until it was a small compressed square. His wary eyes never left George's face. "Don't you wonder what might be in the other andiron?" he said with a glint of mockery. "You have the poker. Why not open up the second Hessian and have your fortune doubly made?"

The struggle was almost visible as George mentally weighed his chances of breaking open the andiron before Adam tackled him.

"No," he finally said reluctantly. "Too risky. Besides, I think I have enough here to set me up rather tidily. Two against one is a little too much giving you the edge."

"What you need is a third party," said a cool voice from the doorway. A tall figure stepped into the lamplight, calmly pointing the pistols which Clarissa had thrown through the window directly at the three of them. The weird light from the floor cast grotesque shadows on the lean face, underlining its features like a death's mask.

"Augusta!" George cried eagerly. "You've found the guns. Quick, give them to me." Without loosening his hold around Clarissa, George began sliding toward his sister-in-law standing in the doorway.

"Don't do it, Augusta," Adam pleaded. "The bastard is

218

trying to get away with Reddick's fortune. Give them to me, Augusta. Hurry!"

"Don't listen to him," George urged. "You know what he is. Come on, old girl, help me out. You won't regret it. I promise. I'll make it worth your while."

"Augusta, hand me those pistols. Can't you see what he's trying to do?"

Without taking their eyes from the other's face, they both reached for the guns. When Augusta spoke finally, the depths of contempt in her voice brought them around to face her astounded, unbelieving.

"If either of you two silly men so much as moves an eyebrow, I shall blow a hole through both your chests with the greatest of pleasure. And I think you both know that I am a very good shot!"

Sixteen

"Augusta! What on earth are you talking about? Come now and help out your favorite relative." The smile on George's face was not half so assured as he tried to make it look.

"Don't waste your famous charm on me, George. I'm impervious to it. I long ago took your measure."

George stared unbelievingly at the glinting barrel of the silver-mounted pistol waving under his nose. This was incredible. The look on Augusta's face gave him the uneasy sensation that something had got beyond his control. "Now Augusta, I know you are a determined . . ."

"That's right." The detached air of the sophisticate was gone completely from the hostile green eyes which watched the three of them like a cat eyeing its prey, hoping for a movement so it could pounce.

"That's right," she went on. "It took a long time and a lot of determination to come to this moment, and I intend to savor it. One of these weapons has not been fired and the other is reloaded. So you see, I might even enjoy putting two bullets through that manly chest of yours, if need be."

"Augusta," George started again, inching toward her and loosening his hold on Clarissa.

"She means it, George," Adam spoke quietly. "You'd better believe her." For once all trace of artifice was gone from Adam's voice. He stood as still as the frozen china figurines on the mantel behind him, his eyes riveted on the taut figure of his sister.

"Thank you, Adam," Augusta replied with the air of one who has just been passed the sugar. "You were always honest. Disgustingly rude, but honest, which is more than can be said for our hypocrite brother-in-law.

With the dogged stubbornness of one who sees a fortune slipping from his grasp, George still refused to believe her. "Augusta," he said unctuously, one graceful hand outstretched. It froze in midair as the pistol flamed with a loud report.

To the end of her life Clarissa would never forget the look of startled disbelief on George's face before he slumped to the floor, nearly pulling her down with him.

Scrambling aside, she saw Adam kneeling beside George, looking at her with a question in his eyes. She nodded that she was not hurt, then watched as Adam with deft fingers lightly felt George's neck and wrist and pulled his coat away from the red stain on his chest.

"My God, Augusta, you've killed him! Why? Why?"

Clarissa covered her face with her hands. Just a moment before George had been a familiar living, breathing man. Now the vacant gray eyes stared up at the ceiling like holes in a mask, and a thin, red line trickled from the blue lips and down the white skin. She was overwhelmed with the horror of it.

She looked from that awful white face up to where Augusta stood in the doorway and felt a cold seeping horror creeping up her back. Augusta was smiling—a vacant, cruel smile. She might have just swatted a fly for all the emotion she felt at snuffing out George's life. My God, my God, Clarissa thought. She is as crazy as her mother!

Adam read the same sentence in the expressionless face in the doorway. Very deliberately he stood up, watching his sister and trying to second-guess what was going on behind that demonic mask.

"I knew I would have to do that," Augusta said coolly, in a voice that raised the hairs on Clarissa's neck. "Too bad. I only intended to graze him. All that blood and all over the Turkey carpet too. Papa will be so distressed." She shrugged. "And now, dear delicate cousin, lay that cravat with those lovely jewels on the table here by me—slowly!"

Careful not to make any sudden moves, Adam studied his sister. "How fortunate that we discovered Mr. Reddick's horde just when Papa was away. Or did you plan that too?"

"Some things are just pure luck. But I knew one of you would eventually locate the fortune if it was here at all. I've watched every move you made."

"I think we are seeing a new side of you tonight. I would never have suspected you capable of such intrigue."

"How would you know what I'm capable of? How would any of you know? Have you ever cared how I felt about anything? Ever wondered what I wanted? Particularly that loathsome hypocrite on the floor who talked Papa into dragging me out to this decaying place away from everything that mattered to me. It wasn't enough that he had already taken away my girlhood and made me the mother of the family. The two of you made me old before my time. You turned me into a spinster wasting away in this rustic hole when I should have been surrounded with beauty and suitors."

"Papa wasn't responsible for Mother's illness," Adam answered quietly. "Why didn't you say how you felt?"

"Why didn't he ask?" Her voice rose with rage. "No, he was too busy with prayers and legal briefs and hovering over a crazy old woman's every senile breach of manners. Pulling us out here because of Mother when we are the ones who matter. I am the one who matters! Well, I hereby claim my inheritance, the meek can have the earth. Take that poker, Adam, and break open that other andiron. And one wrong move in any direction while you're doing it and you'll join George on the carpet."

Clarissa stood quietly to the side, as still as Adam. Like him, she had come to the conclusion that Augusta should be taken very seriously indeed. Her green eyes had a manic cast to them, and the high sharp laugh held a mean ferocity. Disjointed pieces were beginning to fall together in her mind. When she finally spoke, it was with a hesitancy that is afraid of what the answer might be.

"What have you done with Hannah?"

Augusta glanced up at her quickly. "Hannah? I only locked her in her room, just as I did the children and the servants. She is probably waiting patiently there like the little sparrow she is." She smiled contemptuously. "It seems, my little cousin, that you have a few more brains than I gave you credit for."

It took several blows on the andiron before Adam was able to dislodge the head. He swiveled around. "Sorry, sister, but this one is empty," he said, upending and shaking it. "Too bad. One fortune is all you get."

"Then I'll have that one," Augusta said politely, waving the end of the pistol toward the table.

"I didn't think wealth interested you, Augusta," Adam said, anxious to keep her talking.

"Oh, I have a great many talents you don't suspect. For instance, I have made quite a scholarly study of toxicology."

"I made it easy for you, didn't I, being always so suspicious of George. And all along it was you."

Triumph touched the strange smile on Augusta's face. "Oh, yes, it was me. I slipped dear Miss Evans her dose of eternity. That old fool Stubbs thought the tea had killed her, but that was only secondary. It was the water hemlock—one teaspoon ground into the gruel. Very effective, water hemlock."

"And the tea was merely for Clarissa's benefit, wasn't it?"

"How clever you are, Adam dear. Naturally I knew Clarissa's background— Oh, don't look so shocked, Miss

Shaw, we all knew. You can't keep a juicy thing like that quiet. I planned for suspicion to fall on you."

"But why?" Though she knew the best thing would be to keep silent, Clarissa could not hold back her indignation. "Why me? I never knew any of you before I came here. I was no threat to you or to George. Why involve me at all?"

"Let me guess," Adam spoke up. "It was part convenience, very handy to have someone around who had already been suspected of using poison to murder her brother, and partly because George was showing a little too much interest in our new cousin. Isn't that it, Augusta? Good old-fashioned jealousy."

"Stupid! Both of them. Dear George was so afraid he might not get his hands on the Granville money that he would have sought out Clarissa even if she had been convicted of killing her brother. And silly Clarissa! Another empty-headed pretty face, swooning all over the house when George so much as crooked a finger at her."

"Like Jenny?" Adam's voice was suddenly very cold. "Did you slip Jenny water hemlock too?"

Augusta looked startled for a moment; then the smirk returned. "I told George all along that he should have married me instead of Jenny. We would have got on well together."

"Perhaps he drew the line at some things—"

"You'd better be quiet, Adam," Augusta said, circling the long barrel of the pistol. "The next time it will be you."

Clarissa felt her knees trembling. Slowly she sank down on the settee behind her. "And I suppose it was you, then, who put the bur under my horse's saddle. I was supposed to get my neck broken, wasn't I? How disappointed you must have been."

Augusta smiled, her eyes glinting in the lamplight. She looked to Clarissa like a cat who had just swallowed a pet bird. Then a sound on the walk outside drew all their eyes to the window. It was the gig Adam had left waiting near the stables rolling down the graveled walk, followed by footsteps running up the porch stairs to the front door.

224

Clarissa caught her breath, praying silently that perhaps she was wrong and it was not the gig but Judge Granville returning early. He would be able to control his daughter if anyone could.

"That mystified you, didn't it," Augusta went on. "Very convenient that Adam happened along just at the right time." She glanced quickly toward the hall. "Come in, my love," she said, motioning, while behind her, Simon Edwards stepped into the room, his huge bulk filling the doorway.

"Here is another of my many talents," Augusta crowed. "He put the cocklebur under Russ's saddle—and who should know better just where to place it?"

Adam was the first to recover his voice. "You used Papa's groom, poor old Edwards, to try to kill Clarissa? I would have thought better of you, Augusta. What's come over you?"

"He is extremely devoted to me, aren't you, Edwards?"

The dull face looked down on her with a slavish devotion. Calmly he draped her cloak around her shoulders, then, in front of their startled eyes, leaned down and placed a kiss on her long neck. Augusta's eyes never left her victims, but she almost purred with delight.

Adam looked away in disgust. "For God's sake, Augusta. With Papa's groom? Have you no pride?"

"Why are you so shocked? Remember those long rides we took every day? Did you think we spent all our time galloping around the hills? Why some of our best gallops were on the ground, weren't they, Simon?" Her eyes darkened. "And you're hardly the one to talk of pride, tossing in the hay with that Dawson woman! Besides, Edwards is a man of many talents. One of them is impersonating you."

"So it was Edwards who was after Clarissa in the arbor. I thought it was George trying to make her think it was me."

"It was Edwards trying to make her think it was you. You and George were so ready to believe the worst of each other I had only to play you off one against the other."

"What are ye going to do with 'em?" the groom asked. "We can't just leave 'em here."

"Oh, I've got a plan. I've had a plan for everything. Did you bring the horses?"

"The gig was standing ready, so I brought that along instead."

"Clarissa, very slowly give that cravat with those lovely gems to Simon. That's right, no sudden moves. Now, stand over there, not so close to Adam. Simon, you take this pistol which has been fired and put the handkerchief in my hand. That's a good boy."

The groom followed her every command with obvious relish. In his stupid way he was utterly delighted to have the upper hand over two of the Granvilles, and Adam's one fear was that Augusta might not be able to stop him if he should decide that they should leave no witnesses. Yet, looking between his sister and the stolid features of the groom, his fears began to ease. She was in complete control.

"All we need now is one small thing in parting. Some small diversion which might give me a few minutes' grace to get safely away, although if Edwards followed my instructions you won't find a horse in the stables, not even Hannah's ridiculous pony."

"Oh, I did 'em all right. They won't be rounded up till noon tomorrow, if then."

Augusta lifted the barrel of the still-loaded pistol and moved it slowly, deliberately, back and forth between the two people standing in front of the hearth.

Adam's fear came rushing back. "For God's sake, Augusta," he cried, "we're your family!"

Clarissa knew the terrible concern on his face was not for himself. She could feel her hands growing clammy as she looked blankly into the small, deadly, black hole at the end of the pistol pointing straight at her. And behind it, to the murderous eyes of the regal woman she had once so admired as a perfect lady.

"So sorry, cousin dear, but it will keep Adam from following me," Augusta said in her carefully enunciated phrases and fired the pistol. Clarissa barely saw the quick burst of flame before she went smashing into a wall of pain and darkness and felt her body falling, falling into empty space.

"Clarissa! My God, are you all right?"

Her eyes opened a moment to see Adam bending over her and the doorway empty. Then, thankfully, the darkness closed around her.

Cursing Augusta, Adam gently turned Clarissa over to see that she was still breathing and to be reassured by her soft moans. A slow stain was spreading around the hole in the fabric of her shoulder, but it did not look like a fatal wound. Outside he could already hear the carriage rolling down the walk and, gently laying Clarissa on the floor, he dashed up the stairs, forcing his crippled leg. By sheer power of desperation he broke open Hannah's door and had a brief glimpse of her white face before he hurried back down the stairs.

"Clarissa's been hurt—take care of her," he cried over his shoulder and then was out on the veranda. Precious minutes hed been lost; yet he might be able to catch up with them if only he could find a horse. Damn it that Augusta should be so thorough.

His leg was beginning to send throbs of pain through his body, but he pushed on anyway, limping clumsily down the graveled drive. It was hopeless. On foot he could never hope to catch up with them. Then he remembered the High Road. They would have had to go left or right, and if he could make out which way they had taken, it might help later in the pursuit. He set off down the drive, cursing the cruelty of his crippled leg, then stopped in disbelief as he heard horses approaching. Two men on horseback were racing toward him. Shouting and waving his arms, he brought the lathered horses to a sudden stop. He didn't recognize one of the men, but the other was Robert Peckham, the magistrate. Adam had never been happier to see anyone.

"Did you pass a carriage?" he called.

"Going hell-bent for leather. Who was it?"

"Augusta and Edwards—our murderers! Look, give me your horse. I have to follow them!"

"Take Callem's. He's my deputy. Hurry. I'll go with you."

At the urgency in Adam's voice the mystified deputy did not pause to ask questions but slid from the saddle almost the instant that Adam swung up. In a thunder of horses' hoofs the men drove back toward the High Road where at the gate they stopped and circled, unsure of which way to go.

"So it was Augusta. Think they might have headed for New York?" Peckham asked.

"It's their best chance, but . . . I don't know." Adam studied the road carefully. It was too dark to see tracks, but far down near the corner where the smithy's stood next to the dilapidated meetinghouse, a lantern hung on a post before the church door. In its thin bronze glow there seemed to be traces of restless dust recently stirred from its sleeping roadbed. He made a sudden decision.

"I think they took the road north along the river."

"Let's hope you're right," answered Peckham, and they flew off again.

After they passed the smithy's, the road angled toward the river where it was deeply covered by a leafy tunnel which was almost pitch black. Once under the thick trees Adam slowed his mount almost by necessity and relied on his knowledge of the familiar road to make his way. Finally breaking clear of this tunnel, they could make out the dark outline of the countryside around them—the dark hills and the gray moonlit road reaching out before them. And far ahead, the tiny swaying carriage standing against the pale horizon.

"There they are. Come on!" Adam cried, spurring his horse ahead. Good horseman that Edwards was, he was driving wildly now, spurred by some sixth sense that he was being followed. The carriage swayed wildly from one side of the road to the other, balancing on one wheel then the other. As they drove nearer, Edwards began frantically whipping his horse, and the uneven road with its rocks and holes sent the carriage careening wildly in the air to land shuddering against the clay. Adam could see he was gaining on them; yet at the same time he knew that if they reached Sing Sing before him, they would have several roads to choose from and only two men to follow them. It was their best chance for escape. It was not Reddick's jewels Adam wanted that drove him so urgently, he knew, but the need to at all costs keep Augusta's baseness from the rest of the world. He had to bring her back with as few people as possible knowing the truth. And he had to keep her from causing any more harm. Yet with only a few more curves in the road they would be at the crossroads, and with a sinking heart he began to fear that he would never be able to catch up.

Suddenly he saw a yellow streak shoot across the road before the careening carriage, crashing into the driving horse. The terrified beast stumbled and reared, amid a furious clamor of wild equine screams and wild snarls and barks. Adam got close enough to make out the driver, half-risen in his seat, trying desperately to control the plunging animal while the spindly carriage clattered around the road like a toy.

He tried to reach them, frantic to grab at the rearing, backing horse, but before his own mount could cover the distance he saw with a mounting horror that the big black stallion, trying to escape its furious predator, was backing both the carriage and himself over the edge of the hill.

"Brute! Stop!" Adam called wildly, but, too late, he saw the black mass of the gig go careening down the hill, pulling its screaming horse with it. There was a horrible spewing mess of metal and flesh crashing down the ravine, carrying with it the splintered bushes and gorse of the hill, until shoved by its momentum, it fell out over the shallow banks to sink slowly into the dark waters of the Hudson.

By the time he reached the edge of the cliff where the gig had gone over, Ellie's big yellow mastiff Brute was balanced on all four powerful legs, looking placidly down on the shattered debris of the havoc he had wrought. Adam left his foaming horse and stood looking down into the darkness, dimly aware of the thumping against his leg where Brute was wagging his heavy tail in expectation of praise for his night's work.

He wanted to kill the animal, to choke the life out of

that massive throat with his bare hands. God knows he had wanted to stop Augusta, but not like this. Not like this!

"Adam! Are you all right?"

He recognized Morgan Dawson's voice and, turning back toward their cottage, saw that Ellie too had come out of the house to stand next to Robert Peckham. Morgan had the collar of the big dog tightly in his hand now—now, when it was too late.

"There's been an accident," he muttered. "Augusta . . ."

"Augusta!" There seemed no element of surprise in the way Ellie echoed the name.

"And Clarissa's been hurt up at the Hill. Do you think you could go up and help Hannah? She's going to need it."

There were reams of unspoken questions in Ellie Dawson's eyes, but she only nodded silently. "Of course. What about a doctor? Morgan can go for Stubbs, if you like."

"Yes. I think that would be a good idea. Peckham, you and I had better go down there and see if we can recover the bodies."

"The tide is strong there, but we'll give it a try. Mrs. Dawson, you'll find my deputy at Zion Hill. Send him along, will you?"

"Of course. Just let me get some decent clothes on." She almost turned to leave, but hesitated. "Adam—" Her voice faltered. "My dog. I'm so sorry."

He laid his hand on her shoulder. "I know. They were driving very fast and they must have forgotten that Brute is turned loose at night. It was an accident."

And who knows? Maybe it was for the best. That thought at least made it all bearable.

Seventeen

⁓   Sensations, all colors and forms; a blur which slowly, gradually worked its way into comprehensible patterns of faces and things; following on its heels an awareness of searing pain, at first dim, then growing into an agonizing, enveloping fog that blotted out everything else.

Clarissa fought against consciousness, inwardly pleading to be allowed to slip back into that shadowy world where pain was lost in nothingness, where her body ceased to be, while her mind wandered the gray valleys of oblivion.

But consciousness would come and with it the terrible hurt that finally localized itself in her shoulder and arm. Finally she knew she was lying in her own bed with Hannah's familiar face bending over her. The face faded and a strong arm lifted her head while something searing went down her throat and spilled out on the bedclothes. Some remembered panic swelled in her chest that Hannah was forcing tea down her throat—foxglove tea. No, not Hannah, but Philip, her brother, standing tall and wickedly handsome and pouring the bitter dark liquid into her mouth. She fought against it, trying to call for help.

Adam! Adam would help her if only he could hear her, but her voice refused to work. She would open her mouth and silent screams would strain from her throat; then the shadows would close around her and the grayness would claim her again.

One morning she opened her eyes to see sunshine streaming through the window, dappling the faded flowers on the carpet. Her shoulder was bandaged and hurt dreadfully, and there did not seem to be strength enough in her body to turn her head on the pillow. But she was alive and the world was warm and the spring birds were raising a ruckus outside her window. She closed her eyes and listened gratefully, just resting.

When the door opened she looked up to see Ellie Dawson entering the room, her yellow braids wound around her head and a neat starched apron over her brown serge. She was holding a red enamel tray with a bowl that gave off long trailing whisps of smoke.

"I hope that's not tea," Clarissa tried to say and was surprised at how much effort the words needed.

"I thought you were waking up," Ellie said as she set the tray down on the table by the bed, "so I sent down for some soup. It's a very thin broth and will give you more strength than tea. How do you feel?"

"Terribly weak." She made a motion to reach for the bowl, but her arm refused to work.

"Here, let me help. I'll spoon it for you, if you like."

"I don't think I can handle it, I'm so exhausted."

"This will soon have you feeling better." Ellie seated herself on the side of the bed and fed the invalid a few spoonfuls of the hot liquid. Clarissa could feel the warmth of it spreading in her chest.

"What happened?" she said weakly, touching her bandage with her good hand.

Ellie sat the bowl on the table and settled back in her chair. "How much do you remember?"

"It's coming back. The jewels, the pistols, Augusta . . . But how did you get here? I don't remember you . . ."

She gave a short laugh. "I wasn't here. Evidently Augusta shot you as she was leaving, thinking to keep Adam from following her."

Clarissa lay back on the pillow and closed her eyes, "Augusta—she's mad! As mad as her mother. She shot George, Ellie—she killed him with no more feeling than if he'd been a snake. Then she pointed that thing at me. I remember thinking, 'well, this is it.'"

She waited to catch her breath, then turned back to Ellie. "And did it detain Adam?"

Ellie smiled, and Clarissa noted something new in her face—a contentment and warmth that before had been hidden under the sadness. "I think he waited long enough to know you weren't dead; then he took off after her."

"Did he bring her back? I hope so, because she has to be stopped. She's dangerous, Ellie. Terribly dangerous."

"No, he didn't. There was an accident. Augusta's carriage went over the hill near my house. She's dead, Clarissa. She won't hurt anyone else, ever again."

The little strength Clarissa had left seemed to drain from her body. "Dead! Oh, Ellie, not dead! Poor, poor Augusta!"

"Poor indeed!" There was no trace of sentiment in Ellie's voice. "Think, Clarissa, what her life would have been. A trial and a scandal that would ruin her family or else to rot the rest of her life in one of those houses of horror they call asylums for the insane. She was much too dangerous to keep at home like Mrs. Granville."

In spite of herself Clarissa felt the tears running down her face. "Perhaps you're right but—such a terrible waste. She could have been so much more."

"I think she could only be what she was—the victim of her own distorted will." Impulsively Ellie reached out and took Clarissa's hand. "Clarissa Shaw," she said, "you have a warm heart. You weep for a man who tried to use you and a woman who tried to destroy you. It's more than I could do. I think you may deserve him after all." Rising quickly, she took up the tray and started for the door. "I'll send you up some tea."

Clarissa didn't really understand her words. She only knew that the oppressive sadness she felt over the way

233

things had turned out was almost harder to bear than the pain in her shoulder.

Her strength returned very slowly, but she was soon able to get back on her feet, though her first trip downstairs left her limbs trembling and her chest heaving. She sank into the wing chair before the parlor fire, determined to spend the rest of her life there.

Ellie Dawson soon returned to her cottage, leaving Clarissa in Nancy's capable care. Like Ellie, both Hannah and her father seemed to have been changed by the events of that night, although the subdued, haunting sadness that never left their eyes was very different from Ellie's quiet happiness. Judge Granville had returned from his trip to find the fabric of his family completely shredded, while Hannah seemed weighed by grief—too strong a grief, considering the fact that the sisters had never been close. Unexpectedly her eyes would fill or she would leave the room quickly as though fleeing from some specter of her own private tragedy.

One morning Clarissa finally broached the as yet unspoken subject of Augusta and found that it was not grief but fear which was the specter.

"I shall miss Augusta, though of course it was quite wrong, all those terrible things she did, even if she couldn't help it." Hannah's pretty face with its distorted, swollen eyes and puffy cheeks showed the signs of her suffering. She looked years older than her twenty-five. Clarissa wisely kept silent and let her talk.

"But, oh, Clarissa! What frightens me is . . . first mother, then Augusta— What is this terrible weakness in my family? Is it inherited? Sometimes I feel so confused and then I think, is it happening to me too? Am I growing like them?" She put her hands to her face and sobbed.

Comfort and reassurance were what she most needed, and Clarissa tried to supply them as best she could. After all, Hannah was quite a different kind of person from her older sister, not nearly so aggressive and much more attuned to the feelings of others. It was just impossible to imagine her deliberately hurting anyone.

Yet it was not hard to understand her fear. "I think this is something you are just going to have to learn to live with, Hannah, dear, hard as that is. Time alone will help you to find a way."

By the time Hannah left her, Clarissa was so drained of emotion that she gave up on the rest of the day and just went off to bed.

One of the worst things about being an invalid, Clarissa decided, was that it was so confining. She was especially anxious to talk to Adam, but his visits to her bedroom had been so brief and cursory that there was no chance to do more than exchange pleasantries. By the time she was able to spend her afternoons in the parlor, he had gone away for two weeks. She was lying half-asleep on the sofa one afternoon when she opened her eyes to see him standing in the doorway, intently observing her. With a leap of her heart she tried to sit up and, smiling, reached out her hand. He moved forward, a scowl on his dark face, and almost grudgingly raised her fingers to his lips.

"How are you?" he asked, standing awkwardly over her.

"Much better," Clarissa answered. She longed to add, "now that you're back," but she sensed the constraint in his manner. "Won't you sit down and tell me about your trip? We've had so little time to talk since . . ."

"No, no." His hand fluttered nervously. "I don't want to tire you, and there are any number of matters to which I must attend. I've been trying to spare Papa as many of the difficult details as I can—seeing to Augusta's burial, settling the legal matters, all those kinds of things. It keeps me quite occupied."

Clarissa looked quickly away. All at once the memory of all they had experienced on the night she was shot became an unpleasant, painful bond between them. No wonder he was so distant.

"I suppose there was a lot to settle," she said lamely, thinking how unpleasant all of it must have been. "What of the diamonds? Were you able to recover them? Perhaps there will be a reward."

Adam shifted his weight, leaning on his elegant new slim mahogany cane. "No, there is not even that satisfaction to be had from this dreadful business. We were able to recover the bodies from the river, but, unfortunately, the cravat in which the diamonds were wrapped came open with the movement of the water and the stones were lost. I would put some of the river boys diving there to search along the bottom, but the currents can be treacherous at that point. Besides, if word got out that Augusta had those stones in her pocket when she accidentally went over that hill, half the population of Westchester County would be swimming about in the Hudson. I think I would prefer to let the whole thing die an obscure death."

He was so obviously uncomfortable standing there trying to discuss a subject which was so blatantly painful that Clarissa almost pitied him. The memory of the warmth and affection they had shared was like a knife in her heart. Now all that was a lost shadow compared to the heavy burden of death and misery which lay like a mountain between them. Through a long silence, while the gentle ticking of the ormolu clock on the mantel resounded through the room, Clarissa sought desperately for something to say that would dispel the barrier separating them. If only he would reach out to her; but instead he turned away, looking almost longingly through the doorway to the hall beyond.

"Well," he said hesitantly, "I don't want to tire you . . ."

"I am rather tired," she heard herself answering.

"You must rest. I'll stop in again."

"Yes, please do."

Her head sank back on the pillow as he limped from the room. In a way it was a relief to see him go, so difficult and wearying was the effort to understand his unexpected coolness. She simply did not have the strength to handle it now. Time enough to work it out tomorrow, she thought, blinking back the tears that would come in spite of all her firm efforts to keep them locked away.

Judge Granville was particularly solicitous of Clarissa's convalescence, stopping in every day to talk for a moment and to inquire how she felt. One afternoon a few days after her conversation with Adam, she looked up from her chair to see him standing in the doorway with a vision in black taffeta on his arm.

"I've brought someone to see you," he said proudly, handing his wife forward. With her hand resting in quiet dignity on her husband's arm, Amelia Granville resembled a drawing out of the *Ladies' Book* come to life for an afternoon stroll. She made a neat figure in a wide-skirted buckled dress with puffed sleeves and a matching pelerine trimmed in velvet. Her lustrous white hair was waved back from her forehead and tucked in a wide chenille net. Behind her Clarissa caught a glimpse of a small, rotund nurse in a starched cap, her cheery face the complete antithesis of Martha Evans.

"My dear, I heard you were ill and I wished to see how you got on," said Mrs. Granville, sweeping graciously into the room to bend over Clarissa's chair. She laid her small hand lightly against Clarissa's forehead. "Oh, yes, you are quite pale. I must make you some of my valerian root tea. The very thing for a weak body."

Judge Granville beamed at his wife, and Clarissa for a moment almost believed some transformation had taken place. If it had not been for the blank eyes, she might have been convinced of it.

Amelia Granville pulled up a stool near the invalid's chair and leaned over her hand. "I must tell the queen that you've been ill. She will be so distressed."

"I'm feeling much better, thank you, Mrs. Granville. It's good of you to be so concerned."

"Oh, indeed a queen must care for all her subjects. That is part of the responsibilities of her office. Though," she added, sighing, "I do find at times that it grows burdensome and tedious in the extreme."

"My dear," said the judge, laying his hand on his wife's shoulder, "I must get back to my study. Nurse Donnely will help you to walk outside after your visit with Miss Shaw. Pray be careful not to tire her."

Amelia Granville drew herself up in her most regal manner. "I'm sure I shall be the best judge of that."

"Of course, my dear. Of course." The judge gave the new nurse a glance full of instructions, then left the parlor. He had hardly passed through the door before Mrs. Granville was leaning close to Clarissa's ear.

"Who *is* that handsome gentleman?" she asked in a loud whisper. "I declare but he is a dignified figure of a man. Do you know his name? I do think I should like to get to know him."

But Clarissa was growing accustomed to Mrs. Granville's startling ways, and she humored her along, encouraging her to talk, and picking up on what she could that made any sense. After a few minutes' conversation the elderly lady grew weary of the effort and was glad to go along with her nurse to walk the paths in the garden. Clarissa watched her leave, thinking if only the daughter had suffered from premature senility in the same way as her mother, how much misery could have been avoided. Amelia Granville was certainly mindless, but she was also harmless, while Augusta . . . Augusta had gone the way of the furies and left death and misery in her wake.

It was on one of her exhausting trips to the parlor that, late one afternoon, she had a surprising visitor. She was sitting quietly in the wing chair trying to get engrossed in *Northanger Abbey* but finding that her eyes kept straying to the new brass andirons gleaming on the marble hearth, when Magistrate Peckham was announced. Gratefully laying aside the tribulations of Jane Austin's silliest heroine, she welcomed him, extending a hand which he raised to his mustachioed lips. While he folded his long frame in the opposite wing chair, she rang the little china bell for Nancy and asked for tea for them both.

"You are looking very well, Miss Shaw. Do you object to my pipe?"

It was the largest, heaviest pipe Clarissa had ever seen, but he took it out of his pocket and cupped it with such an affectionate familiarity that she would never have dared object.

"There is a tobacco humidor on the table behind you,

if you'd like. Please make yourself comfortable. I'm delighted to have company."

Robert Peckham settled back in his chair, obviously very comfortable indeed. She did look well, he thought. Her cheeks had a little color now, not so pale and drawn as they had looked the night of the accident. She was wearing a dark green dress which set off the brown of her eyes and the red in her hair which was softly waved and caught at her neck in a handsome chignon. Her white linen collar was caught by a large enameled painted brooch, a lovely thing which he recognized as Morgan Dawson's handiwork. Around her shoulders was a wide kerchief that looked to be of Spanish embroidered white silk—very pretty against the dark green of the dress. Robert Peckham liked to see young ladies dress with style.

"Yes, you are much improved, I must say." He struck a match to his pipe and puffed it into life. The pungent tobacco fragrance drifted across the room. "However, this is not purely a social visit. I want to discuss this affair of Augusta Granville with you—there are still a few loose ends. And I have some good news to relate to you along the way."

"Oh, please tell me the good news first. It would be so welcome."

"No, I think the loose ends first. That shall be your punishment for withholding evidence."

"Oh, dear. You've found out about the riding accident."

Peckham's face took on a stern severity which was not matched by the twinkle in his eyes. "Yes. And no thanks to any of the people involved. I believe there were two attempts on your life. One at Andre's Cave and one out there in the arbor the night before the shooting. Is that correct?"

Clarissa kept her eyes on her glass. "Yes, that's correct. We didn't tell you because . . . well, because the first time George said that he would handle everything, and the second because there wasn't time. Adam had to go into New York the very next morning, and after we returned everything seemed to happen all at once."

"Well, while Adam and George were suspecting each other, I was after Augusta all along. So you see, if you had confided in me, we might have spared you a hurt. One that could so easily have been fatal."

"You suspected Augusta? Whatever . . ."

He had her attention and he was enjoying it. Crossing one leg over the other, he puffed at his big pipe contentedly.

"Oh, yes, ever since Miss Evans' death. I had been doing a little digging of my own (hoping to prevent another 'accident') and I uncovered several interesting facts. The first thing I learned was that George had hired Martha Evans' brother to find Mrs. Reddick, trying of course to lay his hands on Reddick's money. But somehow murder didn't fit George. Vain and greedy, yes, but violence didn't seem his kind of thing. I discovered that he knew all about you—as a lawyer he would, of course, and that he had made sure the rest of the family knew about it too."

"So you can add gossip to his list of faults. Judge Granville assured me no one here knew of my background. George himself acted surprised when I told him about it."

"The judge is inclined to be naive at times. The point is that Augusta knew suspicion would fall on you when that cup of foxglove tea was found. Stubbs and I knew from the beginning that the tea alone would have never done away with Miss Evans. Somehow she had been slipped a spoonful of water hemlock mashed in her food. It's as lethal a root as can be found anywhere and a cruel way to die. Between that and the foxglove, coupled with her bad heart, Martha Evans never had a chance."

Clarissa winced at his mention of foxglove. "Augusta must have been mad all the time and we never suspected."

"We found out later that she had made a study of poisonous plants. It took me quite a while to dig up an
240

apothecary whom she had asked for advice down near New York. We also found a notebook in her room with notes quite beautifully illustrated and documented. Had she been of a better turn of mind, she might have done something constructive with that little book. As it was, well, the way she went about poisoning Miss Evans shows how far her murderous instincts had taken over."

"But, Magistrate Peckham, I still don't understand why she would want to kill Nurse Evans and try to incriminate me. Neither of us was any threat to her."

"Martha Evans wasn't, but you most decidedly were." At the consternation on her face he waved his pipe. "Oh, I'll explain, just be patient. I mentioned finding a journal of Augusta's. In our devious, underhanded way we searched all the rooms in this house—yours included."

Even knowing she had nothing to hide, this piece of news made Clarissa uncomfortable.

He went on. "We found a lot of interesting papers among Augusta's things—poems, diaries, that kind of thing. It was enough to let us in on her little secret. Evidentally she had long ago achieved a grand passion for George Clarendon."

"In love with George—Augusta?"

"Yes. And had been for years. She was convinced that she understood him better than anyone and could help him get what he most wanted—wealth. She was beside herself when he married her sister. After Jenny died—and I don't suppose we shall ever know the truth about that—her hopes bloomed anew. Then you arrived, and she saw herself losing out again."

Clarissa spoke almost to herself. "So she was jealous of me." Then she turned her luminous eyes on the magistrate. "But Mr. Peckham, I wasn't promised to George and I doubt that I ever would have been. Why didn't she simply wait?"

"Ah, that involves that good news I mentioned to you earlier. You see, my dear, both George and Augusta knew something about you that you didn't know yourself. You stand to inherit a great deal of money very soon."

He grinned at the pure astonishment on her face. "You must be in error," she finally managed to stammer. "My father had very little, even after the farm was sold—"

"It was not your father. It was your grandfather in England. Your father did come from England, did he not?"

"Yes—but—I never even knew my grandfather."

"Well, almost a year ago the old gentleman died and left several thousand pounds to be divided among his sons, including the one in America. That son being dead, the money was to go to his heirs—which means you."

Clarissa had barely heard a word after "several thousand pounds." Then they all tumbled out at once, excitedly jumbled. "What, how much, who, when . . ."

Peckham laughed, enjoying her pleasure at her good fortune. "Just a minute, I'll go over it all again. The main thing is that four thousand English pounds comes to just about ten thousand American dollars, and that is quite a tidy sum for a single young lady."

She watched him in a daze. It was as though he were discussing someone else, some person far out there in the world who had been unexpectedly showered with fairy gold. Certainly not herself for whom so long every penny had had to be carefully counted. She had never longed to be rich and never considered that she would be. Money had not seemed as important to her as peace of mind for a long time now. Yet, the thought that she would now have the means to support herself, and in some style, gave her a delicious, magical joy. She began to giggle, like a child who has just been handed a gorgeous new toy.

"Ten thousand dollars! Why, it's a fortune!"

"You will have to recover your health now just so you can go out and buy yourself a new bonnet. Several new bonnets!"

"I can't believe it," Clarissa exclaimed. "How did you find out about this? Why didn't I hear?"

"Well, the fact is that it was this inheritance which set George to pursuing you and which drove Augusta to fear that she had lost her chance again. Here was a rich, pliable, and eligible young heiress living right in the house

242

under George's nose. A temptation he would never let pass. It must have been the last straw to an already unbalanced mind."

"But how did they know and not I? I still don't understand."

"The letter from England came to George's office inquiring to your whereabouts. He had handled your father's estate; so they had his name. You had virtually dropped off the earth, and he didn't bother to inform them that you were living here. He was waiting until the two of you were legally bound. Augusta knew everything that went on, as we could tell from her journals, and she was avidly interested in George's business."

"She must have wondered why such a man as he would have begun showering me with so much attention. I wondered at it myself. Although at one time he had me half-convinced that he was in love."

Peckham struck a match to the bowl of his pipe. "I imagine George Clarendon could be pretty persuasive when he wanted," he said between puffs. "And you shouldn't underrate yourself so. A girl who would go down into an abandoned mine in the dead of night is not exactly a mouse."

"That mine!" Clarissa exclaimed. "I still wonder at our actually going searching there at midnight. Looking for treasure and all we found was an old bunch of bones. No doubt Adam has already told you about them."

"Oh, yes. And they've been identified and properly buried by now. What you found was the body of Phillipe Durand, an itinerant painter who lived briefly in this area some years ago."

Clarissa started up from her chair. "Ellie Dawson's painter! That was his body?"

"I see you know the story. Yes, it was Ellie's young man. She made the identification for us from some bits of cheap jewelry buried with the body. He hadn't deserted her after all. We'll probably never know the details, but we surmise that Reddick had one of the andirons secretly recast and hid the jewels in it, then had Durand paint it to

243

match the other antique one. He must have been killed right after that, either by Reddick to keep his secret, or by Mrs. Reddick and Allen in an attempt to find out where the money had been stashed. Whoever did it must have felt a glimmer of conscience and scratched that cross on the stone over the grave."

"So that explains that new look on Ellie's face. She wasn't disgraced by deliberate design but by an accident of fate."

He reached over and knocked his pipe against the fireplace. "You're beginning to look very tired, Miss Shaw. I hope I haven't wearied you. There's not much more to add. Miss Granville had made a lackey out of the half-witted groom who half saw himself already as one of the judge's heirs. She put him up to spiking your horse."

"Yes, and it was Edwards who attacked me and tried to make me think Adam was trying to kill me that night."

"That's right. Augusta probably wrote the note, but it was Edwards doing the skulduggery. Clumsy efforts, both of them; yet they almost worked."

"They would have if it hadn't been for Adam."

"He was trying to catch George, but he was also trying to protect you in both instances."

Rising from his chair, he reached for her hand. "I must go now, Miss Shaw. Get yourself well soon so you can begin to enjoy your new-found wealth. No doubt you will want to consider new horizons when your health permits. This house—" His glance took in the room. "It's not always been a happy place."

She glanced at the hearth, recalling the painted Hessians marching in frozen tread across the fireplace. "Thank you, Mr. Peckham, for your good news, your explanations, and for just coming to see me. You are always welcome."

"Miss Shaw, one last word. You must not think that you are not a pretty girl. Money aside, George Clarendon would have been a lucky man to have won you."

Clarissa felt the warm color rising in her cheeks. "What a lovely compliment. Now you have really made my day."

There was a flirtatious twinkle in Robert Peckham's eyes as he bent over her fingers, so small in his large brown hand. "Then I consider mine well made also." He turned and left her to her contemplations.

Eighteen

Painful as the thought was, Clarissa finally had to conclude that Adam was deliberately avoiding her. More than once after their uncomfortable conversation early in her convalescence, he entered the parlor to find her ensconced on the sofa and almost turned on his heel in his haste to flee the room. She had welcomed his appearance with such a warm stirring inside and such a happy anticipation of his company that she found she was disappointed and hurt by his brusqueness. Once, as she was walking outside, she saw him approach until he caught sight of her, then turn abruptly off. She began to feel that she must have offended him in some way. She also began to grow angry—at Adam for his rudeness and at herself for caring.

She tried to make the excuse for him that he was just lapsing back into his old selfish ways, until finally she had to admit that she was actually very sorry that such a promising friendship had died aborning, while she did not even know why.

In her restlessness she could not get involved with her embroidery or tapestry work and so found the long hours of enforced idleness tedious in the extreme. As soon as she was able, she went back to spending some time each day with Mary and Georgie. She read a good deal and took long walks, which were very pleasant now that summer was in its full formal dress. Twice she took a trip into Sing Sing Village with Hannah, which helped to make those particular days bearable. But most of her hours were long and barren, and she was left with much time to think. Over and over she debated leaving Zion Hill, thinking perhaps to set up a house in New York now that she had the means. As Adam continued to be aloof, she became more and more convinced that here was no place for her and she would be better off to begin to build a new life somewhere else. Yet something held her back. The thought of leaving this house and these people filled her with a nameless grief, as surprising as it was undefined.

One afternoon she took a leisurely walk down to the river where, for the first time since that terrible night of her accident, she found herself standing near the old mine entrance. It looked small and forbidding even in the warm afternoon sunshine, and she wondered how she had ever had the courage to enter it at night. She never could have, of course, except for Adam. What had happened to the closeness, the support, the shared friendship of that strange evening?

I can't leave like this, she thought and realized that perhaps that was why she had not already left Zion Hill. However tenuous, there had been something between them. Where had it gone? If she left without knowing, she would spend the rest of her life wondering why.

Wandering back up the green rise, she sought out one of the benches in the arbor, grateful for the cool shade it offered. The still, quiet air was embedded with the summer fragrances of honeysuckle and jasmine. A cicada snapped its complaint from the grass at some disturbance of its afternoon slumber. She leaned back against the latticed wood and closed her eyes, letting the warm air envelop her in its languid cocoon. Footsteps on the path woke her from her reverie, and she looked up to see Adam Granville standing almost at her elbow.

He had not noticed her there until he was almost upon her, and then, thinking she was asleep, he had stopped and quietly watched until her eyes suddenly opened and looked into his own. Confused, he began to murmur words of apology and made to leave.

"Adam, please don't go."

The words were out almost before she thought them, and they left her horribly embarrassed. Yet she was not sorry. Better to face this and be done with it. Knowing it was over, she would be able to leave Zion Hill without looking backward.

His lean, strong back looked stiff with shock. It was a long minute before he turned, leaning on his stick, his face blank.

Clarissa stammered: "I—that is—I was hoping we might have a chance to talk. We haven't for such a long time."

He sat down on the far end of the bench, his hands on the cane between his legs. "I know we haven't. I didn't want to bother you."

He was so solemn. Clarissa longed for the old acrid banter. Even his sarcasm, given as it was with smiles, was preferable to this.

"It's no bother. I have very little to bother me right now. I've—well, I've missed you. I suppose it isn't lady-like to say so, but it's true."

The cold distance between them seemed to visibly lengthen. "I've been around," he answered without warmth. "I even inquired as to your health a few times."

"Yes, you did. I didn't mean that." He avoided looking at her, staring in mock concentration at the fields that sloped away toward the stables where gray dabs of sheep dappled the grass. "I meant—just to sit and talk."

"Well, here we are. Let's have a conversation. What shall we discuss? The weather is safe. Or the price of wool. Or the outlook for the harvest. Just pick a subject."

This was horrible and Clarissa was sorry she had stopped him. He had an invisible fortress around him built from the wattle and daub of his own defenses. She

248

saw herself beating on its surface, clamoring to be let in, while he sat within, cold, oblivious, silent, and alone.

Anger swept over her. It was on her tongue to tell him to go on then, that she was sorry she ever spoke to him at all. But when she looked back at him sitting there, staring out unseeing at the meadow, pity washed away her anger. His face was suffused with a terrible sadness, his body was stiff, unyielding. Whatever it was that gripped him she was suddenly able to see that he was alone and he was suffering. She blinked back the tears that filled her eyes. What did it matter if she had to swallow her pride? The important thing was that they should know the truth.

"Adam," she finally spoke, "what is wrong? Have I offended you? If I have done so, I am sorry. It was not intentional, I assure you."

This was the last thing he expected to hear, and he seemed to wilt under the generosity of her words. He turned his face away, leaning his cheek on his hands without answering.

She went on: "I had thought we could be friends, but now it seems that we cannot. I should just like to know why, since your friendship had come to be important to me."

She paused. "I should like to know, you see, because I have to decide what to do with myself. I may leave Zion Hill and go to live in New York."

He got up suddenly and walked to the edge of the flag-stones, still not looking at her. "I heard that you were an heiress," he said. "Now you have the means to do whatever you want. The world has opened its doors for you. That's good fortune and I'm happy for you. After all, New York would offer you all kinds of diversions which you would never find out here in the country."

Clarissa tried to laugh. "I could go to Niblo's Gardens every night," she said in an attempt at gaiety, "and ride the steamer all the way to Albany once a week. And——" The caricature of gaiety died on the air.

His stiff back remained unmoving, and his voice was hollow when he spoke, breaking the silence.

"Go to New York, Clarissa. Go and live where there is
249

light and laughter and happiness. Forget Zion Hill and the Granvilles."

She felt the tears begin to course down her cheeks. Her confused feelings crystalized, and all at once she knew clearly what had only been shadowy and dim before.

"But I don't want to go," she cried, trying to choke the sob from her voice. "I don't want to forget the Granvilles. I don't want to forget you. I was just getting to know you . . ."

"Oh, God, Clarissa! You don't know me at all." He turned to look directly into her face for the first time. Her eyes mirrored the suffering in his. Moved by pity and something more than pity, he sat down beside her and took her hands.

"My dearest girl, don't you see? Far from offending me—it's because I care so much that I've kept away. You are young and lovely and now you have an inheritance as well. Every kind of happiness can be yours. And what have I to offer you instead? The heritage of madness, the body of a cripple, the mind of a cynic! I want you to go out and find the world. It was for your protection that I stood back, and for my own as well. I am sorry if I hurt you, but it seemed the best way for both of us."

Because I care so much. His words kept reverberating in her mind, so that she hardly heard anything else he said. So it was not because he didn't love her that he had turned away. He did love her and now he had said so. And it filled her soul with joy and relief.

"But, Adam, I don't want the world. I want you—our friendship, your family, this home. I'm terrified of the world, don't you know that? What do I want with gaiety and excitement? I've had enough excitement this last year to last a lifetime. I want only quiet and peace and your strength to lean on."

"Clarissa, think! Look at my family. A mother with no wits and a crazy murderess for a sister. How can I offer any woman such a heritage? How can I ever have children to pass on such posterity? It would be wrong! Sinful!"

In his urgency he gripped her arms with his hands.

"And look at me. A cripple, dragging one useless leg through life. What woman wants that?"

This at least she could answer. "Another cripple might," she said candidly. "Look at me. You forget that I was broken by adversity. My wounds don't show, but they are here in my heart and they will never completely heal."

He leaned forward, his head in his hands. "They will heal. Wounded hearts always improve with time, but no amount of days will ever make my leg whole again." He pushed his fingers nervously through his long hair. "I am trying to send you away because I know it would be best for you. Don't make it so hard for me!"

"Because he was looking down, he did not see the flush that colored her white cheek.

"You have decided what is best for me without even asking what *I* want. You would push me out into a world I hate, a world I fear to face alone, because you think it is what I need. I tell you, I don't want to face any world without you beside me. You are offering me as bleak an existence as the one you would be left here to face, and all for my best interests! I had hoped that you loved me . . ."

"I do love you," he said, distressed by the emotion that threatened to break her voice. Turning his head away, he looked back at the old house standing framed in the wide, leafy archway of the arbor. What she said was true. If Clarissa went away, Zion Hill would become a bleak, empty place where he and Hannah and their father would shuffle the silent halls, letting the shadows gradually close in around them. Such a gray, desperate future was all that would be left to him.

Clarissa dug her fingers into his sleeve, forcing him to face her and look into his eyes. "Listen to me, Adam," she cried, blinking back her tears. "If you send me away, you will break my heart as well as yours. What does it matter that you have a crippled leg? I love *you*—the person you are. I love your family, even with its problems. Zion Hill is my home now and I don't want any other." She tried to smile. "Who was ever perfect anyway? Every-

251

one—every place has some defect. What matters is that we care for each other."

Looking deeply into her eyes, he seemed to hear her for the first time. "But would you really want to stay?" he asked incredulously. "Would you want to marry me and make a home in this place? Could you spend your life here in this tragedy-filled house, caring for a man who can't even walk properly?"

"Oh, Adam," she sighed. "Just ask me!"

At her words and the look on her face, his defiant resolve withered. He had neither the wish nor the heart to fight against her any longer. He took her in his arms, not with the urgency of passion but with the tenderness of a loving concern.

"Oh, Clarissa, my dear girl." His lips brushed her thick coil of hair. She leaned her cheek against the roughness of his coat, filled to overflowing with a sense of perfect contentment. She could hear his heart beating and his long back felt strong against her arm encircling his waist. She felt no overwhelming passion either—that would come later, she knew from the dim stirrings far back in her mind. There was only this wonderful happiness, this closeness, this man. And for now that was enough.

At length he sat back, taking her face between his hands and looked wonderingly into her eyes, shining with happiness.

"Clarissa Shaw," he said, "I love you. I love you with all my twisted body and heart. Do you think two cripples can build one whole life together?"

She had never seen his face so softened. She laid her hand against his lean cheek. "They might try. And with a little grace and a little luck, they may well succeed."

He moved her hand to his lips and kissed her palm. Then, holding her tightly, he added, "And the taint of insanity? Can grace overcome that?"

Clarissa sat back and looked into his eyes. "What can I say? You think of Augusta and your mother. I see Hannah and your father, Mary and Georgie, and you. I believe that good is stronger than evil and love stronger than

252

death. Can we live with that belief and love each other and then take what comes?"

He smiled down at her. "We might try. Perhaps that is what grace is all about."

And drawing her to him, he kissed her full on the lips, soft and tender and delicate as rose petals, and sweet as the morning dew on a thirsty ground.

It was that evening before they found a few moments to themselves after the happy, excited congratulations of the family. Hannah had wept with pleasure at the thought of Clarissa's staying on with them and had already bestowed on her the accolade of a new sister. Some of the sorrow had melted from Judge Granville's eyes at the thought that something good had come out of all this trouble. A glimmer of faith was restored to his tired, saddened demeanor.

Clarissa herself had not believed that she could be so happy again. She felt the healing quiet of a journey accomplished and a shore reached. The trouble that had begun with her parents' unexpected deaths seemed finally to have been resolved, and a new complete structure had grown from the demoralized ashes of the old.

They stood on the veranda in the gathering dusk, breathing in the summer scents on the cool night air and watching the red disk that was the sun slip behind the dark, mysterious silhouette of the Palisades. Now and then a yellow spark illuminated the graying dusk as fireflies circled under the trees, while from the woods the noisy chattering of the locusts was at full blast.

Adam slipped his arm around her shoulders as she leaned against him. Contentment settled around them like a gauzy veil. "It's a beautiful valley, isn't it, when you stop to look? Puny people with their puny concerns tramp it up and down, but the seasons come and go and come again, and the river is forever."

Moving away a little, she leaned against the thick, white porch column flaked with pealing paint and spotted with mold.

"Adam, do you want to stay here at Zion Hill? We

253

could go somewhere else—New York Town or another house in this neighborhood. Or we could move farther up-river."

He sat down on the steps at her feet, his face blurred by the shadows. "I thought of that too," he said at length. "But before I answer your question, you tell me how *you* feel. Is there too much behind us in this place?"

Clarissa stared back at the broad, tired facade of the old house. Through the window the warm, mellow glow from the oil lamp in the parlor dappled its gold on the porch floor. Inside she could see Hannah sewing in a chair near the curtains. Within the depths of the house, she faintly heard the silver shower of Mary's laughter.

"If it had a new coat of paint and a few loving touches here and there, I think it might make a very nice home. Perhaps the demons have been exorcised once and for all, and the cobwebs swept clean. Perhaps we can fill their spaces with something more healing and lasting. The structure is sound, I believe."

Reaching up, he took her hand; he was obviously relieved. "And we can perhaps bring something to it that it has not known for a long time—the absence of hate and a surfeit of love.

"But I think we'll give the old place a new name," he added, looking around. "Something to do with all these beautiful trees that stand court around it. Linden Hall, perhaps. Or Birch Manor? Beechwood?"

"A new name for a new life." She smiled down at him.

Across the shadowed river the sun dipped behind the hills, leaving a peaceful darkness to descend over the valley.